HEXED

A HELL ON EARTH NOVEL

A.C. MELODY

License Notes

Hexed

ISBN: 9781092425483

Copyright © 2019 A.C. Melody
All rights reserved
Published by A.C. Melody

This is a work of erotic fiction and contains graphic depictions of sexual acts, which may offend some audiences. Names, characters and incidents depicted in this book are entirely fictitious. Any resemblance to actual events, locales, organizations or persons, living or dead, is entirely coincidental and beyond the intent of the author and publisher. All characters portrayed as participating in sexual acts or sexually explicit discussions within this book are 18 years of age or older.

This book was edited by: Monique the Editrix

Cover design by: Deranged Doctor Design

Dedicated to my very own Zoe Bankes and all the other strong, sassy women out there keeping it real. May you always have happiness, snark, and cinnamon rolls.

CHAPTER 1

Pervy

Zoe's ears pricked with awareness in the dead of sleep, a continuous noise luring her from the depths of a fading dream. Whispered conversations overlapped one another, fading in and out, swelling and ebbing in volume. At the first stirrings of wakefulness, the overwhelming sensation of someone standing right beside her bed startled her so much, she jolted halfway across the mattress, twisting to see who it was.

But there was no one.

Her heart pounded so fast and hard, it tracked pain across her chest. Panting from the sudden fright, her eyes darted all over the room. Nothing was out of place. There was nowhere for an intruder to hide. Her closet was a door-less, rectangular hole in the wall across from her, vulgarly displaying all its contents. No boogeyman under the bed, either, because it wasn't even on a frame. Just a mattress and box-spring on the floor, that's how anti-adult she was.

Zoe settled on her ass and brushed tangled curls from

her eyes. The more she calmed, the more her certainty of a presence ever being there began to fade—along with the sensation of it. She could almost laugh at herself, really. It must have been one of those vivid dreams that felt so real, it had tricked her mind and body into believing it. Like the flying and falling dreams. With a tired groan, she scrubbed her hands over her face. It wouldn't be the first time her own brain had victimized her. To say Zoe Bankes had an overactive imagination was like saying Quentin Tarantino films were a little violent.

A shiver coursed through her relaxing muscles, and she finally gave in to that laugh, as sardonic as it was. Preparing to slide back down to her pillow and reclaim sleep, she stopped when the strange presence returned, ten times stronger than the first time and a hell of a lot closer. Zoe didn't jolt this time, but her immediate reaction was to move away from it. She scrambled to the wall at the head of her bed, and despite there still being nothing to see, her eyes wouldn't stop roaming.

Because she could *feel* it.

The very air was thick with the presence, charged with a certain kind of energy. It felt as if someone were stretching over the side of her bed to get a closer look at her, and nothing about that idea made her feel okay. All her sixth-sense alarms triggered, because Zoe no longer had the luxury of blissful, human ignorance. The things that went bump in the night had names, faces, and motives. Yet, something stronger and more intrinsic than her apprehension compelled her hand from the mattress, her fingers tingling with the urge to touch what she couldn't see.

They connected with some sort of density, and it resulted in a surge of power that rippled up her arm and through the air. It wavered like desert heat over asphalt. The presence expanded all around her, and her entire body heated with unexpected desire.

Her mouth popped open with shock from the intensity of it, then she felt something move downward between her and the presence, followed by a slight tug in her very soul. There was no time to freak out about that, though, because everything came to an abrupt stop. The desire, the presence, the charge in the air—everything just vanished, leaving her mind reeling.

Only Zoe didn't cycle through the same hysterical questions every other human would have, because she already knew too many of the answers. She didn't feel like laughing at herself anymore, nor did she doubt the authenticity of what she'd felt. It had been very real. She wasn't the least bit crazy or confused, her mind was quite clear on what had taken place. The only questions remaining were who—or *what*—had just visited her, and most importantly, why?

For the remainder of the night, she slept in short patches of muddled dreams, startling awake and unable to doze off again until she was absolutely certain the presence hadn't returned. At some point, she'd gone from hugging her pillow against the wall, to fully stretched out in her bed like usual. That's the position she found herself in when she woke to the sound of incessant pounding on her front door. She was so exhausted that lifting her head proved challenging. Zoe squinted at the alarm clock until the digital numbers blurred into view, then scoffed in disbelief when they told her it was already a quarter to eleven in the morning. Her hand must have smacked the dials in her sleep, which she could have sworn she'd just fallen back into.

The pounding came again, and Zoe heaved out an angry groan, shoving the blankets away. She snatched up her phone and robe as she stormed from her room. If they could, the multiple locks lining the doorframe would've filed for harassment by the time she was through with them. A familiar cologne blew right into her face when she swung the door open and glared at the tall, well-dressed man blocking her view of the hallway.

"Doll face, you look like hell," Lemar greeted.

Zoe's only response was a middle finger, before she pivoted and huffed her way into the kitchen. It was a row of appliances against the wall to her left and a small island counter to her right. She'd seen toddler play kitchens bigger and better equipped than her real one. The glowing green numbers on the microwave mounted above the stove matched her alarm clock's claim, and she groaned again. How could her body feel completely deprived of rest when she'd slept in so late? Her head was fuzzy, and she fought to keep her heavy eyelids open as she smacked the espresso machine around with no result.

Lemar came to the machine's rescue, taking Zoe by the shoulders and redirecting her to the loveseat in the living room. He'd already raised the shades to let the cheerful, New York morning inside and if it wouldn't have been such a waste of energy, she totally would've flipped that off, too.

"Okay, sugar, you just settle down right here and let Uncle Lemar take care of you," he said with nauseating pleasantry.

"Don't call yourself uncle, Lemar, it makes you sound pervy," she grumbled through a yawn, curling up on the sofa without a fight.

"If that's the best you can do, we're gonna need something a lot stronger than a triple-shot Americano," he muttered on his way back to the kitchen.

Zoe managed an amused snort, then pulled her phone from the oversized pocket of her threadbare robe. She waited an entire minute for the screen to come into focus, before remembering she was blind. With a sigh, she reached over her head and felt around on the end table for her reading glasses. It was one of several pair she kept in strategic locations around the apartment. Like magic, the phone's screen became crystal clear once she slipped them on. After locating her and Kami's message thread, she opened it and got to texting, because somewhere between assaulting the espresso machine and sniping at Lemar, she'd remembered exactly why she was so fucking tired.

"Please tell me this is because there's a naked man in your bed," Lemar inquired, his perverted interest the opposite of subtle.

"Please tell me you didn't just waste a whole fifteen seconds asking, instead of seeing for yourself," she countered as she finished typing out her text to Kami.

Curious: is the demonic security system equipped

with 24-hour monitoring? Emergency call buttons? Is there a code I should be carving into the floorboards while chanting under a full moon to activate?

Zoe *could* just come right out and ask if Saphiel's so-called security system came with a sleazy, Peeping Lee, but she was leery about alarming her best friend without good cause. Mainly because causing Kami to worry had a tendency to trigger bad reactions from her fine-ass Devil, who still intimidated the shit out of Zoe for all the obvious reasons.

The aroma of strong, brewing java hit her nostrils and perked her senses up a little more. Her mouth began watering, so she glanced up from her phone only to find her would-be hero MIA.

"Lemar, caffeinate me!"

He emerged from the spit of alcove her bedroom door was sunk into and folded his arms, giving her an unimpressed look. "One of these days, I'm not even going to bother checking, and that will be the day I've given up all hope for your vagina, Zoe Linnae."

She scoffed. "No, that'll be the day there's a naked man in my bed and you'll be S-O-fucking-L."

"Oh, thank God, you're feeling better." His shoulders sagged with relief. "I was about to call for backup."

Zoe snickered and opened Kami's reply.

Why, what happened? Did someone break in?

Awww, her bestie still worried about her.

I wouldn't be texting if someone broke in. *eyeroll* I said curious. Can't a girl get some deets?

It had been a little over a month since Zoe had resettled into her apartment after the psycho-douchebag-paparazzi-stalker, Jake Sanz, had broken in and met his just demise at the hands of before mentioned fine-ass Devil. Still, she hoped Kami would see her curiosity as natural and nothing more. If it turned out to be something menacing, then damn right she'd run her little ass off to the Monarchs of Greed. She wasn't too proud to hide behind those far more powerful than herself.

Once Lemar brought their coffee into the living room, Zoe sat up to start on hers right away. She needed the fogginess in her brain to take a hike, pronto. Her business wasn't designed for the sluggish. In the world of social media, there was no room for mistakes or procrastination. One typo could mean hours of cleanup. One missed opportunity could cost clients. Hashtag trends, celebrity gossip, scientific breakthroughs, pre-release gamer tech, global activism—all of these things changed with rapid-fire succession. If Zoe wasn't right on top of them for her clients, then her competitors would swoop in and steal valuable prime slots with the most current headlines. If that happened too often, her clients' followers would jump ship and leave a wreckage of smack-talk in their wake. Nobody could blackball a company, product, or up-and-comer faster than a pissed-off avid tweeter with a blog following. Just as Zoe got her laptop fired up, Kami texted her back.

Saph said it's working just fine, not to worry. It's only designed to keep those out who wish you harm. If someone did manage to get through, he'd know about it right away.

Zoe mulled that over for a moment, wondering if Saphiel would consider a demonic Peeping Tom someone with harmful intentions, when he'd spent twenty-four years stalking her best friend before making his move.

Okay, thanks. Feel free to send over the mockups for the wedding invites when they're done, so I can approve.

Knowing that would have Kami replying with a middle finger emoji, Zoe grinned and set her phone aside to contact the next person on her list. Like Lemar had already done, she grabbed her headset and put it into place, opening a video chat in one window, then clicking on every social media icon on her desktop. They popped open in a blink, because if there was one thing Zoe spent a ridiculous amount of money on outside of her Star Wars collectibles, it was her electronics.

"Zo–whoa, what the hell happened to you?" Byron asked when he answered her video call.

Shit. She'd forgotten she'd just rolled out of bed without so much as a jaunt to the restroom yet.

"No questions, I need you here ASAP," she returned.

"Uh, I can be there by four," he replied, bewildered.

"Four? How is that ASAP?"

"That's the best I can do on a Friday, Zo, you know

that."

How was it already Friday? Zoe frowned, then waved her hand. "Fine, see you then."

She ditched her headset, downed the rest of her coffee, then rose from the sofa to smack Lemar on his muscular bicep on her way to the bathroom. "You let me go on a video chat looking like this? What kind of pervy gay uncle are you?"

"The kind that didn't find a naked man in your bed, that's what."

His lingering disappointment gave her something to smile about, at least. She felt even better after a quick shower, followed by her normal morning routine. Tossing her dark curls up out of the way, she took the time to apply her usual cosmetics for those inevitable video calls. What she looked like from the neck down only ever mattered when she was planning to leave her apartment, but since that wasn't on the calendar today, she emerged from her room wearing whatever clothes she'd found first. Plaid skinny jeans, Uggs, and suspenders over a black, fitted t-shirt with the Cheshire Cat's grin on the front and his eyes on the back.

"Lemar, picture," she demanded, posing with her coffee cup in one hand, middle finger flying on the other and a cherry-red grin. "And print!"

After snatching the picture from the printer, she set her mug aside and disappeared into her bedroom again. Lemar didn't even bat an eye when she dragged her life-sized Yoda doll out, taped her picture over its face and aimed it toward the front door.

"There." She smiled. "That's better."

"Oh, sure," Lemar grumbled. "Everyone else gets a warning."

*

The absolute best thing about running your own online business, was having the ability to send employees home early while still demanding more work get done. The only reason why Lemar and Franki worked out of her apartment rather than remotely was because it allowed them to communicate as things were happening, keeping costly delays at a minimum. Plus, they made an amazing team. Zoe wasn't a bleeding heart, but she knew she'd lucked out with her two employees. They were brilliant and a constant source of creative inspiration.

She just hadn't wanted Lemar there during her meeting with Byron. After the way he'd found her that morning, still asleep and dragging ass, she knew he'd be concerned enough to ask questions she couldn't answer. Kami and Saphiel's secrets were now Zoe's burden, but she wouldn't have it any other way.

As she waited, Zoe began her own research into the night's incident. She didn't have much to go on, and it took revisiting the encounter to recapture details that sleep had hazed over. An invisible entity that triggered desire had Google sending her on a wild goose chase, until she plugged in the one word she figured was the most relevant: demon. Article after article popped up about all kinds of lust-inducing demons from almost every culture. The most prevalent seemed to be the Succubi and Incubi. Zoe lost track of time as she dove into the results, learning more about the lilu and lili demons than she'd ever wanted to know, including the various legends surrounding Lilith, the Mother of All Demons.

And that was lovely, because she couldn't discount any of it as just myths now that she knew better. The most intimidating aspect was that these particular demons were ancient—older than Christianity, featuring in Mesopotamian, Akkadian, and Sumerian tales long before they'd appeared in the Hebrew texts of Babylon. It was one thing for Zoe to know that Saphiel was a real-life Devil surrounded by real-life Legion, but the idea of being stalked by something older than the pyramids was a whole other kind of mindfuck.

It was just shy of four-thirty when Byron knocked on her door, startling her. Zoe quickly locked her screen and closed her laptop, shoving the research to the back of her mind. She'd never been the type to worry without just cause, let alone fly into hysterics over a mere possibility. Especially considering the subject matter. In the grand scheme of things, would it really freaking matter how old the demon was?

She opened the door and scowled. "You're late."

Byron's gaze swept over her and his shoulders relaxed with relief. "Thank God, I wasn't sure what to expect when I got here," he replied. He towed a wheeled trunk behind him and paused to smirk at the improved Yoda doll. "Cute. Relative of yours?"

Zoe snorted. At four foot nine, it didn't take much to be taller than her, but Byron's five-four frame wasn't that much bigger. "Why, were you hoping for an introduction?"

He chuckled and made his way to the coffee table. It was a large square because Zoe liked having an adequate workspace and it could fill up really fast with drinks and snacks on one of her foodie or book club nights, since her apartment lacked a separate dining area. After setting the trunk on its bottom, Byron pulled his laptop case up over his head and sat in the armchair to get it set up.

"So, what's the emergency?"

Zoe had been racking her brain about how to approach him all day. In the end, she'd decided to appeal to the paranormal side of his geek. They all had that side, of course, but it varied in types. Zoe's was everything supernatural and science fiction. Byron's just happened to be the kind she needed. Maybe. Hopefully.

"Before you break out into fangirl screams or whatevs, let me preamble that this is purely curiosity based and not in any way a concession to your wholehearted belief in the existence of ghosts."

His face lit up like she was handing him the key to the underworld.

"What did I just say?" she snapped.

"Zoe Bankes, interested in the paranormal outside of fiction?" He grinned. "I'm allowed to revel."

She rolled her eyes. "Sure, vamps and werewolves are a stretch, but Grandma sticking around to bake cookies twenty years after her funeral is completely acceptable."

"Uh yeah, because I have proof that Grandma existed in the first place."

"Okay, can we skip the part where you try and fail,

yet again, to turn me into a true believer and just get to the techy bits?"

Byron copied her eyeroll and opened his trunk of goodies. "Since this was the last topic I expected you to bring up, I'm afraid I didn't bring any ghost-hunting equipment with me," he said. "Ah, except my EMF reader, which I never leave home without."

"Right, but what all does that bad boy cover?" Zoe asked. "I know it's the go-to tool for all ghost hunters, but I live in a large apartment complex with plenty of electromagnetic distortion, so how would you know what's what?"

"Process of elimination." He shrugged. "If you get a big spike, you check for any power sources in the immediate area that could be causing it. If there aren't any, then you have to assume you've found a concentration of spectral activity."

"I don't *have* to assume anything," she corrected him.

"Yeah." He deflated. "Look, Zo, this is stuff you could've just researched online, so why am I really here?"

"You're a tech genius," she answered, trying to ease the sting of his disappointment, because she had no one else she was willing to turn to. Yet. "I was curious if there were other kinds of gadgets, something that might pick up on things more powerful than ghosts?"

He eyed her with a mixture of curiosity and skepticism. "Like what, vampires and werewolves?"

How about real-life fucking demons, hater? Zoe shrugged a shoulder. "Wouldn't supernatural creatures emit a different kind of energy signature than regular people or their ghosts?"

"I'm sure they would, if they actually existed," he deadpanned. "Zoe, I don't expect you to believe in the paranormal, but I do. And not from some romanticized fan-club viewpoint, either. I've actually experienced a haunting before. I don't study it to try to convince others, I do it to try to understand it better for myself and why it happens so irregularly. For me, it's more of a science than a quest to find proof."

Stunned, Zoe chewed on that for a moment. She hadn't meant to offend him, but it appeared she had. "Was it a good haunting or a bad one?"

"Neither, it was just unexpected," he answered, his tone still miffed and defensive. "Up until then, I'd never given any thought to ghosts, but they're kind of hard to dismiss when they suddenly appear right in front of you and your brother. When you aren't the only one who saw it happen, you can't blame it on a trick of the light, your own mind, or poor vision."

His words trailed off as he rubbed his hands down his denim-clad thighs in a way that spoke of discomfort more than irritation.

"Sorry," she said, feeling a little awkward. "I honestly wasn't trying to discredit your belief in ghosts. I really am curious about the equipment involved, how it works, and everything it works for. Aren't there different kinds of ghosts?"

Byron studied her for a moment, only relaxing again once he seemed convinced she was being serious. "Yes, there are a few different kinds of ghosts and hauntings."

"Which are the most powerful? Poltergeists?"

"Many people think that, and there are a handful of reports that seem legitimate, but I've yet to come across any evidence that angry ghosts can physically harm the living. The most they seem capable of doing is manipulating energy in order to move items and slam doors . . . that kind of thing."

"Was that a yes?"

Byron chuckled and shook his head. "In my personal experience, the most powerful hauntings are the residual ones, where something so violent happened at the moment of death, it left a high concentration of energy behind. People also refer to it as the stuck-in-a-loop haunting, if that clarifies things."

"Oh yeah, like when they have to relive the moments leading up to their deaths over and over again." Zoe nodded, not that she knew anything about hauntings, but she did know scary movies.

"Right, but it's largely debated on whether or not the ghost is really still there reliving it, or if it's just the energy of the event itself," he elaborated. "As far as equipment goes, you can use infrared video combined with motion-sensor cameras, set them up overnight or whenever the activity is known to occur. And know that the most important tool you can have, is a ton of patience."

"What about noise?" she asked, thinking about the whispering that had woken her up. "Like in that Michael Keaton movie?"

"*White Noise*?"

"Yeah whatever, it's Batman." She dismissed with a

wave of her hand.

"Actually." Byron laughed as he started tapping away at his keyboard. "I've been working on developing an app that will turn my cellphone into a better EVP recorder than any other currently on the market."

"Really?" Zoe perked up. "EVP is ghost talk, right?"

She wondered if her pervy peeping demon was snickering and making lewd comments about her while being all . . . pervy. Ugh, she really needed to find a better insult.

"Electronic Voice Phenomena, but yes, pretty much." He nodded. "The problem with typical EVP recorders is that there's no way to know if you've picked anything up until after you're done with a hunt and listen to the playbacks. I'm trying to develop an app that will alert me to EVPs as they're happening, so I can stay in that area and maybe even get a running dialogue going."

"That's kind of brilliant," she replied, impressed.

Byron pointed at his temple. "Tech genius."

"I'll have shirts made," Zoe laughed. "So, how far along are you in the development process?"

"I'm using the beta version right now, but can't say I've had any success with it. Haven't failed, either, though."

Zoe opened her mouth to respond and then frowned. "Huh?"

"The app hasn't alerted me to EVPs happening, but I haven't picked any up on the traditional recorder," he explained. "I've been running both simultaneously, because that's the only way I'll be able to test it with any accuracy."

"Ah, gotcha. The ghosts just aren't cooperating. Well, hey, I'll be a beta tester for you. You just have to show me how to use it."

Byron blinked at her in surprise. "You . . . want to go on a ghost hunt?"

"Not even a little." She shot that idea down right away. "But do you have to go on a ghost hunt to pick up EVPs? I mean, are ghosts really that boring?"

He opened his mouth to respond, but Zoe plowed onward. "See, this is one of the things I've never understood about the whole process. In my mind, it would make far more sense that if ghosts were sticking around, they'd be spotted in a larger variety of places at all hours of the day. They're ghosts. Are they really afraid of getting a sunburn? Some people claim that ghosts are attracted to the living, yet all the haunted places are abandoned. It seems to me, if that were true, then ghosts would leave the empty houses and go where all the people are—like every pedestrian-packed sidewalk during rush hour. Are structures the only things ghosts are allowed to haunt? Do they have to follow rules like in *Beetlejuice*?"

Stunned, Byron shook his head, appearing to be at a loss for words for a moment. "Another Keaton movie?"

"I have a thing," she confessed.

"You've actually given this a lot more thought than I ever would've given you credit for," he admitted.

"My brain doesn't have an off switch. You should hear my contemplations regarding the spontaneous birth of fruit flies and why it always triggers a chain reaction of more. Because you never get just one," she said. "This building is over a hundred years old, Byron, I'm fairly certain at least one person has died here since the foundation was poured."

"All right." He chuckled. "I can't argue with that logic. Give me your phone and I'll get you set up."

It didn't take him very long to download the app onto her phone and explain how to use it. Not that there was anything for her to do, except have it on when she wanted to give it a go. After seeing him out, Zoe popped a noodle bowl into the microwave for dinner, then dug back into her research. Afterward, she went through her Friday-night routine of switching all her clients' social media accounts off on all her devices, praying they didn't fuck something up over the weekend and leave her with a giant mess come Monday morning. Some people should never be allowed to write their own tweets.

By nine, she was more than ready for bed and happily turned down Franki's invitation to go to Zappa's. She wasn't feeling the club scene with so little sleep and a possible demonic stalker on her hands.

Despite her exhaustion, though, Zoe struggled to find sleep. The anticipation of possibly getting a result from Byron's app was too consuming. She kept checking her phone to make sure the program hadn't stopped running and that the volume was still turned up all the way. With any luck, the demon would be a no-show. Zoe laughed at herself over that, then gave up and closed her eyes.

She didn't know how long it took her to fall asleep, nor how long she'd been there, before her phone went haywire on the nightstand. Her eyes flew open, breath rushing from her lungs as she grabbed the beeping, flashing thing. For a suspended moment, she was too shocked that the app actually worked to worry about why it was.

"Shit!"

Zoe clutched the phone to her chest and peered around her room. Once again, nothing seemed to be there. But both her phone and the undeniable sensation of another's presence said otherwise. Adrenaline was a sluggish serum through her veins, because she was almost more exhausted than fearful. Maybe she wasn't dealing with a lust demon after all, but one that liked to steal people's sleep. Either way, it had to end before it could get any worse.

"Cut the crap, I know you're there," she snapped.

Though she sounded agitated, inside she was shaking, because who was she kidding? Demons were real. Her half-demon bestie was eternally engaged to a King of Hell. There was no passing anything off for an overactive imagination anymore. That ship had sailed six weeks, four pepperoni pies, and two bottles of wine ago. But if Zoe Bankes was going down, it would not be lacking in epic!

"Way I see it, you've got two choices. Save yourself now or find out just how fast Avarice can get here."

Zoe opened her contacts and pulled up Kami's number. Her thumb was hovering over the dial icon, when her phone went completely dead. The screen went black, stopping Byron's app cold, which left a ringing silence in its wake. With a frown, she slapped the device against her palm, as if that might jar it back into working order.

"That won't help."

"Oh, son of a—"

Wall. Zoe jolted backwards, right into that hard surface when the demon appeared beside her bed. He wasn't at all what she'd been expecting, though it was difficult to really see him. Beyond some kind of black fog that swirled all around and over him, was the silhouette of an imposing, human-shaped male. Transfixed, she wondered what the fog was made out of, and if it had been the very density she'd touched the night before that had triggered her body to heat with lust.

The silence stretched for a moment as she waited for hellish alarms to start going off or a raging Saphiel to burst through her door with Kami hot on his heels. Neither of those things happened. Did that mean her intruder held no ill intentions? Whether he did or not, it appeared she was on her own.

"If you think killing my phone will save you, guess again. All I have to do is scream and you'll be answering to one pissed off Devil, so give me a good reason not to, and make it snappy!"

Her mind raced through countless scenarios of how this could all go down, and she didn't care one iota for her mind's offerings. Zoe made a solid decision right then and there to cut all religious-themed horror movies from her entertainment diet immediately.

The demon tilted his head, regarding her from behind the shifting shadows. Was it some kind of demonic forcefield? Wow, her geekdom knew no bounds. Now she was just blending genres.

"Because *he'll* come next and you won't like it when

that happens," he replied.

Oh God, that voice. Zoe fought the delectable shiver his raspy baritone incited. Between that, the dark mysterious hotness he was portraying and the memory of their previous encounter, the demon was hitting high on her fantasy Richter scale.

"He who?" she asked, doubting her actual desire to know.

Saphiel was intimidating as all get out, and he was only Greed. She knew there were far worse beings in Hell.

"Abaddon."

Zoe wasn't completely successful at stopping her snort of laughter, but it seemed her uninvited guest didn't see the humor in it. "Oh, you're serious. That's a real thing?"

"He is quite real, yes."

"He? Okay, wow, some shows really enjoy their creative license," she muttered to herself. "So, is he like Avarice?"

The demon shifted, the shadows moving with him, rippling like silk. Or rather, like he was on the other side of its surface. That could explain why Saphiel's alarms weren't going off, because the demon wasn't actually in her room per se. Zoe tried not to get too overconfident, because if she was right, she had no idea how quickly that could change.

"You want to know if Abaddon is a Fallen?" he inquired.

"More curious to know if he's wielding some of that deadly sin stuff," she answered.

"You are peculiar," he remarked after a moment. "But to answer your question, yes. Abaddon is the Demon of Wrath. I'm here at his request."

All the humor in Zoe drained, along with some of the blood from her face. She knew all about Kami's demon Pheldra, and that she used to be a Solider of Wrath in the Abyss. It was easy to forget her own trepidation when concern for her best friend came into play.

"Why?" she demanded, sitting forward from the wall. "What does he want?"

He peered through her open doorway, which had a direct visual line to Kami's old bedroom. "Her," he answered. "He wants his perfect weapon back."

Oh, hell no!

"That's why you were here last night? To pull a snatch-and-grab on my best friend?"

"Snatch and grab mean the same thing," he pointed out. "I was tasked to come here and retrieve Wrath's missing soldier now that she's been released from Limbo, and return her to the Abyss where she belongs."

"Oh my God, are you watching this?" Zoe pointed to her own face. "Because I'm about to take immense pleasure in bursting your creepy stalker bubble. Pheldra's the new Queen of Avarice. She doesn't work for Abaddon anymore. Didn't he get her two weeks' notice?"

In a blink, he was in her face, leaning over the side of her bed in the hottest, craziest case of déjà vu Zoe had ever experienced. Her reaction was absolutely ridiculous —pulling the covers tighter around herself, as if they had the ability to shield her. Like they were still imbued with the same magical properties they'd seemed to possess when her parents had tucked her safely into bed as a child. Yet, it wasn't him she feared as much as that inexplicable lust he'd stirred within her the night before. She eyed the dancing shadows warily, praying they wouldn't touch her. She didn't need proof that damn bad.

"Perhaps you should take her place," he suggested. "Your tongue cuts like a sword."

Oh, buddy, you have no idea. At the moment, she was tempted to show him in other, much naughtier ways. She shook her head to dispel those thoughts and tried to scoot further away from him.

"Come any closer and you'll learn just how much," she vowed, impressing herself by just how convincing she sounded. "I wasn't kidding. All I have to do is scream and the race is on. Who do you think will get here first? The Devil or his wolf?"

"You know too much for a Daughter of Eve," he growled, leaning closer and effectively cutting her breath short.

"Helps to have friends in the lowest of places," she retorted, trying not to scowl when her desire to scream continued to slip further away.

"It's dangerous," he warned. "You should never reveal how much you know to demons. You could be viewed as a threat."

Zoe's pulse kicked up, yet strangely, she still didn't feel threatened by him. At least, not in the way she should. "Why do you care?"

He stared at her; she could feel it. That's all it was with him—feelings, impressions. There was no seeing through the ever-shifting shadows between them. And it didn't appear he was going to answer her, either.

"Fine, forget I said anything," she said. "Just let your boss know he can find himself a new WMD."

"WMD?"

"Weapon of Mass Destruction, Mr. I-Don't-Get-Out-Much." She sighed. "Why didn't you just deliver this message last night, instead of rudely waking me?"

"I had no idea you were aware of our existence, until you threatened me with Greed," he answered. "I thought you were merely a sensitive."

"A what?"

"A human who is sensitive to the Veil," he explained. "I think they're called mediums in these modern times."

"Like a ghost whisperer?' She crinkled her nose in distaste.

Surely there was something far more spectacular to be compared to than that? It also dawned on her that if her only points of reference for speaking with a real-life fucking demon was a bunch of TV shows, then she needed to find a new hobby ASAP. Zoe scrutinized the swirling darkness around him with narrowed eyes and wondered if that was the Veil he was talking about. The way it rippled almost mimicked the surface of dark water, yet when he moved, the seemingly liquid ripples changed to something more reminiscent of fog or smoke, wisps of black curling out and all around. It was hard to admit, but she was utterly fascinated.

"Some humans are still born with the gift, though most who claim to have it, do not."

She wasn't sure how to absorb that, nor could she really let it matter more than the threat of his purpose for being there. "You're going to deliver the message to Wrath, right?"

"I have no other choice," he replied after a moment's consideration. His tone reflected something darker and more troubling, triggering her next question.

"He's not the kill-the-messenger type, is he?"

"Hm." It was a single sound. A dark humph of amusement that managed to convey so much more. "Worried about me, little doe? But we've just met."

Holy . . . breathless. *Breathe, Zoe!*

She didn't know if it was the blood rushing through her ears or really happening, but she swore she heard the same faint whispers that had woken her the night before. After a moment, she was sure of it.

"What is that, what are you doing?" she demanded, peering around as the sound seemed to move.

He continued to study her, his head tilted as if he were trying to work out a puzzle. "Is there nothing you want?"

The funny thing about Zoe and nervousness was that it had a tendency to trigger the worst of her sarcasm. "Oh, there's plenty. The Giants to win the Superbowl, no more hunger, child abuse, or human trafficking. The ability to sleep without interruptions," she rattled off. "And if you want to throw in a lifetime supply of coffee, I wouldn't stop you. Why, are you a genie?"

"A Jinn? No."

"Well, thanks for getting my hopes up," she replied dryly. "Now you can explain how you got past the security."

She said it as if she knew exactly what that was,

when she really had no clue.

"Don't worry, it's still in place," he evaded. "I thought Pheldra had erected it to protect herself or her belongings, but I see now it's far too powerful for such a lessor demon."

Zoe ground her molars, understanding he hadn't meant it as an insult. Probably. "Good for you. Ease my mind a little more because you got in, so who else can do the same?"

"Without Greed knowing? No one."

"That's why Abaddon sent you," she deduced, watching the black fog floating around him. "That stuff cloaks you somehow."

He didn't seem to like that observation, because he stiffened before he withdrew. "Go back to your dreams, little doe. I'll not disturb them again."

What?

"Wait!" Zoe panicked for no sane reason. Earlier, she'd just wanted her uninterrupted sleep back. It was harder to feel disgruntled about that now that she knew who'd been disturbing it. "Haven't I at least earned the name of my stalker? I mean, you've robbed me of a lot of sleep these past two nights."

He probably wasn't even allowed to give her his name, considering what had just happened to Saphiel with his Seal. Demonic names were undoubtedly far too powerful to just give away.

His face was a hair away from hers in less than a heartbeat, the air clogging somewhere between her lungs and her throat. Heat spiked through her body, and desire purred like a jungle cat deep in her sex, so incredibly ready to pounce.

"Incubus," she whispered before she could stop it. Her earlier research rushed to the forefront of her dirty mind.

She felt him smile, and though she didn't have visual proof, it was impressively wicked. "You're getting warmer," he answered. "Hex. That is the name you will call me when you're ready to tell me what you want, what you truly desire more than anything else. And then, little doe . . ."

"Then?" she hesitated.

"Hmm. Sleep."

"I'm not—" Zoe cut herself off with the biggest yawn as a sudden lethargy seeped through her body. "Tired. Oh, you . . . fucker."

The deep caress of his amused laugh followed her right into a powerful sleep she couldn't fight, no matter how loudly her brain screamed at her to stay awake. Somewhere in her fading consciousness, she was aware of two important things. One: she was an idiot for forgetting that demons had the ability to make humans fall asleep. And two: the mild disappointment of knowing Hex wasn't even his real name. Though, she supposed it was easier than calling him *that hot, shadowy demon guy* in her head.

CHAPTER 2

CLEVER

Zoe woke the next morning fully rested, clear headed, and royally ticked off. She knew a total of two demons, outside of Saphiel, and both of them had forced her to take naps when she didn't want to! But hunting Hex down in the bowels of Hell to kick his ass would have to wait. She had to warn Kami and Saph of Wrath's plans. There was no way she was going to let some Abyss dweller up and ruin all the happiness her best friend had just found. For years, she'd helplessly watched Kami circle herself, being her own worst antagonist. Even if she hadn't turned out to be half-demon, it wouldn't have surprised Zoe in the least that Kami would only find true love with a Devil. Seriously, Zoe should be a hundred percent certifiable by now, but she was perfectly settled with the evidence that demons existed.

After almost dialing Kami's number a hundred times, she decided the news was simply too delicate to deliver over the phone. Mostly, she was worried that Saph might test his security system in some demonic way she'd never be able to explain to her neighbors or landlord. Becoming homeless just wasn't on her to-do list this weekend.

Though it still irked her beyond belief, whatever mojo Hex had used to make her sleep had left her feeling better rested than she'd felt in days. Her mind was working at warp speed, going over every little detail from the night before in case there were clues she wasn't aware of, but that Saph or Kami might catch when she told them. After a quick shower and making sure her clothes matched, Zoe armed herself with tech and caffeine, then left her apartment.

She gnawed on her lips and thoughts with equal persistence, fretting over what the news might stir up. Her brain envisioned a horrific hellish battle between Greed and Wrath. As entertaining as that would've been to the Zoe of two months ago, it now filled her with dread. Being the only human caught in the middle, she really hoped epic battles weren't in their near future. Or ever.

"Get back inside your apartment right now," Hex demanded, appearing directly in front of her without warning.

"Holy fucking shit fuck!" She jolted like a startled cat, hot coffee sloshing out of the lid of her travel mug, scolding the back of her hand.

Her heart didn't even pause to cop a feel in her throat before landing right in her mouth, where it obliterated the rest of her profanity and ability to breathe.

"Are you okay?"

She whirled wide eyes toward her neighbor, who'd apparently gotten a front row seat to her freak-out. He was busy locking his door, his expression managing to

look both offended and concerned at the same time.
Mark that off the bucket list!
"He can't see me," Hex supplied, though it felt as if he were staring the man down like he could.

Lovely. "Yeah, just clumsy. Burned myself, nothing to worry about," Zoe rambled, knowing she sounded as crazy as she looked and unable to stop it from happening. "Just remembered something important, don't mind me!"

She rushed back to her apartment and unlocked the door, giving her neighbor a mega-watt grin that undoubtedly screamed 'whack-job', before stumbling inside. Zoe slammed the door and collapsed against it for a second, because that's all it took for Hex to appear in her living room. The summer morning streaming through her windows dimmed like a storm cloud passing over the sun. The shadows stretched until the whole room was cloaked in darkness, yet they never abandoned Hex.

"Are you nuts?" she burst out, pushing away from the door and storming towards him. "You can't just do that, they're gonna lock me away in a loony bin!"

"You can't go to Avarice," he stated, unaffected by her outburst.

"My best friend has the right to know that Wrath is looking for her," she countered. "There's no way in hell I'm keeping that from her. It goes against every friend code ever written. Not to mention, I'm not ready to jump right to the top of Saphiel's hit list, fuck you very much!"

"Little doe," he growled quietly, the shadows expanding and darkening.

Foreboding and lust played a xylophone up and down Zoe's spine. His pet name for her was something she was desperately trying not to have a reaction to, because it was the wrong kind. Instead of finding some way to be insulted by it, her dumb ass actually liked it. A lot.

"Hex, I'm serious."

"A boat we're both in. Things have changed," he replied. "I can't let you go through with your plan."

No matter how tempting the demon was, or how much she never wanted to stop hearing him talk, Zoe couldn't allow herself to lose focus. Not when there was a massive threat hanging over her best friend's life and happiness.

"You can't stop me, Hex. You're not even here."

She had no way of proving it, but she had a hunch. The combination of the wave-like shadows and the fact that he hadn't set off Saphiel's alarms were her only scraps of circumstantial evidence. Zoe prayed she was right, because she'd already sent for the cavalry.

"But, I am so much more powerful than you." He sighed with regret rather than arrogance.

"Perhaps, but I am so much more clever," she returned, holding her phone up to show that she'd already sent a text to Kami without even looking, because she was the Goddess of All Things Media. Honest, she had a crown and everything.

For a moment, he remained perfectly still, and she could feel his gaze boring into hers. Then he vanished. Zoe couldn't explain the instant remorse that filled her. As the sunlight filtered through the receding gloom in her apartment, she blinked at the spot Hex had just been and felt her chest tighten with acute disappointment. Her phone vibrated, pulling her out of the confusing aftermath of emotions. Hex believed she'd sent a cry for help, but she really hadn't. Her text to Kami had simply asked if she could come over to hang out, because she missed the pub and wanted another chance to switch Saph's Manchester United flag out for a New York Giants pennant.

Lee's on his way to pick you up. Please refrain from sexually harassing him . . . again.

Zoe grinned and replied with a devil face emoji. After taking a healthy drink of her cooling coffee, she decided to leave it behind. She was going to need something a lot stronger to look a Devil in the eye and tell him his brother was hoping to steal his woman away from him. Zoe hadn't been kidding when she'd mentioned the whole killing-of-the-messenger fear to Hex, nor did she need to see Saphiel in action to believe it. She was a hundred percent content with taking Kami's word for his knack of killing first, asking questions never.

Unable to fight the restlessness, she decided to leave her apartment again and wait for Lee outside in the fresh air. She was one flight down when she heard people coming up the lower levels. Even for a Legion, it would be too soon for Lee's arrival.

Zoe was a serious bad ass, it wasn't just for show. She wasn't easily intimidated, because she'd learned how to scrap her way through a large, loud and crazy family as the youngest of eight kids. That didn't mean she was stupid. Her size always made her aware of her surroundings, and she didn't like being on the losing end of the odds in places without escape routes. Like stairwells. The situation always made her a little nervous, so she carried pepper spray in her purse at all times. She palmed it now, just in case.

As the approaching footsteps grew louder, she found herself fighting a slight chill. She didn't realize the threat was coming from the other direction until it was too late.

With one step to go to the next landing, Zoe was caught mid-air from behind, her right foot never making contact with the metal. Arms banded around her, lifting her back into a solid body. Her startled scream was muffled by a hand that clamped over her face, filling her nostrils with the scent of sexy male and wicked, midnight fantasies.

The stairwell dimmed, fading to black in a hurry, but she wasn't losing consciousness—she was being devoured by shadows. They snuffed everything out around her, and the sound of the other footsteps disappeared along with the stairwell. Everything seemed to slip far, far away, yet it wasn't soundless. The rush of wind was undoubtedly caused by their momentum. She and her captor were moving super fast, but she couldn't say in which direction. Her equilibrium was confused without anything for her eyes to latch on to, so Zoe gave in to her next instinct. Fight like hell. She started kicking and jabbing her elbows into the unyielding body behind her, screaming profanities, threats, and demands into his hot palm. The only reason she'd yet to lose her mind to real fear was because she knew exactly who it was.

Hex.

The bastard was abducting her, proving himself more powerful *and* more clever. *Fucker!* He'd purposely waited for her to leave her apartment where he wouldn't have to worry about setting off Saphiel's alarms, and failing to foresee that possibility pissed her off. She should have just waited for Lee where it was safe, and now she had to suck that up as her own mistake.

Zoe paused in her mental ass-chewing when they stopped moving. The shadows thinned enough to reveal the interior of a house where the darkness appeared natural, even though Hex's shadows still danced over her limited vision like a gossamer veil. She went back to struggling and cursing him. Beyond his enticing scent and the warmth of his defined body were the aromas of a floral sweetened breeze, the ocean, and a kind of humid heat that brought tropical islands to mind. It settled on her skin, heavier and damper than she was used to. Where in the world could they be?

"It had to be this way, doe, you left me no choice," Hex said. "I told you to return to your apartment. I thought you'd understand the importance of staying there."

Zoe fumed, but stopped fighting. After several moments, he hazarded pulling his hand away from her mouth. She remained still and quiet. When he released her the rest of the way, she whipped around and released a stream of pepper spray right at his eyes. The shadows instantly solidified like a wall to protect him, yet she kept on spraying, hoping at least some of it managed to get through. When the can was depleted, the shadows began to recede, going beyond their usual state to where Zoe could actually see Hex, despite the nighttime darkness. She could see the definitions of his prominent cheekbones, his hard jawline, the way his dark hair fell over his forehead and his eyes, which appeared light in color. Where the shadows had made him seem quite large in build, she found he was a tad leaner, but still packed with muscles and broad shoulders. Hex lifted his hand and traced a finger over the bridge of his nose, where a drop of pepper spray had successfully landed before the shadows had solidified all the way. He stuck the drop into his mouth and immediately made a sour face.

"That's disgusting," he remarked. "What is its purpose?"

"AAAAAAAAAAAAAAGGGGGGGHHHHHHHHH!" Zoe exploded, throwing the empty canister across the room.

Hex's hand fell to his side. "It was not my intention to frighten you—"

"I'm not frightened, you asshole, I'm pissed," she managed, her voice hoarse from the excessive fuming she'd already done behind his hand.

His expression was contrary as he shook his head. "I can hear all the layers of your voice, little doe."

"Zoe! My name is Zoe. I'm not your little anything!" she spat, turning from him to put some distance between them as fast as possible.

She dug her phone out of her handbag, never hearing him move. The second she had it in hand, Hex was right there to snatch it away from her.

"No," he said.

"Excuse the fuck out of you, who the hell do you

think you are?"

"The one trying to keep us both alive and in one piece," he answered, holding her phone up too high for her to reach.

Zoe was shorter than short. She'd already spent a lifetime having this game played on her. Cruel older siblings who thought it was hilarious to play keep away from her with various belongings. It had never gotten old for them, but Zoe had gotten sick of it right quick and learned that no one could hold anything out of her reach if they were doubled over in pain. Before she could devise the best attack plan, she watched in horrified shock as the shadows thickened around his hand and swallowed her phone from his grasp.

"NO! What have you done?" she demanded, her chest tightening so bad it brought tears to her eyes.

"Don't worry, it's safe. Just beyond your reach for now."

"Hex!"

Her anger lost to grief. Yes, she grieved for her electronics, for Zoe Bankes was nothing without them, but it went deeper. There was an immense need to warn Kami about Wrath's plans and he'd just taken her only chance away.

"No harm will come to your phone, li—Zoe," he amended, when she shot him a death glare.

"No, just my best friend!" she choked out, her eyes brimming with tears, which only pissed her off more.

She wasn't a crier, damn it, but when it came to those she loved, it was difficult to keep her emotions in check. There were few people on earth she loved as much as

Kami, who was more like family than a friend. The kind of sister Zoe wished she'd had growing up.

Hex gave her a puzzled look. "You're worried about the Queen of Avarice."

"Her name is Kami," Zoe fumed. "And yes, how could I not be? She's . . ."

Zoe realized she was trying to explain friendship, something so fundamentally human, to a goddamn demon and ground her teeth.

"She's what?"

"Just forget it," she snapped, rubbing at her cheeks to erase all evidence of tears. He didn't deserve them. "You couldn't possibly understand. I doubt you have a single fucking friend."

It was harsh, but she couldn't care less. He'd gone from hot and mysterious to her number one arch-nemesis in zero-point-two seconds. The fact that he remained hot, tempting, and mysterious despite it, only added insult to injury.

"Friends," Hex muttered to himself.

Zoe looked at him, ready to launch another snappy retort, only to watch him disappear into the shadows again.

"Hex?" she gasped in utter disbelief, rushing to the spot he'd just been. "Hex!"

He'd left her. *Un-fucking-believable!*

Irate, Zoe turned to search for the closest exit and rammed her shin into a piece of furniture. The instant pain throbbed up and down her leg.

"Oh, ooh, ow!" she hissed and seethed through clenched teeth, clutching the wounded spot with both hands.

Once the ache subsided, she inched around the space with extra care until she located the first lamp. Illuminated, the room turned into two—a living room opened to the kitchen and a hallway leading straight back from the former. It was a small house with unadorned picture windows showcasing a moonless night sky beyond. Zoe hit every light switch she came across until the interior glowed.

The furniture was basic, the décor non-existent. There were no personal items anywhere to indicate that anyone actually lived there. Even the air smelled a bit stale and musty, despite the sea breeze sneaking in through gaps in the windows and under the door.

A quick search through all the rooms turned up zero communication devices. No phones, fax machines or Wi-Fi modems. How did people live that way? Zoe shuddered at the thought and poked her nose around the kitchen, but there were only expired cans and boxed goods. The fridge boasted an open box of baking soda and a half-empty bottle of water.

The only exterior door was between the kitchen and living room and she was really surprised to find it unlocked. Then again, there was nothing in the house to steal. That didn't stop the New Yorker in her from cringing over the practice. Outside, the scenery was breathtaking, though familiar enough.

Across a deep deck, she paused at the top of wooden stairs that zigzagged to the sandy beach far below. They'd been built to follow the natural descent of the rocky outcropping the house had been built upon. A dark ocean stretched as far as the eye could see, and Zoe could just barely make out the distant shapes of either large rocks or maybe islands. The beach continued beyond her sight to the left, before creating a natural bay and jutting forward to a point, where it disappeared again.

She had to be on the other side of the globe. It was the only explanation for how they'd gone from morning in New York to middle of the night in this tropical mystery land in less than ten minutes. Talk about gaining frequent flier miles in a hurry. It sucked that she felt envious for the kidnapping bastard's ability to travel anywhere at any time without the typical hassles. On second thought, that just made him more of a bastard.

The lush, tropical surroundings could belong to too many different locations to give her any clues. As she descended the stairs, her eyes wandered, searching for lights or any other signs of life. It was either too late at night, or—her worst fear—she was the only person there. Was it an island? Ugh, that would figure. After Zoe made it down to the beach, she noticed there wasn't even a dock or shored dinghy. No evidence that anyone lived on or visited the place. Of course, if it truly belonged to Hex, then he would have no need of those things.

With some effort, she shoved the frustration of her circling thoughts away, knowing she wouldn't get any answers unless the demon decided to come back—and his ass *better* be coming back, or she would have no qualms taking advantage of her connections to an actual Devil to see him hunted down and skinned alive!

Satisfied with that conviction, Zoe toed off her shoes when the sand got too thick to walk through. Since it was mid-June, she was already dressed for the weather, thank goodness. Nothing would've been worse than landing on Gilligan's nightmare in a parka and snow boots. Zoe reveled in the feel of her bare feet sinking into the warm grains of sand. It had been too long since she'd felt that sensation, having grown up on the Golden Coast with her large, unruly, and superbly poor family. She was surprised to feel the hint of nostalgia, to discover that a part of her might have been missing her birthplace in some way without even being aware of it.

For as long as she could remember, Zoe had been in love with the idea of living in New York. Even though California was teeming with people, it was such a different atmosphere. She'd been dazzled by the thought of living in a city where innovation and history stood shoulder to shoulder. Where the most diverse population in the country influenced entire neighborhoods, as if they were chunks of foreign lands plucked up from around the world and quilted into the fabric of the five boroughs. She thrived in the chaos, the constant noise and movement.

Everything new happened in the Big Apple first, then spread to the rest of the country. By the time trends made it to SoCal, they'd already been seen in L.A., and passé in Manhattan. Zoe had wanted to be a part of—and in—the moment at all times. Even Hollywood hadn't been enough to keep her on the west side of the country, despite being a major Sci-Fi fan. Besides, she was so much more than her geeky pastimes. It was just easier to let people take her at face value.

And to be honest, her face value was pretty fucking

awesome.

Zoe glanced around again, but the scenery hadn't changed. A breeze rustled the tropical vegetation her little prison was nestled into, drowning out her sigh as she plopped down on the sand. The warm tide rolled over her toes while her concern grew deeper that Hex had just up and marooned her on a deserted island without so much as a coconut radio to call for help.

She couldn't stand the thought that while she sat on her ass in the middle of someone else's version of paradise, her best friend could be getting the worst surprise of her life. Why hadn't she just called Kami when she had the chance? Zoe could kick her own ass for that decision now. She'd wasted so many opportunities to warn her bestie out of some stupid notion that the news would've been better received in person. The news would've been better received, period!

Ugh.

Zoe dug up a handful of damp sand and flung it toward the receding waves. The breeze picked up in the forest surrounding the beach, but she couldn't feel it. She kept waiting for it to caress her skin or play with her hair, yet it never did. It took her a moment to realize that it wasn't wind at all, but the same whispers she'd heard in her room. She glanced over her shoulder toward the nearest outcropping of trees to see if the leaves were even moving, and got a small start to find Hex there, and a lot closer than she would've believed.

"Jesus, could you find a creepier way to make an entrance?" she griped.

Zoe fought a shiver even as she ignored the relief

coursing through her. She didn't want him to think she was happy to see him, no matter the truth.

"I can't make noise walking on a beach," he countered.

"Not that," she sighed, standing and wiping the sand from her clothes. "The whispers, it's just eerie."

Hex froze in his tracks and stared at her with such intensity she had to repress a shudder. "You shouldn't be able to hear that."

"Yeah? Well, you might want to have that looked at, because my hearing works just fine."

"What do the whispers say?"

"Nothing. It's just a sound, but I can never make out any of the words."

That seemed to trouble him even more. "You've heard it before?"

Zoe narrowed her eyes. "I don't think I like where this interrogation is going. If you're about to call me some kind of ghost whisperer again, I think we'll have to bump our argument up to a fist fight."

"Whether you like it or not is irrelevant. Your answer is important," he stated.

"Ooh, you know what else is important? My phone. Contact with the outside world, my best friend in particular. Not being kidnapped and then abandoned on a deserted island with no Wi-Fi!" Zoe argued back. "You want answers, how about coughing up some of your own first?"

All she did was blink, and Hex was gone. Her mouth dropped open, pure disbelief paralyzing her for a moment. Then the anger started boiling toward the surface. Zoe was two seconds away from unleashing it when he suddenly reappeared right beside her. She yelped, jumping in the opposite direction as her heart tried to launch out of her chest.

"Fuck, Hex, for God's sake!" she exploded. The instant shot of adrenaline made her feel dizzy. "Are you trying to kill me?"

"On the contrary, I'm trying to keep you very much alive," he answered, disappearing again directly afterward.

Oh, she was on to this game now and couldn't wait to drive her fist right into his gut for scaring her on purpose. She whipped around, her eyes darting through the darkness in preparation for his reappearance. The whispers came first this time, forewarning both his arrival and general location. Yet, he still managed to surprise her somewhat when he changed direction at the last second and appeared right behind her. He gripped her shoulders to keep her steady, and heat erupted through her skin on contact, making a beeline right for her sex.

"And now I have my answer," he said, tucking his head beside hers, his warm breath playing along the side of her neck and ear in the most damaging way.

The totality of his presence vanquished her irritation and reignited the lust she'd been ignoring since the night before.

"Good for you," she forced out, proud when it didn't emerge as breathless as she felt. "I'm still waiting for mine."

"I told you," he reiterated, turning her to face him. "I brought you here to keep you safe."

"I don't care about that, Hex!" She was exasperated for so many reasons.

One, his steady calmness only made her more antsy, and two, she was getting real tired of trying to see him clearly though the constant haze of black smoke. There was no light on the beach, but her eyes had adjusted to the dark, allowing her to get more impressions of his features, like the fact that his mouth was both full and wide, making it a dangerous seduction without even trying. But it was still all too fuzzy, and she was already farsighted, as it was.

"You don't care about your own life?" His tone was skeptical.

"I'm obsessed with it, but I think you're just using that as an excuse to keep me away from the one who's life is really in danger, for no logical reason."

"Zoe, you are very much in danger," he affirmed. "Do you really think those were humans racing up the stairs to get you? Those were Legion, and they didn't belong to Greed, who, by your own admission, is protecting your friend and keeping her safe. That makes you the only leverage Wrath has to get what he wants. Abaddon is not a Devil to be forsaken, especially when it comes to rare and irreplaceable weapons."

Zoe's brows creased at that last bit, because his tone had taken on a darker, more bitter edge. Still, the need to convince him of his stupidity outweighed her curiosity.

"Kami would never let anything happen to me. If you had let me go to her, I would already be just as protected by Saphiel as she is."

Something dark crossed his features. "No." His tone

was severe. "I do not share your faith in that. Not when I am well aware of Greed's predilections."

"What's that supposed to mean?"

"That means your friend does not have the final say in that relationship, nor will she ever. I refuse to bet your life against the notoriously merciless Greed on the odds that he can be swayed by a subjugated concubine."

The shock was immediate, like a bucket of ice water to her face. Zoe wrenched out of his hold, her hands curling into fists at her sides. The desire to slap him came over her so strongly, it was startling. Instead, she jumped up onto the tips of her toes and stuck her finger in his face, like she wasn't a whole foot and half shorter than him.

"I don't fucking care who or what you are, you don't *ever* talk about my best friend that way!"

She stormed off in a spray of sand before she did something she'd regret, and couldn't recall ever feeling as disgusted or incensed as she did in that moment. It made her feel sick to her stomach, that's how strong it was. How dare he talk about Kami that way? He didn't even know her! Zoe was left to wonder just what kind of women Saphiel had been hooking up with before her bestie saved him from the dumpster diving. She paused to collect her shoes where she'd kicked them off and shook her head, immediately regretting those thoughts because it wasn't fair. None of Hex's issues were Saphiel's fault by any stretch of the imagination. Not only would he never treat Kami in such a horrible way, he'd been kinder to Zoe than any Devil had to be.

Hex wanted to talk like he knew better than she did,

when he was really quite ignorant. Perhaps, that had been the darkness she'd seen crossing his features—the idea that a mere human could be more knowledgeable about a Devil than a demon was.

Back inside the house, she slammed and locked the door, then dumped her sandy shoes on the hardwood floor beside it. During her earlier search for a phone, she'd noticed that the only bathroom was an en-suite in the only bedroom. She made her way to it, locking both doors behind her. After ensuring there were clean towels available, she peeled her sandy clothes off and tugged the band free that had been keeping her curls out of the way. She set the tap to lukewarm and climbed under the spray, letting it clean her skin and cool her temper.

The lousiest part was that Hex's slanderous insults couldn't even top what bothered her the most, which was the sheer helplessness. She couldn't stand it. It felt like her insides were churning with razor-sharp rocks. It grated on every single one of her natural instincts. Not being able to do anything to help herself or Kami was like being slowly crushed under a sinking weight.

Once she had all the sand and sticky humidity washed from her skin, Zoe turned off the taps. The towels were average-sized, which on her, was the equivalent of a beach towel. She was just wrapping the soft material around herself when a knock came at the bathroom door, causing her to jump.

"For fuck . . . Go away, Hex!" she snapped. His sneaking up on her all he damn time was getting old fast.

Hadn't she locked the bedroom door? Her head snapped up when the light fixture above the sink's mirror flickered and dimmed. Then her mouth dropped open when Hex walked right through the solid door, the shadows swirling like mad around him.

Seriously?!

"Not until you explain what just happened."

Astounded, it took a few seconds for Zoe's brain to snap out of it. "Are you serious?" she demanded, gesturing toward the door. "GET OUT!"

"I wouldn't be here if I wasn't serious," he said, once again completely unaffected by her emotional outburst. "And this is where you are, I want to talk, so no."

"Haven't you ever heard of privacy?" Zoe snapped, then held her hand up and took a breath. "Never mind, I forgot I was talking to the pervert that's been spying on me for at least two days. I don't even want to know what you've seen, let alone how many times you've already watched me shower."

"I've never watched you shower, nor am I doing so now," he pointed out. "I waited until you were covered. I'm well aware of humans' strange behaviors and practices when it comes to their bodies."

"If you weren't watching, then how did you know when I was covered?" she countered.

"I heard you," he replied, as if that should be obvious.

"Uh-huh," she scoffed, unconvinced. "Move."

To her surprise, he stepped aside and allowed her to exit the bathroom, though he didn't hesitate to follow her. He brought the shadows along with him, dimming the bedroom lights next. The annoyance of that gave her an idea.

"You want to talk?" she asked, turning to face him.

"I already said as much."

"Then lose the shadows," she leveraged. "And give me five minutes to get dressed, not necessarily in that order."

Hex just stood there, and she could feel his gaze roaming over the parts of her damp body not covered by the towel, but she was not affected.

Liar.

"Hello? Earth to demon boy," she snapped her fingers.

"I have not been a boy for longer than the last thousand generations of your family have been on Earth," he remarked. "I will lose the shadows when you lose the attitude."

Zoe's brow arched in displeasure, even as her mind raced. Did that mean he'd been human before becoming a demon? Was that even possible?

"I'll lose the attitude when I'm damn good and ready," she returned. "I am not now, nor will I ever be, yours or anyone else's subjugated concubine!"

The shadows raced for the corners and crevices of the room, which brightened with a quickness. Before she could really claim to be ready, Zoe came face to face with the full power of Hex's wicked grin. The palest of pale blue eyes glinted at her with sensual contradiction. When he stepped forward, his muscles rippled under the material of his shirt. Heat unfurled through her chest and spread, encompassing her naughty lady bits. What had she just claimed?

"Mmm, I'm not sure you believe that, little doe," he

observed. "I brought you some clothes. They're in the closet. You have five minutes, after which I will return, whether you're dressed or not."

Neither his tone, nor the dirty smirk on his full mouth, left any doubt as to which he'd prefer. When he exited the room the conventional way, Zoe noticed the ink along his arms and neck. It looked like some kind of dead language. Symbols she didn't recognize in truth, but found familiar due to those supernatural movies and shows she loved so much.

She needed a moment to catch her breath and remember why she was supposed to be infuriated with him, rather than picturing him naked.

As much as it went against everything she believed in, Zoe made sure she was dressed and out of the room in under five minutes. The comfortable, loose-fitting tank top and denim shorts were her exact size. She didn't even want to know how he'd managed that. Nor did she want to picture him picking out the bras and panties she'd found, either. Since each article of clothing still had their tags, she was quite content theorizing that he'd used his shadow mojo to rob a department store.

Finding Hex in the kitchen making a sandwich was the last thing she'd been expecting when she emerged from the room. Her relief was undeniable that he was still shadowless and didn't seem to mind all the lights in the house blazing.

"So, you ditched me to go shopping," she observed. "I don't suppose you picked up a laptop, tablet, cellphone and Wi-Fi router while you were out?"

"That would've been pointless," he replied. "We're

on an uninhabited island in Papua New Guinea with no cell towers."

Zoe gaped at him. "Then why the hell did you take my phone?"

"Because we're not staying, and it was distracting you. I left to get the provisions you needed." He looked up at her and there was no mistaking the unbidden desire in his eyes. "Food and water. The clothes are only for your comfort, not something I would deem a necessity."

Zoe snorted and climbed onto one of the bar stools at the counter. "Oh, buddy, you have no idea just how far away you are from ever seeing me naked by my choice."

Damn, she was getting good at this lying shit. Someone should give her a fucking Oscar.

"Hm." He made that same amused sound he'd made in her room the night before. It was no less appealing the second time around. "Eat."

He slid the plate toward her, then put the ingredients away. When he returned from the fridge, he set a bottle of water in front of her.

"How do you know I even like this or that I'm not allergic?" she asked, just to be stubborn.

"I watched you eat one of these yesterday. I noticed that you don't eat well or often."

"First, I eat just fine," she returned. "Second, thanks for confirming your spying habits."

"I never denied all of them," he replied, unrepentant.

Zoe gave him a scowl she felt conveyed her thoughts well enough. Then she picked up the peanut butter and peach jam sandwich to take a bite and almost blew her own ploy of reluctance by moaning. Why did food always taste better when someone else made it? She couldn't hide the grumble of her stomach when the creamy peanut butter and sweet jam hit her taste buds, which had Hex's brow rising slowly in a smug way.

"I believe that's my point," he commented, as if anyone was actually keeping score.

Bastard.

After taking a long drink of water, Zoe recapped the bottle and tilted it. "You could have at least gotten soda."

"You drink enough caffeine as it is."

She gasped and gave him the dirtiest look she could muster. "That's blasphemy, take it back."

"No." He smirked, appearing amused despite how much she wasn't joking. "Finish eating. You agreed we'd talk."

"Oh, my God, I can talk and eat at the same time, I'm not five," she said. "Are all you demons so damn bossy?"

"Are all you humans so damn mouthy?"

"Oh no, Hexy, there are no other humans like me. You can't top this, buddy. You lucked out."

He grimaced. "Don't call me Hexy."

"Why not? It's not like it's your real name anyway," she countered with an arch of her brow, daring him to say otherwise.

He studied her for a moment, before looking down at his upturned hands. More tattoos lined the outside of them, all the way up to the tip of his pinky fingers.

"It's the only one I remember." His tone was solemn, cutting through all the humor right away. "And the one I've had the longest, so in truth, it's more my real name than any I had before it."

Well, shitballs. So much for going at him with guns blazing. It was a little difficult to take jabs at him in the wake of a confession like that. Zoe set the remainder of her sandwich and sarcasm aside and released a heavy sigh.

"Hex, what you said about my best friend . . . that was really awful," she stated. "I mean like really, *really* awful and not even remotely true."

He frowned. "Everything I spoke was the absolute truth, Zoe, as it will always be truth. Lying is a human invention designed to protect fragile egos. Demons have no need of such things. Like all Angels, Saphiel is dominant by nature, he would never have a mate unwilling to submit to him. Like all mates of Devils, that makes your friend a concubine. Please explain how this information is making you angry."

"Well, for starters, it's the twenty-first century, no one uses the degrading term concubine anymore. Then, there was the whole deliverance," she explained. "You know, when you spat *subjugated concubine* like it's the worst kind of insult, after denying her ability to have any sway over Saph whatsoever."

Hex shook his head. "It was never meant as an insult. I was merely stating the facts of the situation. Concubines are revered in Hell. They hold the same powerful status as their kings to all other demons, but they cannot overrule their Devils. Devils aren't known for taking pity on the plights of humans. Especially against one of their own. Abaddon and Saphiel are brothers. So, I stand by my original statement. I am not wagering your life against those odds."

"I trust Kami with my life above anyone else on this planet," Zoe argued. "Which means I trust Saphiel with it, too, because if he ever let anything happen to me, she would never forgive him for it."

"Never?" he questioned. "Zoe, I think you're forgetting just how long that is for demons. Even in a human body, your friend is going to outlive you by centuries. Her Devil will be forgiven."

Zoe's mouth fell open, undeniable hurt cutting through her chest. "Are you trying to make sure I hate you, Hex? Because you're doing a bang-up job of it."

"The last thing I want is for you to hate me, Zoe. I speak truths you don't want to accept, that is not the same thing. Nor does it change the fact that they are, indeed, truths."

"You can't speak the truth about people you don't even know," she corrected. "You've never met Kami and I'm beginning to doubt you've ever met Saphiel. Perhaps the real problem here is that you can't accept that I might be the one speaking truths. That Saphiel's love for Kami has changed him into something better than whatever demon mommies tell their demon babies at bedtime."

"It doesn't matter either way," he stated. "You're not going to them. You are staying with me until the threat is over."

"The threat is to Kami—"

"No!" Hex slammed his hand on the counter, startling her. "Wrath knows he can't touch Avarice's queen. I reported as much back to him as I told you I would. I had hoped that would be the end of it, but he will not rest until he gets what he wants. He sent me back —for *you*, Zoe. I was meant to abduct you for Abaddon, to use as bait or leverage, but instead, I chose to risk *everything* to keep you safe. So, I don't want to hear another fucking word about Kami!"

Stunned, Zoe's mind circled his words like a coyote circled a rabbit den. It was the everything he'd emphasized that stood out the loudest, his tone indicating there was so much more to it than just putting himself in danger by going against his boss's orders.

"Why?" It was the only question she could think to ask. "Why would you risk anything at all for a human you don't even know? Why not just let Wrath try to use me to get what he wants, so everyone lives happily ever after?"

It didn't sound sensible, no, but in her mind any scenario where Saph and Kami were able to save her would result in everyone living happily ever after. She thoroughly believed and trusted in that.

"You would not live at all, let alone happily."

"Why do you care? What is it about me that would force you to make the decision to risk everything—which is something major, Hex, I'm not stupid. There's a bigger game being played here. If I'm some kind of pawn on a demonic chessboard, then I damn well want to know what the prize is!"

"Your life is the prize, Zoe, is that not enough?" he bit out. "Do you value that so little?"

"No, I just know when I'm being denied the whole story, and I'm warning you right now, Hex, I'm not the type to sit by quietly. If you want my trust, you're going to have to convince me that you actually fucking deserve it."

"I just saved your life, I'm the only one who fucking deserves it," he growled.

When the shadows billowed around him, Zoe couldn't get off the stool fast enough.

"Oh, the hell you will!" she declared, scrambling right over the island counter and lunging for what little of Hex she could still see, just before the shadows swallowed them both.

CHAPTER 3

TEMPTATION

Something in Hex shifted when Zoe rushed over the counter and lunged, her arms wrapping around his neck just in time to be shut up inside the Veil along with him. She'd kicked her plate along the way, sending it crashing to the floor and knocking her water bottle over in the process. In the darkness of the Shallows, their breaths mingled. Zoe's was labored, but Hex's was a rush of quiet awe.

Then, she started slapping at his chest.

"You don't get to run off the second the conversation doesn't go your way!" she accused. "What kind of pussy ass shit is that?"

Utterly undone, Hex laughed. The feeling sprang up out of nowhere, overtaking him with its complexity. Happiness, awe, admiration, fear, arousal—so many emotions he hadn't felt in too many centuries to count, and never all at once.

"You're laughing at me?" Zoe balked in disbelief, her sable eyes filled with the ire of a goddess.

Hex had never wanted to kiss anyone as much as he

wanted to fuse his lips to hers and dive into that hot little mouth that could grind a man up like a shredder. But he wasn't a man and she would find out soon enough that he couldn't be pulverized by her sharp, cutting words, either.

He didn't think twice about tightening his arms around her when she tried to push free of him. It didn't matter how angry she was, she wouldn't survive in the Shallows without him as her anchor. He hadn't sacrificed everything to save her, just to lose her to the fucking Veil.

"At you, no," he answered, still grinning, still captivated by her. "But Hades' breath, Zoe, you're a firestorm of fury and righteousness, who just ran headlong into the Veil after a demon. I don't know if that makes you brave or reckless, but you're absolutely right; there is no other human like you."

"Duh, dumbass!"

He laughed harder. She couldn't even give him that. Couldn't accept it as a compliment rather than an astute observation, even though she felt it. Zoe tried to feign indifference, but he knew better. He could hear, see, and read every layer of her—that hadn't been a lie. She wanted to fight, to cling to her anger, but she felt the connection between them. Hex had felt it the very moment he'd entered her apartment, drawn not to Pheldra's energy signature, but in the opposite direction, to where this petite creature lay sleeping all snug in her bed.

"You need to stop laughing," she warned, but there wasn't much grit to it anymore.

Hex could see Zoe was fighting her own smile and that had something strange expanding in his chest. He studied her face, too contrary and bold to be beautiful. Like her, everything was blunt. Her nose, her cheekbones, her chin. But the whole of it, framed by those dark brown curls still damp from her shower, was nothing short of riveting. In his arms, she felt even smaller than she looked, and he marveled at how something so tiny and fragile could house so much courageous fire.

"And why is that?" he challenged.

He enjoyed how much she thought she was the boss. He didn't mind letting her think it—most of the time. But Hex wasn't one of the many human boys that he imagined tripped over themselves to get on her good side. He hadn't missed the way she'd taken notice of that whenever he gave her a taste of his confidence. It was there now, as he slipped his hand into her hair to feel the contrast of cool silk slide through his fingers, before cradling the back of her head. Her body stiffened, her eyes scanning him with uncertainty and wariness. She thought he meant to kiss her, but he wasn't, no matter how much he burned for it. They had some serious conversations ahead of them first, and he refused to allow their intimacies to become one of her regrets.

Hex formed words in his mind, trying to put things he'd never spoken aloud to anyone in order. The crux was that he couldn't say the most important things he needed to. He was physically incapable of spelling out what might be their easiest escape route—Abaddon had made sure of it as an insurance policy against Hex seeking the only thing that might guarantee his freedom. That's why he had to get Zoe to understand the extent of danger they were in. He very much needed her on his side, because she might be the only one who could save them both.

Hex lifted her a bit higher and walked out of the Shallows, releasing the Veil completely as he carried her to the island counter. He sat her on the edge, tucking himself right in between her thighs where he longed to be the most, then settled a firm grip on her hips to keep her in place. What he was about to reveal wasn't going to just anger her this time, it might actually make her hate him.

"I didn't leave because the conversation wasn't going my way, Zoe," he confessed. "I left because I don't know how to convey honest, vitally important things to you without making you angrier than you already are."

"Presumptuous much?"

Hex just stared at her rather than repeat his earlier words about all the things she could never hide from him. "There is a bigger game at play, of that you're absolutely correct. Abaddon has been orchestrating his own end game for eons and wouldn't think twice about sacrificing a human to get what he wants."

"And what does he want?" she asked. "Aside from my best friend?"

"To win. To fulfill his destiny by leading the battle against the unworthy on Judgment Day. In order to do that, he's convinced he needs every powerful weapon in existence at his disposal."

"So, still my best friend," she remarked.

Hex wished he could share her humor. Especially when he looked into her eyes and couldn't claim to recognize his own reflection there.

"She's not the only powerful weapon in existence,"

he said. "Abaddon is a collector, and he's been at it for a very long time, but not all of them are like Pheldra. Not all of them found a happy home in the Abyss, Zoe, only a prison. While she enjoyed living and fighting with the other soldiers day in and day out, while she found purpose there, everyone else was kept like relics in a museum. Weapons, locked in cases in Wrath's armory with nothing but the slow drag of time to keep them company."

"I have a strange feeling this is leading to an actual point," she said, though it was more apprehensive than sarcastic.

"You deduced it yourself, already," he reminded her. "Abaddon sent me to collect Pheldra, because I'm the only demon in existence who could get into your apartment without setting off Saphiel's alarms. Just as Pheldra is, I am one of a kind. An extremely powerful weapon."

Her eyes latched onto the tattoos running up the side of his neck before dropping to his arms. She couldn't see those tattoos unless he were to lift his arms, but then he'd lose his grip on her. It was enough to know she was aware of the sigils eternally etched into his skin, binding him to the Veil.

He watched her throat work as she swallowed heavily. "What kind of extremely powerful weapon?"

"It's complicated," he replied, because it truly was. "Abaddon's sole concern is that I'm the only Veil Strider. Death and the Reapers can pass through at certain junctions, but the only creature to ever exist who can travel every inch of the Veil and survive, is me. I could live in its greatest depths for eternity and never perish."

Zoe frowned. "But I was just in it. You said so yourself."

"The Shallows, yes, because you were anchored to me. And it was only for a short time. But even with me, you would never survive going any deeper than that or staying too long in the Shallows. It's the land of the dead, Zoe. It would poison your mind and drain your health, until you became nothing more than a wraith."

"Then how the hell did we end up on the other side of the world in a matter of minutes?" she demanded.

Hex let out a sigh that was both exasperation and humor. The way her mind worked awed and frustrated him. She saw too much, connected things she shouldn't be able to connect and questioned everything, inspecting each new piece of information for holes or gaps. And she wasn't satisfied until they were all filled.

"Because I'm ancient, little doe. I know every nook and cranny of the Veil, every shortcut and express route to every destination in this realm and all others."

"And use it," she commented shrewdly. "You use it like a shield."

He nodded. "More like a cloak, but yes," he confirmed. "Because it's a part of me or I'm a part of it, I'm not altogether sure which."

Her eyes widened a fraction. "So, you're not from the Abyss at all, you . . . I thought you worked for Abaddon?"

Hex shrugged a shoulder. "When you want out of prison, you're willing to do anything for the warden, and I desperately wanted out of prison, Zoe." He willed her to understand. To *feel* it the way he needed her to. "More to the point, I didn't want to go back once I was out. As far as weapons go, I knew Abaddon would prefer Pheldra over me. Once I had her in the Veil, he would've had no other choice but to exchange my freedom for her return. Pheldra would've been happy with the arrangement, had Greed not found her first."

He'd already felt Zoe stiffen, her gaze piercing into his with clear understanding and banked conviction, waiting to strike at a moment's notice. "And if she hadn't been happy with the arrangement, what then?" she asked, her tone hollow. "You would've bartered with her freedom to gain yours, anyway?"

"Yes."

"You need to move," she hissed through her teeth. "Now."

Though he'd already anticipated that exact reaction, Hex was reluctant to leave it at that. A pattern he didn't like was developing and if things didn't change, they were in danger of running the same gamut over and over —she gets angry and he leaves; he returns, and she just gets angrier. He had nothing left to anger her about, so he could only hope they were going to progress into less hostile territory soon.

"Before I do, I need you to know that I took no pleasure in telling you this. I don't enjoy making you angry, and I still never want you to hate me. I gave you the truth, as you asked. Not only because you deserve it, but so you can finally understand the kind of trouble we're in."

"We're in trouble, because you put us there!"

"To save your life, absolutely, and I would do it again, Zoe," he vowed.

"Why?" she demanded. "That's the one question you can't seem to answer, Hex. Why?"

He stared into her eyes, frustrated with the knowledge that she wouldn't accept his reason if he told her now, but that didn't make it any less of a fact. She was his. He'd known it the moment he'd felt her presence, but she was far from ready to hear those simple, honest words.

"For the same reason why I would never trade *you* for my freedom," he answered, then did as she asked and stepped back, let his hands drop to his sides. "I have to leave to do what I'd been trying to do when you stopped me, and that's begin the preparations for our next location. We can't stay here too long. I've no doubt Abaddon has already mobilized more of his Legion and contacted his spies. I won't be long."

****

For the first time in her twenty-four years on earth, Zoe Bankes didn't know what the hell she was doing. Hex had left her with more questions than answers, making it difficult to settle. She was torn between his blunt confessions and the small insight to his predicament. He'd been Abaddon's prisoner. Despite how much she wanted to dismiss that, she couldn't. She was getting her own taste of lack of freedom and couldn't imagine what it would be like to have it even worse, to be subjected to imprisonment by Wrath, of all Devils. Zoe was going crazy with restlessness after a couple of hours, but Hex made it sound like he'd been in the Abyss long enough to have seen Pheldra there before she'd been sentenced to Limbo. That was, at the very least, twenty-four-and-a-half years ago, and possibly longer.

Zoe wanted to know what kind of extremely powerful weapon Hex was, because it had to be more than just his ability to travel through the Veil, otherwise he wouldn't have said it was complicated. There was still a lot he was keeping from her. Yet, he'd told her things more devious beings wouldn't have. He hadn't just come clean with his confession about his plans to exchange Pheldra for his freedom, he'd revealed exactly why he was so adamant about staying far away from Saphiel. The Devil was going to kill him, and Zoe couldn't even deny it, because she knew it was a hundred percent plausible. Especially if Saph had any inkling of the truth.

She just wasn't sure what she found harder to face—the reason Hex would risk it all to save her, or that she was truly being hunted by an actual Devil from Hell. And not just any Devil, no, because that wouldn't be epic enough—it had to be Wrath of all fucking demons! Why couldn't Hex have ticked off Sloth? At least then they'd have plenty of time to get away.

"That's the most common misconception of all time."

As she was cleaning up her broken plate and sandwich leftovers, Zoe's muscles jerked in surprise and her heart lurched in her chest yet again.

"Hex, for fucking Christ!" she choked out around her stolen breath. "Do you see how small I am? How many more of those do you think my heart can take?"

"I told you I wouldn't be long," he said, waving his arm toward the kitchen. A swirl of black fog swept over Zoe's hands and the floor, removing all traces of broken ceramic and food. He grabbed her hands to inspect them, his thumbs rubbing over her palms in a way that should not make her toes want to curl, yet did anyway. "Do you think you could take my desire to keep you safe seriously by not messing with shit that can hurt you? No one lives here to care if there's a broken plate on the floor."

"Really? But trying to give me a heart attack every ten minutes is perfectly healthy?" she countered, tugging her hands free, though the damage was already done. The lingering sensation of his touch had her fingers tingling and the rest of her body revving with envy. "When you said you had to go prep a new location, I expected it to take longer than five minutes. What else was I supposed to do?"

Partway to the sink to wash the bits of sticky jam off, she recalled what he'd said upon arrival and paused, narrowing her eyes at him.

"Were you inside my head?"

"No, you were complaining out loud," he answered. "I can't read minds, Zoe, nor do I need to. I already told you that I can hear and see all of your layers without it."

The fact that she was starting to believe him didn't help numb the ghostly sensation of his thumbs massaging her palms. She hadn't realized she'd been talking out loud, but it was definitely possible. One of the reasons why she was so successful in social media was because she couldn't contain her own thoughts, and her personalized filter worked at rapid speeds. Her dad used to say it was because she was too small to hold anything inside. Zoe knew that was BS, but it made for a handy excuse.

"What did you mean by misconception?" she asked.

"Humans think the Seven embody the sins they represent, but that's not the case," he explained, standing on the other side of the counter and watching her. "All demons are tasked with taunting the naturally ingrained sins of humans. It's only because those seven sins in particular were deemed the worst of the lot that their demons gained so much power in the minds of mankind, and thus their roles in mainstream religion."

"So, Wrath isn't the walking epitome of rage, that's what you're telling me?" she hazarded.

"Quite the opposite. Abaddon is cold and calculating. His mind only works strategically; everything is a battle to be won. His callous, aloof nature is what provokes the wrath in others so quickly. That, and he treats everyone around him like they're nothing more than objects to be used at his whim. Pawns and weapons, rather than living beings with some modicum of dignity."

Zoe chewed on the corner of her lip and watched Hex carefully. It was obvious that either Abaddon or the Abyss had done a number on him, and she hated how much that made her feel something for him beyond smoldering lust and the desire to strangle the shit out of him, because it complicated matters.

"If what you're saying is true, then why does Saphiel work on Wall Street?"

"That's where he feeds," Hex supplied, his

displeasure over the subject matter apparent by his tone. "Demons feed off the energy produced when humans give in to their particular sin. It's what sustains them, keeps them powerful. The more the humans around them give in to their specific sin, the stronger they become. So, as I'm sure you can imagine, Greed is one of the most powerful beings in existence."

"Oh, yeah," Zoe agreed, not even trying to play it off. Everybody and their mother was greedy for something.

"That's why he has a familiar," he continued. "You mentioned it last night. His wolf. Greed is so powerful, he can't contain it all himself, so his familiar carries the majority of it."

Zoe's eyes widened as she recalled curling up under Wolfe's ginormous head to snuggle beside Kami. She had no idea she'd been holding a nuclear bomb of demonic power in her lap the whole time.

"Jesus." She shook her head. "What's your sin, then?"

When Hex merely stared at her, she sighed and arched a brow. "Come on, you just said all demons have to provoke human sins, and earlier, you said your extreme weaponry was complicated, so cough it up. I already know you're more than just a Veil Strider."

"It doesn't matter," he tried to evade. "It doesn't affect you."

"Hello, I'm stuck here with you for God knows how long, everything about you affects me."

His eyes flashed, expression darkening just enough for her to feel the guilt of her words, but it was too late.

The offense had already been dealt. And honestly, how did he expect her to view their situation? She was not there by choice and he knew it.

Zoe refused to cower when he rounded the island toward her. He didn't move fast. He moved deliberately, stalking her down and framing her between his muscled arms as he braced his hands on the counter.

"No. I mean, it literally doesn't affect you, Zoe. I've tried." Even as the words left his mouth, she heard the whispers, causing her to peer around as if her eyes could track the sound, rather than her ears. "Is there nothing you want?"

He practically whispered it, but everything inside of her was jarred back into the memory of the night before, when he'd done and asked the same thing. Her lips parted as her eyes whipped to his with shock. "You . . . what did you do?"

"What I always do," he answered. "I find the one thing you want the most, the one thing you desire above everything else in life, and I fuel it. Inflame it, like a billows to the embers of your mind, until you can think of nothing else, until it becomes a singular obsession and you're willing to give me anything I want just to have it."

"You're—"

"Pan's shadow, leading the lost boys to Neverland with the promise of eternal youth," he supplied for her. "Men want to be sex gods and power moguls, women want to be beautiful and desired. Both want to be adored and envied by others. But not you."

Startled, Zoe blinked.

"You can't be lured deeper into your desires.

Otherwise, you wouldn't be able to hear the whispers with your ears. You'd hear them as everyone else does, that nagging, festering thought in your head growing increasingly louder and persistent."

"So, you're telling me that every time I've heard the whispers, that was you, trying to figure out my greatest desire?"

He released the counter and straightened. "Last night, yes. On the beach earlier, no. I was just trying to get the answer you refused to give me. And I did. You hear the whispers when I specifically target you, because there's nothing you want that badly."

"Oh, there's plenty I want," she corrected him, the fire of indignation blazing in her chest. "Your blood on my knuckles, for starters. Let me clue you in on how much I will *never* be a target for you or anyone else. I am superbly amazing just the way I am. I'm talking, supreme fucking being of awesomeness personified, this shit doesn't get any better kind of amazing. So, don't you ever use your demon hoodoo on me again, Hex, or you won't like what my greatest desire ends up becoming!"

When he laughed, loud and heartily, she felt the heat of rage rise to her cheeks.

"See? That's exactly what I'm talking about." He grinned, his pale eyes glinting with appreciation. "You actually believe that wholeheartedly. In my experience, humans are rarely that content with themselves. They either wear their insecurities on their sleeves, or hide them behind false bravado."

Zoe nearly faltered, unsure if that statement should make her angrier or not, because she was still justifiably pissed. "I'm two seconds away from throat-punching you, and you're grinning?"

"Yes, because unlike you, I can focus on the whole conversation, rather than narrowing in on one piece of information like a viper," he said. "But on top of all your awesomeness, you are also quite stubborn."

"I prefer dedicated," she corrected him, some of her anger slipping with his acceptance of her awesomeness. "And you're lying."

"I don't lie."

"You said you only used your hoodoo on me last night and on the beach, but the whispers are what woke me up your first night at my apartment."

His brow lifted. "So, you're saying you've heard it from the start, failed to mention it until tonight on the beach, yet I'm the one who gets accused of withholding information?"

Zoe was not amused. At least, not that he needed to know, but damn if she didn't have a weakness for men with quick minds. His humor faded and his expression grew serious, mimicking the look he'd given her just before his blunt confession about trading Pheldra's freedom for his own. Zoe wasn't sure if she could handle any more conflict when it came to her feelings about him.

"That wasn't me trying to target you," he said. "It's a natural phenomenon triggered by instincts similar to the way humans naturally sense out a new environment—looking around, smelling, judging the energies of a room by how it makes them feel. My powers often do the same thing of their own volition, but always when it's a place I've never been before."

Okay, how could she argue with that? *Ugh, damn it.* Now, she was pretty much not angry anymore. "So, it's like a demonic defense mechanism?"

He cocked his head, considering. "No, it's a search for any targets that might be in my immediate vicinity."

"Fucking figures." She laughed, unable to do otherwise.

Hex's grin returned and the study he gave her was enough to light more than just a few fires in her blood. "Say what you will, Zoe. Your acceptance of demons and Fallen speaks for itself. If you truly thought our existence was that deplorable, you'd be sobbing in a corner right now, instead of sassing me."

"Sass is my default setting, there are no other options," she pointed out with every ounce of sincerity she possessed.

Well, sass and naughtiness. Yeah, she was a pervert, but damn if she wasn't funny while she was at it.

"I have no doubt," he replied. "And I have no shame."

"That makes two of us," she responded.

"I'm not ashamed of what I am," he elaborated. "As with my name, I've been a demon far longer than whatever I was before it. I cannot change that, nor would I. The only alternative would've been to spend thousands of years crying over a fate I could neither alter nor avoid."

Ah. So, he hadn't been ready to drop another confession bomb on her, just worried that she didn't approve of his more demonic qualities.

"Why are you telling me this?"

"Because I'm not any kind of good, Zoe. I may not be considered evil in the grand hierarchy of Hell, but I will never be good by earthly standards. And you can't humanize me. I will never stop being who and what I am."

"And who are you, Hex?" she asked, though she was fairly certain she already knew. She wanted to hear him say it. "Saphiel is Greed. Abaddon is Wrath. Who is Hex?"

"Temptation."

"Mm." Just as she suspected. "So, you tempt people until they're begging for what they want, and then?"

"Don't do this," he warned.

"You said you weren't ashamed, so prove it," she pushed. "Fill in the blanks, Hex. It's like ad-libs. I tempt people in exchange for . . . blank—"

"Them, Zoe! What else is there?"

"Their souls, you mean."

"And their obligation to me for the rest of their natural lives. Any time I need a favor," he added, gesturing to her. "Like when I need someone to pick out your clothes or buy your food."

Zoe peered down at the tank top and shorts. Suddenly, the reason they fit so well made sense. He'd obviously asked a woman to do the shopping, because even her undergarments were both attractive and comfortable. She'd just assumed he'd been holding out on some secret skills. "So, let me get this straight. You give people exactly what they want in exchange for becoming your personal shoppers?"

"Eternal damnation."

"Well, there's that."

Hex stilled, giving her a surprised look and Zoe caved, unable to keep up the ruse any longer. It was funny that he'd expect her to want him to change. It had never once crossed her mind. Him being a demon would never register on her list of concerns, especially after getting to know him a little better.

"Hex, I don't give a shit about your demony-demonness. If people want to sell their souls for a boob job, that's on them. I take responsibility for my own choices, I don't lose sleep over people who can't do the same." She shook her head. "What I do stay up all night worrying about is my business. A business that I've spent the past two and a half years busting my ass to get off the ground, which is in danger of crashing into a fiery deathball of ruin, because I don't have access to Wi-Fi."

"I feel regret about that, Zoe, if for no other reason than it means a lot to you, but I'm not sorry," he replied. "I won't apologize for making your life a priority. Your business is nothing without you alive to run it."

She ground her teeth in frustration, because she knew he was right and she hated it, but he was also wrong about her safety.

"Hex, I know you don't want to hear it, and the last thing I want is you getting ticked and disappearing again, but I know with everything in me that I would be safe with Kami and Saph," she said. "If you could just let me prove it."

"How?"

"We could go there then you could see for yourself —"

He shook his head and paced away. "No."

Zoe felt more deflated than angry, but she had to try.

"Look, I know you think I'm being unreasonable, I can hear and feel that coming off you loud and clear," he said, turning back to her. "But let me break this scenario down for you. Say I take you back and Greed doesn't immediately attack me. Say he actually listens to reason when we explain the situation to him, then what? You would still be in danger of getting abducted by Abaddon or his Legion, because nothing Greed says will ever deter him from what he wants. And the minute Abaddon manages to capture you—and he will find a way—then you're dead. He will offer you to Pheldra in exchange for her return to the Abyss, but it's not up to her. Whether you want to believe that or not, it is divinely, cosmically out of her hands. She is predestined to rule beside Saphiel for all eternity now. And even if there was a choice, it would be up to Saphiel to make as her king, and you know, deep down, that he would never choose your life over his mate's return to the Abyss. Then Abaddon will kill you out of spite, for you are of no further use to him.

"That's one possible scenario," he continued. "The other is that as soon as we arrive, Greed hands me straight over to Abaddon and thinks they're all good, but they won't be. Abaddon will keep trying for Pheldra, and if he doesn't manage to capture you, it will only be because you're stuck living with Greed and his queen for the rest of your natural life, or under the constant guard of his Legion. I don't think you'd be happy living that way for long. And I simply cannot return to the Abyss, Zoe. I would rather cease to exist."

Her throat felt tight with all the things she wanted to dispute, but as fucked up as it may be, she couldn't deny that Hex's grim rundown was the most likely outcome. It was an impossible situation, and she hadn't even thought about what might happen if Abaddon didn't take no for an answer. Zoe didn't want to be stuck living with Saph and Kami for an indefinite amount of time, or be imprisoned in her own apartment simply because it was secure. Even to have her Wi-Fi back, there would be no joy or relief continuing to live with her freedom so restricted. They needed to find a way to eliminate the threat altogether.

Hex watched her, as if waiting for a storm to break over his head. Normally, she'd find some amusement in that, but not right now. Instead, she took a deep breath and spread her hands.

"What are we going to do?" she asked. "Just keep running until Abaddon forgets we exist?"

"It would be nice if that were even an option," he deadpanned. "Right now, I'm only concerned with getting you to a more secure location. Then we can figure out a battle plan."

Zoe blew out a breath, because she wasn't crazy about that answer. "I'd rather start on a plan now, Hex. I don't like waiting for bad shit to happen, and honestly, I'm going to die from boredom if I don't have anything to focus on."

Something sizzled in his eyes when they traveled over her. "I can think of many ways to keep your mind occupied," he vowed. "You might not desire any one thing strong enough to be tempted, but I can certainly figure out all the little things that bring you pleasure."

She didn't dare tell him that his voice alone could tempt her to do just about anything, especially when it dropped a few octaves into that raspy purr when he was trying to seduce her into doing what he wanted. Her panties were already in danger of getting soaked with arousal. She needed to redirect him before he could touch her, otherwise it would be hopeless.

"How about you tell me all about Abaddon, instead?"

The mention of the Devil's name made him sneer, killing his flow instantly. "There is nothing pleasurable about that conversation."

"I know," she said. "But it is necessary."

"Only you would think so."

"Humor me, Hex. Give me all the information I want and maybe I'll share the secret to one of my little pleasures with you afterward."

His eyes narrowed, regarding her while he appeared to weigh the deal in his mind. "Fine, but I get to choose the pleasure you're to reveal to me," he bargained. "I already know how you operate, little doe, and I don't trust you not to turn your end of the bargain into some kind of folly."

Zoe was too impressed by his quick study to bother feigning offense, so merely gave him an appreciative smile and gestured to the living room. "Shall we?"

CHAPTER 4

Indulgence

They spent the rest of the night sating Zoe's never-ending curiosity. The moment Hex began painting the picture in her mind with his vivid accounts of the Abyss, she had a string of endless questions. It was a cold, dark realm leagues below the fiery pits of Hell, ruled by the equally cold King of Wrath, Abaddon. Tangled in and around the briars and jagged rocks of the Abyss itself was the supposed palace of Tartarus, that ancient god for which the whole thing had originally been named. Hex described it as little better than ruins, most of it lost to history, save for a massive gallery where statues were once displayed in alcoves between columns, which Abaddon had turned into his armory.

"Those alcoves were our cells," Hex revealed. "Each of his weapons on display, so he could peruse his collection at his leisure. Except Pheldra. She never stepped foot inside his armory."

Zoe wondered if Pheldra had even been aware of the place, or if Abaddon had kept her deliberately ignorant of it. Hex went on to tell her the ceiling was open all down the center, and the air—thickly sweetened from the pomegranate forest that surrounded the courtyard—would drive them mad for freedom. And there stood a well, no more than two steps up from the ground, but that went deeper than any other well in existence. It was filled with pure darkness. Chained at the very bottom of the well was Azazel, one of the Angels who'd fallen the farthest by teaching mankind things they were never supposed to know.

It was just before dawn when Zoe's tired brain couldn't think of anything more to ask. Laying idle for so many hours wasn't something she was used to, and the continuous flow of Hex's husky timbre had acted like one of those meditation albums, lulling her into such a relaxed state, she hadn't even noticed the hours slipping by.

Even though he'd been wise to suspect her initial plans to shortchange him, Hex had ended up telling her so much, she didn't feel right about cheating him out of an honest answer. It wasn't that she was bashful, she was just blatantly attracted to him—so much so, that he didn't need any additional ammunition against her. If it came right down to it, all he'd have to do is seduce her with his voice.

Zoe stretched with a yawn, then rolled onto her side on the sofa, facing him. He sat in the only armchair cocked more toward her than the center of the room.

"All right, Hexy," she prompted, smiling when his lip curled in distaste at the nickname. "What is the one desire you want me to reveal?"

He studied her for a moment, his expression relaxed,

yet giving nothing away. "I already know you desire me, no matter how much you try to hide it."

She blinked at him, unsure of how to play that off or if she should even bother. Maybe it was the sleepiness starting to take hold or the lack of activity, but Zoe just couldn't muster the energy to make a big deal out of it.

"Was that your pick?"

"No." He smirked, lowering himself to the floor to crawl the short distance to her. He knelt beside the sofa and braced his hand against the back of it, covering most of her without even touching. "I want to know one of the areas of your body that arouses you and what you like having done to it the most."

"Technically, that's two desires," she pointed out, though she couldn't keep her mouth from curving up at the corners.

"You and I both know I gave you way more information than you bargained for."

Zoe smiled. "How convenient for you."

His reciprocating grin was nothing short of devious. "Yes," he admitted. "Now, for my reward."

"My neck," she answered. There was no point in delaying the inevitable. "As lame as it sounds, kissing my neck will get me aroused very quickly. Especially when it's nibbled on a little bit."

She watched him drink in that area of her body. Was he imagining what she would taste like, just like she was imagining what his mouth would feel like? The tension between them was palpable and Zoe couldn't stop herself from anticipating some kind of physical contact. A touch, perhaps, or would it be something more damaging, like a kiss?

"You should get some sleep," he said, lowering his arm and sitting back on his haunches so he was no longer hovering over her.

Lucky for him, it was only a suggestion and not a repeat of his demon trickery. But it was a far cry from the response she'd been expecting. He looked out the window behind the sofa, eyes distant, face withdrawn.

"I need to go check on the progress of our next location, but I'll have to wait until you wake," he added. "I can't leave you unattended and defenseless while you sleep."

Can't or won't? "I appreciate that," she said sincerely. His behavior was making her more and more confused by the second.

"You can sleep wherever you want," he continued as if she hadn't spoken. "But the bed is probably more comfortable than here."

"Such a gentleman," she said around another yawn.

He looked at her, expression passive. "I wasn't being nice, I simply have no use for it. I don't sleep."

She propped herself up on her elbow, her brow creasing as she studied him. "Why are you suddenly so grumpy? I gave you an honest answer."

"I'm not grumpy, I'm anxious," he said, rising from the floor and walking back toward the kitchen. "We've already been here too long, and now we'll have to be here even longer, because your human body has to sleep half a day just to function."

Taken aback, Zoe sat up all the way. "Oh, I'm sorry, who abducted who again?"

"I never should have agreed to your idea, you ask too many questions," he ground out.

"I don't recall holding a fucking gun to your head," she erupted, sending one of the throw pillows flying right at his back.

When he turned to face her, his expression was dark. "Go to bed, Zoe, before I make you."

It took her a total of three raging inhales to come to the conclusion that whatever the hell was going on was *his* issue, because she hadn't said or done anything wrong. The fact that he was taking it out on her had indignation straightening her spine and firing up her sleepy brain. She'd be damned if she was going to play along with his temper tantrum any longer.

Zoe stood and crossed the room to gather her purse where she'd abandoned it earlier. She dug around inside it until she found what she was looking for, then walked right up to Hex and slapped it into his hand.

"What is this?"

"It's a fucking tampon, Hex," she snapped. "Apparently, you need it more than I do."

She turned away from him, following the hallway to the bedroom, where she shut and locked the door. If he was as clever as she believed, he wouldn't dare walk through it a second time.

***

Much to Zoe's surprise, she managed to fall asleep quickly, and just as Hex predicted, stayed there almost half the day. There were no working clocks in the house and her phone was long gone, so she had no way of checking the time. Judging by the color of the sunlight, she was fairly certain it was late afternoon. Hex must have heard her moving around, because he was gone by the time she emerged from the bedroom. She'd dressed in another outfit he'd had one of his puppets buy for her. Again, it was both stylish and comfy. If the woman wasn't already an actual personal shopper by trade, she should be, because she was damn good at it.

Oops. Zoe snickered at her own unintentional pun while shrugging it off. Oh, well. They were both damned already, no sense in pretending otherwise.

In the kitchen, there was more food than she'd been expecting when she rifled through the fridge and cupboards, but it was all healthy stuff. Nothing she could grab quickly and eat on her way outside—like donuts or pop-tarts. Hex should have been dubbed the Demon of Nutrition, because that had to be a real thing. Zoe finally settled on toast with jam, reluctantly grabbed a bottle of water and headed out onto the deck.

She wanted coffee so bad, she could feel the withdrawal sinking claws into her brain, fouling up her mood. Another reason why she'd decided on her mission. If she could keep herself busy, hopefully she wouldn't be plagued by the cravings.

After devouring the toast and downing half the water, she descended the wooden stairs to the beach, but didn't head toward the ocean. Rather, she hooked a left and headed for the thick jungle that made up most of the island. She was determined to see what was on the other side, mainly, if there would be more islands close enough to reach with a quick swim, or passing boats—particularly of the yacht variety—complete with satellite and Wi-Fi. Even though she still believed in the plausibility of Hex's scenarios, it had dawned on her that she'd unwittingly made their situation a lot worse by texting Kami the day before. There was no doubt her best friend had spent the last twenty-four hours worried sick about her, and Zoe didn't even want to imagine how Saphiel was dealing with that. If there was some way to get a message to Kami, just to let her know she was safe and would return as soon as possible, then she needed to do it. The sooner, the better.

Not long after she started hiking into the thick underbrush and towering trees, Zoe noticed how quiet it was for a jungle. She paused to listen, but other than an occasional, distant bird call, she heard nothing. Did that mean most of the wildlife in the jungle was nocturnal? She thought back to the night before, when she'd wandered down to the water. But she couldn't recall hearing or seeing any wildlife then, either. That was just odd, even for her, and she was a freaking city girl.

Zoe continued on, trying not to walk through any plants that looked potentially poisonous, but for all she knew, they all were. It would be just her luck to wind up covered in an itchy rash thousands of miles from the nearest pharmacy. Hours passed while she trudged on, the scenery never really changing or offering any indications that it would end soon.

When the first bug landed on her, Zoe dutifully swatted it and then fought a chill, realizing she'd been taken from New York without getting any of the inoculations most people get before visiting foreign countries. What if she ended up with malaria, just because her travel agency was run by Hell?

"Fuck," she swore, looking around as something else buzzed in her ear.

Darkness spread rapidly through the forest, ten times faster than it would have on the beach. That explained it. She hadn't really been hiking that long, had she? Then she remembered she was in the southern hemisphere, which had the complete opposite seasons than what she was used to, which meant June would have shorter days than December.

Damn it! Zoe had hoped cutting through the jungle would get her to the other side of the island faster. Now she was in danger of getting totally lost and probably eaten by some nocturnal predator. Man versus beast was no longer the epic way to go out—it was all so passé and largely relegated to those YouTube vines designed to incriminate the dumbest people on the planet. Which, despite her current situation, was not Zoe Bankes!

Another thirty minutes passed with the rapid depletion of natural light, making it harder for her to stay on what she believed was the exact path she'd created. She was beginning to understand why every real and fictional explorer had that iconic guide at the front, who whacked bushes away with a machete. It obviously served multiple purposes, one being a permanent bread crumb to follow on the way back. Zoe couldn't find any damaged plants where she may have walked through them. She'd either been too careful, or the forest was simply that resilient—the insects certainly were.

Her foot caught on a slippery root and she thought for sure her ankle was in for a hard twist, but then the root gave and snapped. She released a breath of relief, and then whispers filled the air all around her, sending goosebumps all over her skin. More relief flooded through her when she turned to see Hex stepping out of the shadows behind her, though she was still quite ticked at him for his asinine behavior the night before.

"What are you doing out here?" he asked.

The calmness of his tone irked her all over again, so she merely turned on her heels and continued picking her way through the forest. He let her get about two more feet before wrapping his arms around her from behind. In a blink, she was back at the beach where she'd started.

"I didn't ask for your help," she snapped, jerking away from him and instantly regretting it as her head spun.

"You didn't have to," he countered. "I could feel you needed it, and you were dangerously close to stepping on a death adder, which would've been unpleasant for both of you."

Zoe swallowed the delayed fright over that, but it reminded her of all the other animals she hadn't seen or heard. "Are they all that stealthy here, or is there another reason why this island seems so strangely absent of wildlife?"

He glanced toward the forest. "I hadn't noticed, but I'm most likely the cause. I carry the land of the dead everywhere I go. Animals are highly sensitive to it."

That made sense. Not only because of the Veil, but they undoubtedly sensed he was a demon and animals were naturally leery of things they considered predators. Zoe made to turn away from him again and head up to the point of the island along the beach, when he stopped her.

"You're still angry."

"Yeah, because you still haven't apologized for being a total jerk, you jerk," she said, whirling on him. "I don't know what got into you last night, but I didn't do anything to deserve being snapped at!"

"No, you didn't," he agreed. "And yes, you did."

Zoe arched a brow. "Excuse you?"

"You allowed yourself to become vulnerable with a demon, Zoe," he stated. "You have no idea how dangerous that is."

"You better explain a lot better than that, Hex, because the only goddamn thing I did was keep my end of the bargain. Was I supposed to lie and go back on it?"

He scowled. "No."

"Then am I not supposed to trust you?"

He studied her, his expression dark, but not nearly as bad as it had been the night before. "I want you to trust me, Zoe, but perhaps you'd be better off if you didn't."

"You're not making any sense, Hex," she huffed in exasperation when he didn't elaborate.

There was a moment of silence before he spoke.

"Last night when you were in that vulnerable, relaxed state, your mind and body too tired to fight, and you revealed the key to your pleasure, it triggered every single one of my instincts to attack," he said, jabbing his own chest with his fingertips. "You were so primed, ripe for the taking. A few suggestions, a little seductive shove and I could have completely bent you to my will. And for the first time in all my existence it felt . . . off. I still longed for it, my instincts were strongly urging me forward, yet I couldn't allow myself to do it. Not with you."

"Why not with me?" she asked, zeroing in on that. All their arguments seemed to come right back down to the way he regarded her as different from others.

"You have to know by now, little doe," he answered. "You're so much more than any other human."

Zoe had always felt she was different in her own way, but the world wasn't really lacking others like her, despite what she claimed. She just liked to say that for fun. So, she tried to wrap her head around the logistics of it, to help her make more sense of the situation.

"I thought you said I couldn't be tempted," she whispered.

He shook his head. "You can't. What I wanted to do to you last night is different."

"How?"

"Because, it wouldn't have earned me your soul, only your temporary loyalty and obedience," he answered. "It's merely an indulgence, comparable to how you might snack in between meals."

"Ew, what?" she balked. "That just took a left turn out of nowhere, I thought we were talking about seduction, not hunger pains."

Hex didn't sigh but it was something close to it. "All demons need to feed, Zoe, I'm no different. The only way I can sate my hunger is by coaxing humans into giving in to their desires, no matter how big or small. The small desires can sustain me for quite some time, but I do need a main course every now and then. Regardless, I never miss an opportunity to indulge, especially when a human is so perfectly susceptible, as you were last night."

"God, you're like a vampire without fangs," she remarked, wondering why that suddenly didn't sound as hot as she'd always believed.

Probably because the idea of being supernaturally manipulated into becoming a victim had lost all its charm when she'd learned it had almost happened to her against her knowledge or consent.

"Nothing I just described sounded anything like a vampire." He scowled. "I think you mean to insult me because you're still angry."

But, she wasn't. Everything he'd said had sunk in, jumbling around with the rest before settling. It wasn't anger she felt anymore. She couldn't possibly hold his nature against him, and he had stopped himself from 'indulging' his cravings on her, but that didn't mean his behavior toward her was acceptable.

"So, what you're saying is that you were a jerk to me for my own good?"

He stared at her, obviously detecting the dry sarcasm in her tone just fine as she knew he would. "The honest answer is yes. But I do regret the way I spoke to you and didn't like upsetting you, Zoe, I was trying to handle a situation I've never been in before."

She continued to look at him expectantly. "And?"

"I did not handle it well," he admitted. When she continued to wait, he finally added, "I apologize."

"Fine. Apology accepted," she said. "I understand the situation you were in, now that you've explained it to me, but know this, Hex, I don't respond well to being treated badly when I didn't do anything to deserve it. Don't ever do that again or you'll get more from me than just a tampon."

Hex grimaced, the muscles working in the back of his jaw. "I still don't even know what that was for."

Zoe choked out a laugh and shook her head. "Shit," she dragged the word out on a long exhale. It figured one of her more brilliant moments would get wasted on the only being in the universe who didn't even get it. "No time to explain. The sun's almost down and if I hurry, I might still catch a boat."

"There are no boats," he said, stepping forward to stop her. "And even if there were, I would not let you catch one."

"Relax, I don't mean to climb aboard and sail off," she explained. "I just need to find a way to get a message to Kami, which I already know you don't agree with, and that really sucks for you because it would be a lot better for us if I did."

"Explain," he demanded.

"I texted her yesterday, remember?" she said. "She's gotta be scared out of her mind that I've up and disappeared without a trace. And I worry about how much worse that's going to be for you when Saphiel starts tearing the planet apart to find me just to make his queen happy again."

A day ago, Zoe would've expected to feel a smug kind of victory when Hex's face paled, but it didn't feel anything like a win now. After everything she'd learned about his unfortunate imprisonment, and his description of what it had been like in the Abyss, she really couldn't blame him for doing everything in his power to keep his freedom. She was truly concerned that he'd inadvertently made things worse for himself by abducting her. Of course, she hadn't helped matters by sending that text to Kami, but she hadn't been aware of that at the time.

Before she could blink, Hex hauled her up in his arms and then they were in the kitchen. His shadows hadn't even appeared, yet it felt like a part of her equilibrium had gotten left behind on the beach.

"I have to go speed things up for our next location," he said. "Try not to wander too far from the house. With my absence, the wildlife may return and there are a lot of dangerous things native to these islands."

The shadows had already begun swirling around him to take his gorgeous body from her sight again.

"No, that's fine, I'll just be here doing absolutely fucking nothing!" she griped, throwing her hands in the air.

When his mouth slanted into a sexy smirk, Zoe flipped him off and then he was gone.

"Ugh! Demons!" she groaned, frustrated. She wished she had something to kick that wouldn't break her toes.

Suddenly, the whispers assaulted the air all around her, louder than she'd ever heard them before. Zoe spun right into the threshold of the Veil, where Hex's hands caught her up and lifted her from the floor. He set her on the counter and crushed his mouth to hers so fast, it made her head spin. Her breath caught at the back of her throat, heat spiraling from his mouth all the way to her toes. Lust zinged right through her like fireworks, her blood cells popping and sizzling when he cupped her face and his tongue dove between her lips. Currents of arousal traveled right down her body to harden her nipples and drench her panties.

He kissed her dirty, tasting like every favorite food and drink she'd ever consumed. Tasting exactly how she'd expect Temptation to taste. He kissed her hungry, as if she might taste the same for him, but there was something else. Something he was holding back, and it was trying to lure her deeper. After everything he'd just told her, Zoe was startled enough by the urge to follow it that she pulled back. Hex was still covered in shadows, only his face and arms outside of the Veil. His hands sunk deeper into her hair and she fought the shiver it triggered from her scalp all the way to her aching nipples.

"Mmm, little doe," he hummed and leaned in, sucked her lips between his teeth for a nibble. For once in her life, Zoe was utterly speechless. He'd caught her so off guard, taking her by complete surprise. The demon deserved a motherfucking trophy. "Try not to miss me while I'm gone. I'm not sure how long I'll be this time, but if anything happens, scream. Scream your fucking head off, Zoe, and I'll be right here."

It was her turn to bite when he dipped in for another kiss and her eyes were wide open. They'd never been more open. "You really need to work on your sweet-nothings, Hexy."

With a flick of her tongue over his lips, she gave him an air kiss and shoved him into the Veil. She needed to breathe.

Unholy fuck, did she need to breathe.

CHAPTER 5

WHAT THE TIDE DRAGGED IN

It was potentially dangerous and unwise to rush a Voodoo Queen, but Hex wasn't in the position to stop. Not with Zoe's warning digging burs into his brain—a single moment forgotten that should have been at the forefront of his mind, yet wasn't. He'd been too worried about her safety, putting distance between her and Abaddon's Legion. Wrath, himself, never left the Abyss. He'd probably remain rooted there until the end of days. Hex wanted to bludgeon himself for forgetting that detail so easily. Zoe had shown him her phone in her apartment, proof that she'd already made contact with Greed's queen. Avarice could be uprooting every Legion under his command at that very moment to track Zoe down. Hunt Hex down.

That was a lot of fucking demons. And one big ass wolf, he was sure.

It had already been over a day since she'd sent the text. Since her friend would've noticed her missing. That was more time than he was comfortable thinking about. In the Veil, he paced. He watched Farah work, though she couldn't see him. She'd felt him the moment he'd arrived, of that he was certain. But she was too practiced, too powerful to flinch in the midst of her rituals. It was taking too long, despite knowing that was necessary. He'd asked for something huge and that was bound to take awhile. Hex didn't have time to spare, but if she was successful, they'd be set. They wouldn't need time, would no longer need to run.

It's not like he was asking her to build the damn thing, just open the fucking door!

He licked his lips for the hundredth time, and almost groaned. If he were human, they'd probably be raw by now, but he could still taste Zoe there and he wanted more. He wanted to lick every inch of her body, feast on her naughtiest, most delicious parts and then fuck each one until she passed out from the pleasure. And he wanted to do it while she ran her sassy little mouth. Wanted to hear just how creative she could get when describing all the wicked things she wanted him to do to her. He had no doubts her fantasies would be just as blunt and extraordinary as she was. Her fire was Hex's biggest craving.

That, and she'd accepted him. He hadn't expected that. Humans were generally repulsed by the things demons did, or at the very least, disapproving. It had taken him by complete surprise, which should be impossible for anyone to do, but then that was his little doe in a nutshell. Impossible. Impossibly clever, accepting, courageous. Impossibly his. When she'd flipped him off . . . oh yeah, that had been it. There had been no way he could leave her presence again without finally staking some kind of claim. To give in to his least damaging craving by tasting her lush lips and feeling the heat of her pink tongue dueling with his. He'd almost expected it to cut him, but for all the sharp-edged hostility Zoe was capable of lashing out, her tongue was soft and wet and perfectly supple.

He needed to get back to her. The longer he was away, the better the chance of something going horribly wrong. Which could be anything from another demon finding her to Zoe disobeying him, as she was wont to do, and getting attacked by some poisonous reptile. Of course, there was also a chance she'd simply destroy his island out of sheer boredom and rage. He didn't want to keep running into her shield of anger, but each time they ended up there, it seemed to be weaker and took less time for her to lower it. He wanted them to keep moving forward, though he knew the major snag they'd hit last night had been all his doing. He'd just needed to get her away from him before he gave in to the overwhelming pressure of his own instincts.

Hex had no idea what was in store for them. He didn't have any long-term plans percolating, nothing beyond keeping her safe. Her life, just like he'd told her, was his only priority at the moment. Well, that and freedom. He still very much wanted his fucking freedom, but that had been knocked down to second tier the moment he'd chosen to save Zoe.

"Just go on outta here now, if all you're gonna do is plague me with your impatience!" Farah snapped, pausing to glance over her shoulder.

She didn't attempt to find him. Instead, she took a

slow survey of the entire room, because the Veil surrounded her, and his presence along with it. Hex stopped pacing and folded his arms over his chest. He wasn't leaving. With a sigh, Farah muttered under her breath about the dead always being in such a damn hurry, then went back to work.

He'd never given her any reason to think differently, and wasn't going to correct her now, either. Farah, like all of the other practitioners he'd ever worked with over the centuries, believed him to be just another one of their spirits because he was in the Veil. As far as humans knew, only the dead dwelled there. They were willing to work with him, for him, when they believed that. He doubted they'd be so accommodating if they knew the truth.

Most of the world's view on Voodoo was that it was bad shit, but that was a convenient cover that allowed them to be left alone to their craft. Hex had intimate, first-hand experience with truly evil practices not to be an expert on the subject. Voodoo was just another ancient evolution of animism—the belief in spirit and its influence over the living and objects, the power of living words and their usages, and the mutual respect of each. Farah would do nothing to offend her ancestors, her spirits, or her gods. Her life was devoted to them. That's what really frightened people about religions like Voodoo. Its practitioners were true believers with unerring faith. They gave themselves over to their beliefs completely, without reservation, and let it consume them. They didn't live it partway, didn't only practiced it on certain days of the week or spend every waking moment outside of ceremony breaking its rules. In Voodoo, there was no confessional, no scapegoats and often no second chances—self-responsibility was just the entrance fee for learning the traditions. Practicing it, well, that price was usually a lot higher.

Hex persuaded the Veil to solidify against his back, giving him something to lean against to help him fight the urge to pace. The minutes ticked by into more hours. When he felt the sun slipping away from his location and heading toward Zoe's, his gut churned with anxiety. A specter passed about twenty yards to his right and disappeared. It was the fifth specter in less than ten minutes, but far from alarming. He wasn't at just any junction in the Veil; this was one of the most powerful hubs in the world. Over the last couple of centuries, it had become his favorite. Perhaps it was the music.

As the sun slid toward the other side of the world, Hex leaned his head back and willed time to be on their side for just a little while longer. As the city grew darker, the crowds grew thicker. The celebratory din grew louder and the distant sound of a trumpet rose above it, making him wonder what kind of music Zoe liked.

The moment the sun set for good and darkness fell over them, Farah's voice rose steadily louder, her chanting growing faster. Hex felt the gathering of energies from those items she'd painstakingly set into place, those tools of her trade she fussed over. Each one anointed and initiated into the fold by its own little ritual, while adding to the whole of the big one. She didn't use books, had no need of written material. All the words flew from her mouth in a particular rhythm. Words she knew by heart, taught from birth, ingrained by the rights of her blood and those of her ancestors. Her belief was absolute, untainted, pure in its hold over her. It was some pretty fucking powerful shit.

Hex sank a little deeper into the Veil when her spirits started showing up, answering the call to assist her. They filled up the Shallows, coming between him and Farah as her body started moving and jerking, her power too strong to contain. She lifted her head and danced, but it wasn't a dance, it was manic. She flung her arms and hopped on her feet and cried her living words. The spirits grew denser, more detailed in their lack of transparency.

It was time for Hex to leave. He needed to get back to Zoe. If he timed it right, Farah would be finished by the time they returned. He prayed it was with success rather than a denial. He wasn't of her faith, but he hoped one of her gods answered, because his had abandoned him long ago. With one final glance toward the frenzied ritual, he turned to race through the shadows of the Veil only to find them receding from him.

The sound of a collective movement startled him. Hex whipped around to find that all of the spirits had parted, not just their positions, but the very Shallows, itself. They were staring at him, and when his head snapped up to see beyond them, he found Farah staring right at him, too. With eyes of pure white.

"Oh, I see you now, demon." She smiled.

****

This. Fucking. Sucks. Donkey balls.
Zoe lay on the floor of the living room, staring up at

the ceiling. Her brain was dying. That's what it felt like. After spending so many years always doing, thinking, creating, snarking, it was dying a slow, horrible and droll death of disuse. The worst part was that she couldn't even sleep through it, because her internal clock told her it was still time to be awake, despite the never-ending darkness.

Her fingers brushed across her mouth for the millionth time, and like all the times before, she quickly dropped her hand again, lest the demon reappear to find her reminiscing over his kiss. Zoe could still feel his lips assaulting hers in all the best ways, pushing, brushing, manipulating. It was another show of his confidence, the way he kissed. Skilled, a little cocky, and a whole lotta hot. Every time she licked her lips and swallowed, a different flavor made itself known. The best was espresso. God, yes, the demon tasted like freaking coffee and now she craved both with an intensity she could hardly stand.

Hex was just too fucking delicious for her own good. Ever since he'd left, she'd been waiting for her lust to cool down, for the tingling warmth in her sex to wear off, but it wasn't happening. Her body was ready, even if her mind and that big thing thumping away in her chest wasn't. That vital organ he'd jolted so many times with his sudden appearance act, it seemed to think he was the one operating it now. Not romantically, of course. But it sure in the hell wanted to race for his presence. The way his physical presence had felt pressed against hers, in particular.

After growing even darker, the sky began to lighten, drawing Zoe out of her naughty fantasies of what she'd like to do to Hex first. It had been a long time since she'd watched the sun rise and she'd missed the first one there due to her and Hex's last argument. Back home, her work schedule kept her up late at night. Depending on how that went, it usually dictated what time she crawled out of bed in the morning, though she typically never slept past nine. Well, unless she had a hot ass demon waking her up in the middle of the night.

With a final lustful shiver, Zoe abandoned the floor and didn't bother with shoes as she made her way out onto the deck. The sky was a rich, royal blue, and starless. The wildlife was still eerily absent, but after Hex's parting words, that was probably for the best.

The breeze had cooled a little since her last venture outside, but it was still warm and humid. Nostalgia made a nuisance of itself again, once she reached the sand and recalled that it had been in California where she'd last seen a sunrise over the ocean. The same exact ocean she was now on the other side of, assuming Hex had been honest about their location.

After a small debate, she decided he'd have no reason to lie. It wasn't like she could use the information against him. The more she considered his claim about lying being solely a human trait, the more sense it made. There weren't expressions like "the truth hurts" for no reason. Coercion and manipulation didn't require lying even when humans were the ones doing it, so outsmarting a target while remaining honest would likely be more of a turn on for demons, she imagined. And no matter how shows and movies like to dramatize it, humans did not need that much persuasion to give in to their sins.

Hex had been pretty fucking honest with her the whole time. The kind of honest that would get a lesser being's ass kicked on a regular basis. She'd always viewed herself as a pretty blunt person, but he was opening her eyes to a whole new definition of the word.

Try as she might, she was getting worried about him. He'd been gone a lot longer than any time before, and her imagination—that thing overflowing with supernatural fiction—wasn't helping with the onslaught of worst-case scenarios. What if Abaddon had found him in the next location and was even right now, torturing him? That was the mildest of her mind's conjurations, though she doubted Saphiel had found him, otherwise she'd already be on her way to the best unknown English pub in the States.

Zoe released a sigh and waded into the slow rolling tide. Another chord of unexpected longing was plucked in her soul to feel the ebb and flow of the ocean breaking around her ankles. Then she watched the sun peek over the liquid horizon, at last. It wasn't perfect. The little house appeared to be facing southeast, rather than a direct view, but it was damn good enough. For a moment, the light was almost blinding, obscuring that distant point of island jutting out into the sea. She shielded her eyes with her hand, but couldn't bring herself to look away, knowing it might be another decade or so before she ever saw it again. The breeze played with her curls, bringing floral musk and sea salt to her nose. The subtle aroma of green heat, the sunlight filtering through plant life joined the mix as the sun crept higher. It was definitely not a New York sunrise.

As the light faded to a more bearable measure, Zoe blinked. There were spots in her vision now, the perfect negative of the partial sun viewable on the back of her eyelids when she closed them. No matter how much she blinked, though, one spot wasn't going away. In fact, it was getting bigger and coming closer. The moment it reached the island's point, the sound of a boat motor reached her ears, echoing off the land and trees, even while the wind tried to sweep it in another direction.

Zoe froze. Her first two reactions collided head-on inside her, making it impossible to decide which one she wanted to use—instant excitement over a possible way to contact Kami, or the fear that one of Abaddon's Legion had found her. The indecision was enough to have her backing up. Sand clung to her feet as the speedboat drew nearer. It wasn't at full throttle, which was why she remained on the brink of indecision. Had it come barreling down on her, she wouldn't have hesitated to hightail it back into the house. Not that she had anyway to protect herself there, either, but it was better than being in the wide open without so much as a stick.

Shit. Zoe continued to inch her way back toward the steps, which now seemed a hundred miles away for her short legs. She glanced around for some kind of handy weapon nearby, but there wasn't even a sand dollar to be found. *Figures.*

The boat's driver let up on the throttle and coasted closer to shore, the sun still blazing behind them, making it difficult for Zoe to get a good look at who or what they might be. At last, the prow turned, and the boat skimmed past her toward the right. Her jaw nearly dropped when she saw the golden god of a man standing behind the wheel. His hair was shades of blond, raw honey to platinum and naturally wavy, almost curling at the ends. He wore a pair of long navy shorts and a white shirt, open to show off a naked, sun-kissed torso the Renaissance masters would've killed each other to sculpt. Poor David never would've stood a chance.

When he slid sunglasses up to perch atop his head and smiled at her with eyes the same azure blue as the water, one of her brain cells died a little. That just had the rest of them firing up with one singular conclusion: *no way in hell this thing is human.* He made every male model and A-lister look like cheap knock-offs.

After he cut the motor, the waves rocked the boat up onto the beach. At first, she thought it was a natural occurrence, but the tide continued to recede until the boat was fully marooned. That could *not* be normal.

"Beautiful day for a swim," he commented.

The popping sound in her ears were more brain cells blowing circuits when his sexy accent washed over her. She had the sudden desire to go swimming, and that had her taking another step back.

With enviable grace, he launched himself over the side of the boat and landed barefoot in the damp sand. He wasn't Legion—he was too fucking beautiful and alluring for that. And somehow she knew he wasn't Abaddon, either. He smiled too easily to fit Hex's cold and calculating description. Zoe just couldn't fathom why any of the other Seven would be there.

After studying her for a moment, he wiped his hands together and glanced at his boat. "Seems I'm stuck," he said, humor glinting in his eyes like the sunlight danced off the waves. "Mind giving me a hand?"

Alarms sounded loud and clear in her head. Zoe took a few more steps back, but she'd be damned if she would run screaming. Yet.

"How about we cut the bullshit and you just tell me why you're really here?"

His grin spread wicked fast and while it wasn't exactly friendly, it made him that much more attractive, which shouldn't even be possible.

"Bold for a Daughter of Eve."

"Observant for a Devil," Zoe countered. "Now that we've established which side of Hell's gates we're standing on, how about we drop the pleasantries and get down to business. What do you want?"

His chuckle reached her on the breeze, just as gorgeous as the rest of him. "I thought perhaps we could help one another," he said, spreading his hands in offer. "Favor for favor. You come with me willingly, and after I've gotten what I need, I promise I'll take you anywhere in the world you want to go."

"Yeah, I won't be doing that," she said. "Can't even say I wish I could help, because frankly, I don't want to. I'm already a little busy staying alive and healthy, so, pass."

"I promise no harm will come to you," he said. "I just need to motivate your demon into doing me a favor."

"Oh, is that all? Have you ever thought about just asking him?" Zoe countered. "In fact, let me get him for you. HEX!"

"HEX!" he started yelling with her, his expression

filled with amusement.

His laughter was like a siren's song, and it resonated all the way to the marrow of her bones with the promise that he'd reveal secrets of some exotic mystery, the beckoning pull of something too profound to resist. Zoe had the oddest connection to some intrinsic need, a primal urge, but then it stopped. She shook her head to dislodge the strangeness and refocused on the Devil.

"What, no answer?" he grinned.

"What have you done with him?" she demanded, her heart thudding hard.

"I'm merely keeping him occupied," he shrugged. "Just long enough to convince you to help me."

"And why the hell would I do that?"

"Do you know why he brought you to this island?" he asked.

Yeah, there's no freaking Wi-Fi!

"I'm sure you have a theory."

"Theory? No. It's one of the few places he can exist in the mortal realm outside of the Veil. You see, one of his bones is buried here. Just there, under that tree."

She followed the direction he pointed to, where the jungle was the thickest and the trees were the tallest and biggest around, indicating they were the oldest.

"Do you know what would happen to your demon if I destroyed this island?" he asked, when she looked at him again.

Most people froze up when panic struck, but Zoe Bankes lived on the energy of panic. She wouldn't have lasted two seconds in the realm of social media if things like anxiety and fear had the ability to incapacitate her.

Panic only drove her mind to work faster, clearer.

"Oh no," she feigned worry with dry sarcasm. "Please don't threaten the demon who abducted me and is holding me prisoner against my will, whatever will I do without him?"

"If that were truly the case, then why would you choose to stay here, rather than go with me?"

Zoe shrugged a shoulder and gave him the honest truth. "I like my odds better with him."

"Hmm," he mused, appearing humored, yet she could feel his growing agitation. "So, he hasn't revealed who he really is to you yet. Interesting. Well, I suppose if you won't come willingly, I'll just have to move onto plan B."

"HEX!" Zoe screamed, turning on her heels and running, as the Devil strode across the sand toward her. She refused to take her eyes off him and knew, deep down, that she was probably just delaying the inevitable, but damn if she wasn't going down kicking and screaming. "HEX, COME ON! HEX!"

Genuine panic had begun wrapping itself around Zoe's heart and mind, when whispers suddenly caressed her ears, igniting shivers along the back of her neck. It filled her with more relief than she could have guessed at. With a burst of winded laughter, she stopped running and spun back to the face the Devil with a middle finger.

"You lose." She grinned.

He halted, a split-second of puzzlement. Then, he clenched his teeth and his eyes darkened like a storm brewing at sea. Zoe swore the very sun dimmed. The ocean around them began to churn. He took another step toward her and the Veil ripped the air open right between them, shadows pouring out like ink in water. Hex's strong arms wrapped around Zoe to pull her into the darkness with him, and he didn't hesitate to start moving. A hundred different reactions pinged around inside her all at once—relief, lust, admiration, lust . . . yeah, lust.

Maybe it was the close encounter with the fourth kind, but her libido was full on cheerleading with Hex's presence. *Give me an H, give me an E, give me a good reason why I'm turning into Sinister fucking Barbie!* Happy to put the blame solely on the demon heating up her insides like a sauna, Zoe turned in his arms and climbed up his rock-hard body to put her face in his as he sped through the Veil.

"Fucking took you long enough," she griped. "Think you could've cut it any closer there, champ?"

"Sorry, I got delayed," he grit out. "I—"

The rest of his sentence was cut off when he almost dropped her, his body doubling over as he coughed up a bucket of seawater. The Veil thinned around them in a way that made Zoe very nervous, like she somehow knew it wasn't supposed to do that.

"Shit, that's not good," she panicked, clinging to him when it kept happening. "Hex? It's your bone—"

The second he was given a moment to breath, he roared. It sounded both pained and outraged. Then, they were moving faster. The darkness became a wind tunnel of nothingness. Hex was wracked with more bouts of coughing up seawater, and he seemed to be weakening.

"Who the fuck did we just piss off? Poseidon?" Zoe demanded.

She was scared for him and for herself, unsure of what would happen to her in the Veil if he collapsed.

"Worse," he coughed, his voice raw. "Leviathan."

"Holy shit, are you serious?" she whimpered. "Where are we going?"

"City of the Dead."

A shiver ran through her, ominous prospects filling her mind. The lonely little island didn't seem so bad now in retrospect. Before she could say as much, the Shallows pulsed and thinned again. Hex's hold on her almost faltered as he released another howl of pain-filled rage. Zoe tightened her arms around his neck. She knew what was happening. Leviathan was keeping good on his threat and destroying the island, Hex's buried bone along with it.

"Go back, Hex," she encouraged. "Just go back and stop it!"

"Too . . . late," he managed through ragged, audible breaths. "Almost there."

A few seconds later, they emerged from the Shallows at top speed and Hex turned just in time to hit the exterior wall of a building with his back to save Zoe from the collision.

"Fucking momentum," he muttered.

He leaned against the wall with his eyes closed, still holding on to her. Zoe blinked at the nighttime city surrounding them with shocked wonder. She couldn't have mistaken the well-known architecture of the French Quarter if she'd tried. Given he was a demon with the ability to trek through the Veil, she thought he'd meant City of the Dead in a more literal sense, so she was tremendously relieved.

"New Orleans?" she exhaled. "You brought us to New Orleans?"

"Mmm," he acknowledged. "Hope you like jazz."

Before she could reply, Hex collapsed and nearly took her down with him.

"Hex!"

Concern threatened to cripple Zoe when she knelt beside him and found his skin icy to the touch. A look around for help turned up nothing. The city was a ghost town. No sign of people, animals, or movement of any kind. Unable to accept that, Zoe jumped to her feet and barged into the nearest establishment, only to find it empty. She raced back out into the street, her eyes searching for any sign of life, no matter how small or distant. It was dark, her mind tried to reason that as the excuse for the lack of activity, even as her chest grew heavier with the truth. Just like the island, they were completely alone. No one was there to help them, because the city wasn't real. Somehow, it was just an illusion.

"Fuck, Hex!" she raged, dropping beside him once more. "What am I supposed to do now?"

Zoe lifted her hand, torn between stroking his hair and throttling him awake, when he suddenly vanished, robbing her of both. It was startling, but she didn't panic right away. He was always disappearing and reappearing on her. She glanced around, expecting to see some evidence of his shadows. Instead, she found a woman standing in the middle of the otherwise empty street, staring at her with eyes of pure white. Her hair and body were wrapped in a mixture of earthy fabrics with a golden orange that complemented her darker complexion. The question remained of who or what she was, just as it seemed to apply to everyone she'd been meeting lately.

"Hurry, Zoe. Follow the lights."

Taken aback, Zoe scrambled to her feet once the woman also vanished from sight. She tried to overcome the surprise and unease, but ended up shaking her head.

"Hmm-mm, nope," she said out loud. "I do not like that you know my name, lady. Not even a little."

It was obvious the woman had done something with Hex, but where could Zoe even begin to look? She peered down a dark side road first and then back down the infamous Bourbon Street, when a distant streetlamp lit up.

Zoe started, then narrowed her eyes with a frown. "Well, shit."

CHAPTER SIX

DEMIMONDE

Against all logic, Zoe jogged barefoot through the abandoned streets of New Orleans, chasing the light as it jumped from one streetlamp to the next. With the last one already behind her, she didn't need any more direction to find her destination. The storefront advertising all-natural herbs, homeopathic remedies, and spiritual counseling was the only one on the entire block completely lit up. Even the second story windows were glowing in welcome. Zoe was just leery about what kind of welcome that might be.

Windchimes, rather than bells, announced her arrival when she stepped through the front door of the shop. An assortment of aromas instantly invaded her senses, yet most of them were surprisingly pleasant. *Pretty convincing for an illusion.* There was no one on the main floor lined with shelves of bottled herbs and display cases filling up the center to keep the room open and airy. A back door behind the counter most likely led to a storage room, but there was another open doorway to the right, draped in colorful silk. Beyond it was more storage, but also a staircase. As Zoe quietly climbed the stairs, she listened for any strange noises that might alert her to a bad situation. She was halfway up when the woman called down to her.

"You want your demon to wake up, I suggest you choose a different version of hurry, girl. I can't do this on my own."

Despite her lingering wariness, Zoe rushed up the remaining steps and into the second-floor apartment. The glow she'd noted from the street below came not just from the light fixtures and lamps, but countless burning candles. They were set in random places on every available surface, but that was the extent of anything she'd expected to find there. Antique furniture blended seamlessly with modern appliances, thriving houseplants, and various pieces of art. The living room was open to the small, yet efficient kitchen. Exposed posts and beams made the apartment look taller than it should be, and more spacious. She could still pick out the supernatural totems, though—sigils carved into windchimes made of wood and bone, and painted on mandalas struck with feathers and colorful stones. She was even fairly certain that it was what she couldn't see, the things hidden inside the door frames and behind the walls, that made the woman feel more secure in her surroundings.

"You were expecting some kind of movie set?" the woman asked from the mouth of the hallway, a slightly amused smirk curving her lips. Zoe couldn't deny it, so she simply shrugged. "Come on, we're short on time."

Zoe followed her toward the back of the apartment and into the only bedroom, where Hex lay unconscious and mostly naked in the center of a large bed. The latter would've caused her pause—and let's face it, oodles of drooling admiration for his phenomenal physique—had his skin not been so pale it was practically transparent.

"Jesus," she gasped, moving closer to the bed and eyeing the array of obvious ritualistic tools atop the chest of drawers in and amongst more glowing candles. "Let me guess, props?"

Her tone revealed just how much she knew they weren't, which was probably why the woman gave her a hearty laugh before she turned serious.

"We need to sever whatever tie there is that's hurting him," she said, unfolding a square of gold cloth to reveal a very ceremonial-looking dagger. "Physically and magically, in tandem."

Zoe stared at her like she'd grown a second head, before giving the same look to the blade the woman held out for her to take.

"I'm not a surgeon."

"And this is not a scalpel."

"Look, Miss—"

"Farah," the woman offered.

Hex's shoulders lifted from the mattress with a rough, strained breath that didn't sound any better going back in.

"What's the tie?" Farah demanded, her urgent tone spurring Zoe's anxiety higher. "What's the physical link?"

"A–a bone, on the island," Zoe stammered, grabbing the handle of the knife, as she looked the woman straight in her spooky white eyes. "You know, the one you just helped the Leviathan destroy?"

It was just another hunch, of course, deduced from the fact that the woman knew Hex and had apparently been involved in creating the illusion of New Orleans. Who else could Leviathan have used to keep Hex occupied, as he'd claimed?

Rather than respond, Farah's head fell back, and she began a low, guttural chanting. Her arms lifted away from her body, bent at the elbows with palms pointed toward the floor, as if she were pushing down on some invisible force. Then her head fell forward, and all the candles in the room dimmed. She began pushing the force in a sweeping, shoving motion toward Hex, before swaying her entire being back and forth like she was using it to cover him from head to toe over and over.

Zoe would be lying if she claimed not to be nervous when she could actually feel the powers Farah was manipulating in the air. The shit was real. She was definitely worried about the part she was supposed to play in this team operation, because no matter how frustrating or aggravating Hex could be, no matter how much she longed for home, her best friend, and Wi-Fi, there was no going back to a world where he didn't exist. Not without losing some part of herself she wasn't even sure how to examine yet.

Farah's chanting grew faster, and she started bouncing, her hands hovering over Hex. The flames of the candles wavered, some growing taller and brighter, while others remained dim. She shouted a single word, grabbed the unseen force like a rope or chain and started pulling it. Zoe got lost in the act of witnessing, unsure if she was awed or terrified by the amount of strain she could detect in Farah's features and muscles. Exactly the kind of strain one would expect to see a person exert while pulling something heavy and tangible.

It took Zoe a moment to realize that shadows had begun seeping out of Hex's body, where those strange tattoos were carved into his skin all down his sides. Some irrational part of her panicked—he'd told her he and the Veil were part of each other. What if that was the only thing that had kept him alive for all these centuries, and the only thing keeping him alive now?

"Stop!" Zoe cried over the woman's bellowing chant. "You can't take that from him, he'll die!"

But Farah didn't stop. If anything, her ritual was drawing to some kind of crescendo. Zoe tried to grab one of Farah's flailing arms to snap her out of it and damn near broke her hand on another invisible power that felt a lot like trying to punch a jet stream.

"Fuck," she swore, her arm whipping back with enough force to jar her shoulder. She shook her hand, even though it didn't hurt; it was more of a stinging zap. She tested the weight of the dagger in her other hand. "Okay, lady, you wanna play operation?"

Zoe wasn't a killer. Her only intention was to slice through whatever hoodoo magic was protecting Farah, so she could bitch-slap some sense into her. But she was reminded of just how weak and human she really was when Farah caught the blade between her palms, stopping her cold. Zoe panted, stunned and more than a little afraid of what might happen next, when Farah merely started chanting again. She continued to hold the blade, her magical words whispering over the flawless metal.

"We must cut as one," she said abruptly, lifting white eyes to Zoe. "There."

Zoe followed the direction she pointed and saw something glowing in the side of Hex's left arm, under the fog of black shadows.

"Hurry, I can't hold it at the surface too long," Farah urged. "We must slice at the same time."

"Shit." Zoe swore, both her breath and nerves were shaky as she moved into position. Unfortunately, between the rolling shadows and her own faulty eyesight, the area just looked like a glowing blur to her. "I can't see it, I don't have my glasses!"

The woman waved her hand and the second Zoe blinked, her vision was crystal clear. It wasn't just a glowing blur on Hex's arm, it was one of his tattoos. Did that mean each symbol or letter was associated with one of his bones buried on earth?

"Sure, make me feel guilty," Zoe muttered. "Ready when you are."

"I slice," Farah instructed, making a chopping motion with the side of her right hand into her left palm. "You slice."

"Got it," Zoe said, steeling her nerves against what would most likely make her sick.

She nearly jumped when the woman let out a high-pitched battle cry, lifted her face to the ceiling and then swung her arm in a more exaggerated version of her chopping motion. Zoe could feel sweat beading on her forehead as she watched the woman's hand like a hawk, the tip of the blade poised at the glowing symbol. The moment the side of Farah's hand made contact with her palm, Zoe pressed the knife into Hex's flesh. She sliced, and Farah sliced at the same time.

If only that could have been the end of it. If only it had been just blood running out of the incision, but it wasn't. The more the woman sliced, forcing Zoe to do the same, the more of Hex's shadows concentrated in the area around the wound she was causing, becoming an extremely dangerous obstacle. One that no amount of blowing or waving with her hand did anything to move.

"Cut it out of him, Zoe, you must get it out of there!" Farah ordered in between her loud cries and chopping motions.

"The tattoo?"

"What hides beneath."

Oh God, seriously? Zoe tried not to retch as she sliced deeper, or when she had no other choice but to use her fingers to dig into the wound, because she could no longer see what she was doing.

"I feel it," she called out on a breath of surprise and relief.

She hadn't known what she was looking for, but when her fingers found a knot that was not made from anything biological, she knew she'd found it. Slick with blood, it was difficult to pull it away from his tissue and veins, or all the other things she didn't want to accidentally damage. Finally, she was able to get the tip of the knife under one taut side.

"Okay, slice!" she said.

Her fingers trembled, threatening to ruin her hold as she waited for just the right moment. Through clenched teeth, she seethed her own kind of battle cry to keep herself focused and away from thoughts of getting sick. The knot wasn't giving up easily. It took five or six sawing-motion slices to finally cut through just one side of it, which left her without any tautness to use as leverage. The glowing of the knot played peek-a-boo with her through the thick fog of his shadows and it seemed to be pulsing like a heartbeat. It took several failed attempts to fold it just right over the edge of the blade where it wouldn't slide off and she could hold it in that position to wait for the right time. Everything was just so slippery—her hands, the knife, the knot. She was almost glad now that the shadows were blocking her view of the gore she'd caused.

To her surprise, it only took three slices to finally sever the last side of the knot, and she released a pent-up cry of relief when she stumbled backward with it in hand.

"Got it!"

Farah stopped her keening and chanting. Something powerful in the air died like a wind coming to an abrupt halt. Calmness settled over the room and the candle flames returned to their normal, steady glow. Zoe covered her mouth with her forearm to keep the aftermath from spilling out—emotions, nerves, adrenaline, whatever it was that was still churning inside her and making her feel queasy. The knot wasn't glowing anymore, it was just a bloody bit of grossness in her hand. She gladly dumped it into the woman's open palm.

"What is it?" Zoe asked.

"A fragment of a very ancient spell," Farah answered, examining the small object with creased brows and a frown. "The physical manifestation of dark magic."

She raised her head and studied Hex, then crossed to the nearest dresser where she dropped the knot into one of the open flames. It started sizzling and popping, and then, in a sudden change that had Zoe nearly jumping out of her skin, the thing unraveled, screeched and slithered out of the candle onto the top of the dresser, appearing more leech-like than rope-like. Farah picked up a heavy, brass statue and squashed it dead.

"Evil has been done to your demon, girl."

Zoe sucked in choppy breaths and waited for her heart to slow back down again as she studied Hex. She wasn't sure if it was her imagination or truth, but it seemed some of the color was beginning to return to his pallid skin.

"He's not my demon."

"No?" Farah smirked with amusement.

She didn't have to point out all the evidence to the contrary; Zoe was well aware of them and not even close to being ready to weigh in on them yet.

"Is that what the rest of the tattoos are?" she asked instead. "More evil?"

"Stitching at the seams," Farah replied. "Whatever your demon began as in his life, he is no longer. I'm too afraid to guess at how long ago that change took place, but know this. The evil done to him, the evil I fear rebirthed him into this, that is not what's in his heart."

"Is that why you're helping us?" Zoe asked. "Why you let him go, against Leviathan's wishes?"

Farah laughed and sank down into an armchair beside the dresser.

"I do not answer to your devils," she countered.
"They are not mine. Your sea creature merely offered me a truth my curiosity couldn't ignore."

"What truth?"

"That the spirit I was helping was not in fact a spirit at all. To be honest, I always knew there was something different about this one," she continued, leaning further back in the chair. "I suppose I needed to confirm my suspicions."

"But you let him go, anyway, after learning the truth," Zoe pointed out.

"I trust my spirits, I let them guide my decisions. They seem partial to your demon," she replied and then looked Zoe in the eyes. "And warn of what might happen should he perish."

"What would happen?"

"It would all unravel, that's what they said," she answered. "They're not always clear as to what, though. I must go now. I've used too much of my powers opening the door and saving your demon. But I will return."

"The door to what?" Zoe asked, shaking her head in confusion.

"This half-world," she gestured. "One of many demimondes between the realms of the living and the dead. Worry not, your devils and sea monsters are not welcome here."

"Wait, what am I supposed to do with Hex?" she asked when the woman started fading in and out like an apparition.

"Let him rest and heal. He has over two hundred bones left, he'll be fine."

Farah faded completely out of sight, and Zoe ground her teeth on a growl of frustration. She didn't want to be stuck alone in an empty half-world! What if Hex took a turn for the worse and she had no one to help her?

"Great. Just fucking awesome!" she erupted, kicking the empty chair. She glanced down at the knife still clutched in her right hand, and tossed it on the dresser with disgust.

In the bathroom, she scrubbed the drying blood away and couldn't say why she'd been both surprised and relieved that it was red. Yes, she could. Too many damn horror movies tended to depict demons spewing black blood to further emphasize their evilness. Zoe's laugh was miserably self-deprecating. She'd never realized just how many expectations she'd had for the real supernatural world based off Hollywood's version, but Farah's apartment and Hex's blood appeared to be two of them.

She scrutinized herself in the mirror and took stock of her current situation. All the high-strung emotions and adrenaline had all but dissipated and she no longer felt sick to her stomach, so that was a bonus.

"Good job not puking on the patient, doc," she complimented herself.

Unfortunately, that reminded her that her medical duties weren't over. She cursed herself for how much time had already passed since she'd cut the knot out of Hex's arm, knowing he'd been lying there bleeding the whole time.

Good thing med school was never an option.

Zoe gathered bandages and clean cloths from the

bathroom, then quickly returned to the bedroom. At least his color still appeared to be getting better. The shadows had receded as well, now that the ritual was over. In hindsight, it was easy to deduce they'd emerged on their own to protect him, rather than being drawn out to be stolen as she'd originally feared. At the side of the bed, she paused. There was no wound. Dry blood stained his arm and the sheet where it had pooled during the procedure, but otherwise his skin was flawless. Even the ink of the tattoo she'd sliced to hell was completely unmarred.

"Well, shit." She frowned, wondering if it was part of his demonic abilities, or if the shadows had played a part in his super-fast healing.

Either way, it was a relief to know he hadn't been lying there bleeding all that time. Zoe set the bandages aside and cleaned the dried blood from his skin with an alcohol wipe. Then, she carefully lifted his arm and covered the bloody part of the sheet with a thick layer of clean, dry cloths to rest it on. It was hard telling how long it would take him to wake up, but she knew there was no way in hell she could move him to change the whole sheet.

Perched on the side of the bed, she examined his tattoos. The symbols formed a direct line all the way from the hairline behind his ear down the side of his entire body, visible where he wasn't covered with the sheet. It even outlined his foot to the point of his baby toe, just as it did on his hands. Stitching at the seams, Farah had said, but what the fuck did that mean? That Hex was some kind of demonic Voodoo doll? Hell's own

Frankenstein's monster? The more she learned about him, the more questions she had. It was getting to be exhausting.

There were no clocks in the bedroom, but she was fairly certain it had taken a couple of hours for the ritual. Maybe she was just exhausted all around. The sun had already risen in Papua New Guinea, and if it had already set in the real New Orleans as it had in the demimonde version, then it was getting close to her normal bed time in New York. She could feel it settling into her bones and brain, the weariness and need to shut it all down for a while to recharge. The high-octane emotions and events of the day weren't helping her stay awake, either. She was crashing fast. Not wanting to disturb Hex, Zoe forced herself to stand and went about snuffing all the candles that hadn't already drowned their own wicks in melted wax. Though she was fairly certain half-worlds couldn't be burned down by candles, the precaution was too ingrained to ignore.

With a pause at the head of the bed, she gave in to her desire to brush Hex's hair from his forehead, then frowned at the tattoo that had been hiding underneath. It was different than the rest, centered above his brows. It almost looked like a target. A solid circle around a smaller, solid circle, around a smaller circle made of tiny dash marks, and it wasn't black like the others, but a deep, strawberry red. Perhaps it was a scar, rather than another tattoo. She realized she could still see clearly without glasses and was struck with surprised guilt all over again. Zoe couldn't believe Farah would give her such an incredible gift after she'd tried to thwart her ritual.

It choked Zoe up a bit, but she quickly shook it off. There was no sense getting worked up over something that would most likely be gone by morning. She blamed it on fatigue and headed out of the room. At the doorway, her gaze skimmed over Hex's gorgeous body again, then she turned off the light and went about snuffing the rest of the candles in the apartment.

By the time she made it to the long sofa with its throw blanket and pillows, Zoe knew two things with absolute certainty. One, she was going to sleep with Hex. The knowledge was already burning in all her womanly instincts and needy places too strongly to deny, despite everything he'd revealed to her the day before. Or perhaps because of it. She needed to know the decision was hers, and not some demonic coercion. And two, she was going to spend every waking moment ensuring the warning Farah's spirits had given her never came true. Hex would not perish, Abbadon would not capture Zoe, and the fucker would not hunt Kami for all eternity. She would find a way to keep them all safe no matter what. There just had to be a way.

****

Hex's eyes opened to a white ceiling and silence. He closed them again and let his senses take over, expanding them to get a feel for the time and place, the status of all his lost boys and girls . . . the island. Leviathan had targeted his bone, but otherwise, the island had been left intact. He could still feel it there, but no longer his connection to it. Hex would never be able to use it as one of his earthly hideouts ever again. He wasn't nearly as concerned with how quickly Abaddon had turned to Leviathan as he was with how fast the sea beast had come looking to take advantage of the situation. It stunk of desperation, and that was never a good sign when it came to the Seven. Hex had been imprisoned in the Abyss for too long. He needed to get the bigger picture on what the fuck was happening with Hell's most nefarious and narcissistic. With Zoe's connections to the new Queen of Avarice, perhaps she could help fill in some of the blanks for him. If she wasn't raring to kill him first.

He'd already felt her out first thing, sleeping in the other room and undoubtedly exhausted from all she'd been put through over the last two days. It was an uncomfortable feeling knowing he'd caused and played a major part in those things, but he would not apologize for saving her life. The night before was a blur awash in magic, so he could only hope Farah had managed to keep Zoe from freaking out too much after he'd lost consciousness. He wondered what his little doe thought of her new temporary home and then grimaced. She probably hated it for the lack of Wi-Fi, alone.

With a groan, he rubbed his face with his hands and sat up. He was naked, covered only with a sheet. There was blood on the bed near his left arm. He ran a hand over his skin, fully aware of the missing link to his destroyed bone that had been there. He just wasn't clear on any of the details. More blood covered the athame on the dresser. Hex pinched a clean portion of the steel blade so he could inspect the prints along the handle, and an unsettling darkness fell over him. They were far too small to belong to Farah.

"Shit."

He tossed the athame back on the dresser, wrapped the sheet around his waist more securely, and wandered out into the living room. The sun was just coming back around to his beloved city, casting a warm glow over his beautiful girl and highlighting the mahogany shades in her dark curls. Hex sat on the coffee table and lifted her hand, examining the dried blood staining the crevices alongside her fingernails. He swore under his breath again.

"I'm so sorry, doe," he whispered, placing kisses over her knuckles.

"That's a start," she muttered sleepily, her voice husky and as tempting as she was.

"Go back to sleep. I'll get you some food and clean clothes," he said, rising with a burst of need to expel his anger.

"Yeah, get pissed, that's healthy."

Her words stopped him dead in his tracks, and his muscles tensed. "Would you rather I feel grateful? Should I thank you for helping Farah sever the tie to my bone, Zoe?"

He turned while speaking, to find her sitting herself up on the cushions. Her lids were still heavy, but he knew her mind was already growing as sharp and clear as a missile's trajectory.

"That's the usual response."

"You shouldn't have been in that position to begin with!"

"Okay, I get it. I'm the damsel in distress and you're the white knight." She yawned. "The not-any-kind-of-good white knight, rather. If it makes you feel any better, I totally let you bleed out while I cried over my own problems."

"Sure, that really makes us even," he bit out.

"What is this? Do you really want to fight right now?" she asked, lifting her hand to gesture at his rigid stance.

Hex gnawed on his anger. She was right. He didn't want to fight with her, damn it. He'd been trying so hard to move them away from that arena. He forced his muscles to relax and shoved the anger aside for the moment, but the heavy regret and disappointment wouldn't budge.

"I thought that's what we do," he said.

Zoe snorted. "Yeah, I guess it is."

Hex made his way back to the coffee table and reclaimed it as his seat, so he could brush his fingers through the curls framing her face.

"I didn't bleed out. The Veil would never allow that."

Her mouth moved in a way that told him he'd just confirmed her own suspicions, and she nodded. "I noticed," she said. After a moment of staring at her own hands, she looked him right in the eye, her exotic brown irises crystal clear. "What happened to you, Hex? What did they do to you?"

Her words stirred vague memories he was completely detached from. "I don't remember any of the actual details, not of the event. I remember being one thing and then waking up as something else. I imagine I was human once, because how else would I have bones? But I don't recall anything about my human life. Not my name, not my homeland. Nothing."

Zoe studied him intently, then, sighing, shook her head. "I wish I could call your bullshit."

Hex shrugged a shoulder, the aggravation over the ancient mystery of his creation was just too far removed from him. He was no longer emotionally attached to it. The disappointment he felt was only for not being able to give her the answers she wanted. "Me too, baby."

Zoe chuckled, giving her head another shake. "And here I thought demons were supposed to be the masters of deception." She smirked, then raised her hand when Hex opened his mouth to remind her of where he stood on the subject. "I know, I get it. You're happy with the way things are, unashamed to be a real demony demon and stuff. Look, if you don't get me some caffeine very soon, I'm gonna go into the bedroom, grab that bloody knife and see how many more knots I can cut out of you. I'm pretty sure they're all connected to your tatts, but science cannot be proven without the process of elimination first."

Hex frowned at her, his eyes narrowed on her sober expression. Not that he was worried about her mostly empty threat, he was merely contemplating her request.

"All right, I'll let you drown yourself in caffeine at the corner café, only because I need your mind as focused as possible," he agreed. When her features brightened with curiosity more than excitement over his concession, he held up his finger to stop the barrage of questions before they could even start. "But you will eat a full, nutritious breakfast, or no coffee."

"I'll eat breakfast because I'm hungry," she corrected with a defiant arch of her brow.

Hex just grinned and caressed the side of her face. "Whatever you say, boss." He rose and tucked the sheet again, only because he wanted to stay on her friendly and cooperative side. Otherwise, he'd already be naked. "I'm going to go get us both some new clothes, it won't take long."

"It's no fun when you give up that easily," she complained as he started turning away.

"A win's a win. I want you to eat, I don't really care how it has to happen."

"Please don't pretend like you don't enjoy trying to assert your demony bossiness over me," she said, giving him a knowing look.

Fuck it. If she wanted to spar dirty, he'd take that over friendly and cooperative any day. Hex called forth the shadows, opening the Shallows for fast transport, then dropped the sheet and gave his little doe a wicked smirk over his shoulder.

"Please don't act like you don't enjoy the hell out of it," he returned.

Before he could disappear completely into the Veil, she leaped to her feet and smacked him right on his bare ass.

"Like you said, a win's a win." She chuckled naughtily, giving him a wink as she sauntered away.

Hex ground out a laugh through his teeth, his entire body growing rock hard from the feel of her hot little hand on his ass and suggestive behavior. The spanking didn't do it for him in all honesty, but right now, any kind of physical contact with Zoe was enough to drive him wild. He needed to hurry up and convince her of things he already knew to be inexplicably true. That she was his, and that he could show her a kind of pleasure guaranteed to prove that the debate between which of them was boss would never be relevant.

CHAPTER 7

WORDS WITH FRENEMIES

A hot shower and girl-power pep talk hadn't helped Zoe recuperate from the backfire of slapping Hex on his superbly firm ass, so she zeroed in on a new project instead. The sculpted piece of art that was the demon's buttocks hadn't been the only thing he'd revealed when he'd turned his back on her and dropped the sheet. His entire spine was lined in tattoos, all the way down to the delicious plane between his lower back dimples. God, it was almost wrong that someone so ridiculously hot had spent most of his existence hidden away in the pure darkness of the Veil.

Like the mark on his forehead, the ink running down his back differed from those lining both sides of his body. Each was a different color, and they were oddly spaced, rather than connected like . . . well, a seam. Zoe shuddered at that eerie description and hoped Farah hadn't meant it in a literal sense.

"Ready to eat?"

Pulled from her thoughts, Zoe stepped out of the holistic shop and onto the sidewalk, so Hex could follow, letting the door swing closed behind them. She watched him slip on a pair of sunglasses and glanced at the bright, morning sun. The air was just as heavy with humidity there as it had been on the island, and it wasn't even noon yet. One would think a half-world would only have half the realism, but oh no. They were definitely in the south.

"I'm ready to consume ridiculous amounts of coffee," she answered. "Do you need more cover?"

Hex's brows creased in question over the top of his dark shades, so she pointed toward the sun. He scowled and put his hand on the back of her neck to aim her toward the café across the street at the corner.

"How many times do I have to tell you I'm not a vampire? The sun can't hurt me."

"Well, with the way you travel smothered in shadows all the time, you'd think so."

"That's for stealth, speed, and protection, not a sensitivity to the light."

"Noted." She sighed. "Guess I'll have to find another way to kill you."

Hex chuckled and gave her a naughty smirk. "You keep talking dirty to me, we might have to skip breakfast."

Zoe stepped onto the curb of the next sidewalk and gave him a pitying look. "Aww, it's cute how you think I'd actually skip out on coffee for you."

Inside the café, she was again struck by the realism of their environment. The aroma of food and brewing coffee hit her head-on, yet the place was completely devoid of either and the people making it.

Hex gave her a playful smile. "Guess we get to eat

for free."

"Yeah, and make it all ourselves," she grumbled as he headed toward the counter.

"You leave that detail to me," he said. "See those chalkboards on the wall?"

She glanced at the three boards on the wall to her right. They were directly across from the counter and visible to anyone who sat at any of the tables in the large space in between. The largest one in the middle listed the breakfast specials, while the two skinnier boards flanking it listed the various types of teas and coffees.

"What about them?"

"They need to be erased so we can put them to better use."

"Like strip hangman?" she suggested.

Hex stared at her for a moment before narrowing his eyes accusingly. "This is one of those rare instances when I can't tell if you're joking."

Zoe preened, taking that as a win without revealing that it was because she wasn't entirely joking at all. She grabbed a chair and pulled it over to the wall to start on the chalkboards. Once she had everything erased, she cocked a hip and considered the blank slates in front of her.

"Well, now how am I going to know what I want to order?" she asked, looking over her shoulder just as Hex was setting two full plates on the nearest table. Her lips pulled into a mildly surprised frown when he returned to the counter to retrieve a silver coffee pot and two mugs. "How the hell?"

"I'm just that damn good," he said with a naughty

smirk. "Come on, coffee's fresh and hot."

A little mesmerized, Zoe climbed off the chair and studied the loaded table. There was even a tray of pastries in the center, yet she hadn't heard so much as an eggshell crack.

She shook her head. "Hex."

"This place is between worlds," he explained, leaning his hands on the back of a chair. "It's quite easy for me to reach through the thin layer to retrieve things."

"Because of the Veil," she surmised.

He nodded.

Zoe gestured to the food and coffee. "So, you just stole someone's breakfast out from under them?"

Hex gave her a wry expression. "No, I stole breakfast from the kitchen. It hadn't been served yet," he replied. "Maybe the beignets, those I took off a serving table, but there were plenty more I left behind."

"From this café?" she asked, just wanting confirmation.

"Yes, just right on the other side of the fabric of this demimonde," he answered. "Knowing how much you love your questions, I assumed Farah had explained at least that much to you last night."

"She did, kind of," Zoe confirmed, not in the least offended by his remark. "I guess I just didn't realize they were so close."

"Think of the world of the living as a solid ball of wood embedded with speakers, nice and flush," Hex said, holding his hands up in demonstration. "Wrapped around it is an egg crate, only with the holes more spaced out. The Veil is the very material the crate is made out of, but each of the little divots where the eggs sit is a demimonde. Pockets of space, mimicking the environment of the living world just on the other side of the Veil from where they touch. A vibrational replica."

"A what?"

"A carbon copy, created by the energies the living produce, imprinted into the fabric of space and time," he elaborated.

Zoe's mind exploded, as she peered all around her again. "So it ends?" she speculated. "We can't just hop in a car and drive from here to the next town or state."

"Correct," he said, lowering his hands again. "Those walls between each demimonde is the Veil, where only I or the dead can travel. Though, during certain cosmic events, the vibrations can harmonize, drawing demimondes through the Veil to overlap with parts of the land of the living."

As Zoe tried to wrap her head around that, Hex poured the steaming hot coffee into their mugs. The sight and smell of the rich, black deliciousness had an unexpected pang of gratitude hitting her right in the chest. In a strange way, the truth and evidence of all his abilities was like meeting one of the superheroes she geeked out about in real life. That he would use those powers just to get coffee and food for her was so simple, yet insanely touching. Without giving it a second thought, she rose up on her tiptoes, wrapped her arms around his neck and pressed her lips to his. All the hot, midnight sin and dark fantasies he'd tasted like on the island were still right there, waiting to grab hold of her libido and take it for a spin. She used his disorientation to step away before he could reciprocate and really mess with her system.

"No one's ever stolen coffee for me before," she said.

Hex blinked once before coming out of his temporary shock. "Fuck, if that's all it takes."

Zoe laughed and grabbed a beignet off the tray. "Now, you're catching on," she said. "So, what was your plan for the boards?"

When he didn't answer, she glanced over her shoulder. He rubbed a hand over his face roughly and gave her an exasperated look that had her grinning shamelessly. After polishing off her pastry, she plopped down at the table and took a long, deep drink of coffee, letting out a low moan when the dark liquid made its way down her throat.

"Dear God, it's true," she continued after taking another sip. "This city really does make the best coffee."

"Words," Hex blurted, giving her a heated glare for the noises she was making. "Certain words. We're going to make a list."

"Okay," Zoe drug out in puzzlement. "What kind of words?"

He considered it for a moment. "Can you name the Seven?"

"I think so."

"On the board," he gestured. "Without any damn sound effects, if you can manage to contain yourself."

With a chuckle, she approached the boards again, taking her coffee with her. She contemplated grabbing the pot, but decided she'd inflict bodily damage if Hex tried to take it away before it was empty. After moving the

chair to the first narrow board on the left, she grabbed a piece of chalk and wrote out the list.
1. Pride
2. Greed
3. Lust
4. Gluttony
5. Envy
6. Wrath
7. Sloth

Finished, she placed the chalk back in the tray and stepped down, so Hex could see it. He rubbed a hand over his chin and scrutinized the board, as if it were complicated plays to the next football game.

"What's the deal?" she huffed. "It's seven words."

His expression was dark, muscles working in the back of his jaw, as he stalked to the other narrow board and wrote out his own list.
1. Superbia
2. Avaritia
3. Umbrella
4. Gula
5. Invidia
6. Ira
7. Acedia

When he was done, he gestured to his board. "What does it say?"

Zoe blinked at him, stunned that he was being serious. "How the hell should I know? I don't speak gibberish."

"It's Latin," he corrected her. "This is the Seven in Latin."

"Really?" She arched an eyebrow, jabbing her finger at the third word down. "And what was umbrella Latin for, again?"

"What?" He frowned.

"You wrote umbrella, Hex."

He studied it, his eyes narrowed. "It says manacle."

"Yeah, that's much better," she scoffed. "I can see how manacle would be a more favorable option."

"I didn't say manacle," he growled, turning away.

"Then I need my fucking ears checked," she exclaimed, tossing her hand up in the air.

"No, you don't," he said. "I need my brain fixed."

Zoe halted, her frustrated tirade dying before she could make another retort. His tone sounded dark and defeated.

"What are you talking about?"

He looked at her, his expression darker than she'd seen it before. Even worse than when he'd blown up during their argument about her being the one in danger, not Kami.

"It's all messed up," he said, rubbing a hand over his head. "That's why I need your words. Mine are gone."

She took a deep, steadying breath. "Okay, Hex, I need a little more to go on than that. We're talking right now, and have been talking. You have plenty of words and you've been using them all correctly, so I don't understand what you're trying to explain here."

He simply nodded, then instead of elaborating, he asked, "Can you name them?"

"I just did." She waved a hand at the list.

"No, their actual names," he said. "Do you know all

their names?"

"Oh, um . . ." Zoe returned to the board and grabbed the chalk. "Okay, I know Greed is Saphiel and Wrath is Abaddon."

She wrote the names out next to their corresponding sin. Hex appeared at her side with her plate.

"Trade me," he said. "You eat, I'll list the names."

She studied him. Whatever struggle he was experiencing was still evident in his features, but he also appeared determined to fight through it and she admired that.

"Good idea, because I don't think I know them all now that I'm up here," she admitted.

He gave her a quick smile and accepted the chalk from her. "Just read back what I write."

"Beliel," she said, after he wrote the name next to the sin of Pride. "Wait, I thought pride was Lucifer?"

"It is," he replied. "To humans. But Lucifer isn't actually anyone's name. It was a typo made by scribes translating texts from languages they weren't fluent in. The Demon of Pride is definitely Beliel."

"Okay, well at least that one isn't a brain issue."

Hex smiled over his shoulder at her. "Science has to be proven through the process of elimination first," he repeated her earlier statement.

Zoe brightened and pointed her fork at him. "That's genius, Hexy."

"Ugh," he sneered and went back to work.

She snickered to herself and shoveled more food into her mouth—she really was quite famished. The two slices of jam toast she'd eaten the day before may as well have been a single saltine cracker for how hungry she felt now.

After he finished writing out the next name below Saphiel, Zoe's chewing slowed as she tilted her head and tried to sound it out in her mind first.

"I'm not sure I know how to pronounce that," she confessed, pursing her lips. "Neb-u-cad–"

He shook his head. "Stop. It's wrong."

"How do you know if I don't finish?" she asked.

"Nebuchadnezzar was a Babylonian king." He sighed. "Not a deadly sin. I must have still been thinking about the Lucifer typo and my broken brain latched onto the first Babylonian king it could think of."

"Okay, I'm not sure I follow that completely, but this is still good right? Now we know which word is all messed up for you."

"You know," he said. "I can't verify it, but you know which one. Do you know his real name?"

Zoe looked from her list to his and realized they must match, because he couldn't seem to name the third one down correctly in Latin or in English. The name or the sin, she noticed. Lust was the one she'd written for that slot, but no matter how much she wracked her brain and even with all the supernatural TV shows and movies in her memory vault, she couldn't seem to find a name for that particular sin.

"No, I'm sorry. If I had Wi-Fi and my phone, I could look it up in like two seconds." Hex scowled at her, but she didn't back down. "Just stating facts."

He straightened, then perked up slightly. "The library. We can find it there."

"Maybe you should finish the list, in case it isn't just

one of them," she suggested.

"Trust me, it's only the one," he replied darkly.

"Okay, then how about you finish it just to sate my curiosity," she amended, giving him a cheeky grin.

He smirked, but started scribbling out the last three names.

Gluttony – Beelzabul

Envy – Leviathan

"Well, that explains a lot," Zoe muttered to herself. When he wrote out the last one for the sin of Sloth, she stepped forward and wagged her fork at it. "Wait, I think that might be another one. Ba'al Pe'or? I've never heard that name before."

"No, you're right. His name would be modernized now," Hex said, rubbing the name out and rewriting it.

"Belphegor?" Zoe read aloud to make sure it was right.

"Belphegor," Hex repeated in confirmation.

"Man, his parents hated him," she remarked. "So, it really is just the one. Lust."

He gave her a funny look. "Pachyderm?"

Zoe nearly choked on her eggs, but the sincerity of his question had her laughter dying. "Wow, you're not kidding. Okay, how about neither one of us try to say that particular sin?"

Hex frowned. "Yeah, sure."

Finished with her breakfast, Zoe set her plate aside and wiped bacon grease from her fingers on one of the napkins. Hex abandoned the chalk, but he was brooding. She didn't find that as hot as all the supernatural romance novels had led her to believe. It was because she was getting to know him better, and didn't like seeing him troubled nearly as much as she liked seeing him trying to be all bossy.

"Hey, don't worry. I'll find his name," she assured him. "How far is the library from here?"

The shadows and Hex's arms wrapped around her simultaneously. Zoe barely felt the rush of darkness before they came to a stop inside a brightly lit library done in modern colors and shapes. It was just enough to make her feel a little lightheaded, a little off balance, but it passed quickly.

"Well, all right then." She exhaled, peering around. "I'll get started, you get the coffee."

When he didn't budge, Zoe crossed her arms and gave him an expectant look. "I ate my damn breakfast and one lousy cup is far from *drowning* myself in caffeine. Your words, not mine."

He gave her an unimpressed smirk, then disappeared into the shadows again, only to reappear before she could even move an inch. He'd been smart enough to bring the entire silver carafe along with her mug. Zoe grinned, accepting a freshly poured cup from him. With the same gratitude she'd felt the first time, she rose up to kiss him on the cheek.

Hex turned his mouth to hers at the last second, taking her by surprise. It left her mind reeling and her toes tingling. He seemed determined to make a point when he cuffed the side of her neck and plunged deep, turning her small show of appreciation into a steamy seduction. The heat of his mouth tasted like her favorite kind of licorice. Not the twisted vines in a box, but the long, thick rope kind she used to get at the pier as a kid. But when she nearly dropped her coffee without it striking a single chord of concern, the significance of that startled her.

"Hex." It was a breathless plea, though she'd aimed for determined.

"Mmm, now that's how you thank somebody," he said. The thick gravel of his voice did untold, wicked things to her insides as he peppered soft caresses over her jaw and cheek. "I could spend days exploring each and every one of your details, little doe."

A hot shiver of yearning worked all the way down her spine, igniting more of her lust, and that beast was gaining momentum dangerously fast.

"We don't have days, Hex," she pointed out, as much to abort her own fantasies as his. "The longer we stay here, the more vulnerable your witch friend becomes to the Seven."

He straightened and his brows creased with concern, even as he shook his head in denial. "She's a Queen of the Voodoo. Her ancestors were brought over from Saint-Domingue before the rebellion and the Louisiana Purchase. Her family's spirits and magic runs deep here, and they have never wavered from their faith. If anything, it has grown stronger in this hub of the dead."

"Shit, okay." Zoe exhaled. "That's a lot more powerful than I thought. But, Hex, Leviathan already knows about her, and that she's been helping you. After royally pissing him off, how long do you think it will take him to run back to Abaddon with the news?"

He growled, spinning away from her.

Regret tightened her chest. She hated that she was always the one pointing out all the negatives of their situation. An idea struck her, but she was wary of how Hex might react to it.

"Maybe there's a way to stall him or make it up to him," she said, deciding it was worth the risk of his anger. "Before you showed up, Leviathan said he just needed you to do him a favor. What if that favor will keep him from reporting back to Abaddon?"

Hex looked at her, his expression still troubled. Another thought hit Zoe and she didn't like it one single bit.

"Shit, Hex," she gasped. "What if he's out there, right now, hunting down another one of your bones?"

His features grew even darker, his lips curling back in a snarl. "Stay here."

The room seemed to erupt with dark clouds as the Veil opened to swallow him whole. Zoe toasted the shadows with her coffee as they began to recede.

"Yeah, because I'm totally free to leave whenever I want." She sighed.

****

Hex heard her sass, but it only made him more determined to finish what he'd started. His clever little mate wasn't the only one who wanted the freedom to come and go as she pleased. More to the point, he couldn't bear the thought of losing her, and that's exactly what would happen if Abaddon caught up with them now. Even if Greed or his new bride could convince the Devil to spare Zoe's life, Abaddon would never let Hex go. As a prisoner of the Abyss, he would never see her again, and that was too vile a thought to consider. Which was why he was taking her advice. As the lesser of their current evils, Leviathan could, at the very least, be eliminated as a threat. At the most, he may be able to afford them a little more time, so they could formulate a decent plan of action. Or *any* plan of action.

The last place he'd expected to find the Hellmouth was sitting behind a desk inside the home office of his mansion in the Greek Isles. Hex remained hidden so he could peer over the beast's shoulder and find out what he was so urgently scribbling on about. When he saw it was nothing more than notes regarding a new product line for one of his company's many subsidiaries, Hex nearly rolled his eyes. He'd never understood the Seven's desires to immerse themselves in human business. It seemed as appealing as an acid bath followed by rolling down a salt pillar.

Hex moved deeper into the room carpeted in the kind of teal that managed to not be blue or green at the same time, depending on how the sunlight hit it. He compared a priceless waterscape with the very sea it depicted visible through the open French doors. Centered beneath it was an antique side-table full of more expensive nautical relics and a collection of business cards. The companies and their logos differed, but not the name of the being they all belonged to. He released the Veil just enough to be noticeable, pretty much the same way he'd first revealed himself to Zoe—going from completely unseen to surrounded by his shadows. There were no outward signs from Leviathan that Hex's sudden appearance bothered him, but that wasn't surprising. Hex plucked up one of the cards and arched a brow at the beast's bowed head.

"Thirio Pelagos?" he read aloud. "That's subtle."

"Almost as subtle as a living curse calling himself Hex," Leviathan remarked without pausing in his note-taking.

Hex shrugged and dropped the card back into its holder. He didn't bother explaining that it had never been his choice, just the name he'd gotten stuck with for so long it had erased any that came before it from his memory. When Envy continued to be a dick by making him wait, Hex folded his arms over his chest and leaned against the doorjamb of the French doors. He understood the bastard was using it as a form of payback for the island incident, but he didn't have time to play grudge games.

"Let's get straight to the point," he said. "You need a favor that you thought you could threaten my mate into forcing me to do, which went about as well as I can imagine it would've gone for me had our roles been reversed."

There, that got the fucker's attention. The pen stopped its incessant scratching at once and Leviathan lifted his face slowly; his eyes brewing like a pissed off ocean.

"I also know that you have no love or loyalty for Abaddon or any of his ilk."

"I have even less love or tolerance for the Damned," Leviathan replied. "Especially one that's trying to play in the big leagues where he doesn't belong."

It appeared the Devil wasn't as ready to bargain as Hex had hoped, clinging to an offense that could burn like Greek fire if he didn't get a shove in the right direction.

"Well, I know that's not true," he returned. "I've never done anything to alter the entire course of your existence, so I think your hatred for all things divine is so thorough, it's the only reason why you sought me out for help. And here I am, despite your threat against my mate, offering a mutually beneficial exchange, rather than seeking retribution. And we both know you would never do the same, so let's cut the offended bullshit, shall we?"

Leviathan laughed, leaning back in his chair. "My pleasure. No offense, but you're only here offering an exchange, because you've been left no other option. And because you, Strider, will never be powerful enough to bring retribution to anyone's door, let alone mine. How's that for no bullshit?"

"You also get the added benefit of pulling one over on Abaddon." Hex picked right up, ignoring the rest, because it didn't matter. It was all just word games. "I mean, when was the last time you got to take a stab at one of those fuckers?"

Leviathan leveled him with a look that warned he was dangerously close to crossing a line, before seething with reluctant agreement. "Yes, well, there is that."

He stared out at the Aegean through the open French doors to his left. Hex knew better than to rush things now. After several minutes ticked by, Leviathan removed a long, velvet jewelry box from the top drawer of his desk and brought it to Hex.

"I need you to deliver this to the Renner Farm on the outskirts of Liberty, Kansas in two days' time."

"I'm not sure I have two days," Hex replied honestly.

"I'll make sure you do."

"Fine." He accepted the box. "Just to the farm, or someone in particular at the farm?"

"Just leave it with the other gifts, it will get where it needs to go," Leviathan answered.

Hex studied him, but didn't question his information or how he'd obtained it. Instead, he held the box up to seal their deal. "As soon as I deliver this, we're square." It was a statement, not a question.

"Deliver it and I'll go back to forgetting that you even exist."

"Just make sure you forget my mate exists, Levi, and I'll forget I know exactly where to find yours," Hex returned, stepping into the shadows to leave, before every single one of his muscles clenched with rage. Muttering a heated curse, he pivoted on his heels and stormed back into the office. "Which is exactly why you threatened her in the first place, you primordial fucking prick!"

Leviathan merely gave him a smug smirk and headed back toward his desk. "Always level the playing field *before* you enter negotiations, Hex, that's strategy one-oh-one. I thought you would've picked up a thing or two after so many years in the Abyss. You had something I wanted, I had to make sure that went both ways, and there's nothing more effective than a high-risk insurance policy. But don't forget that I could easily tip the scales completely in my favor by adding the rest of your bones to that." He reclaimed his seat and looked Hex dead in the eye, but none of the smugness or humor was there anymore. "I told you, *Strider*, you're not cut out for this league."

Hex called the shadows around him completely, before he could ruin his small victory. He let the Veil whisk him far away from Greece and its ancient sea monster, but he was slightly more perplexed by Leviathan's last words than angry. They almost felt like a warning or hidden message, rather than an insult. The way he kept referring to him as just Strider was both oddly deliberate and frustratingly meaningless.

Still, Hex couldn't believe he hadn't seen Leviathan's ploy from the start. It was so painfully clear in hindsight. He'd just been too distracted with the destruction of his bone and making sure Zoe was safe to pay close enough attention to the blatant use of theatrics. Leviathan was not only ancient and cunning, he could literally bend the oceans and sea life to his will. He never needed to talk Zoe into going with him, he could have had her locked away in his mansion long before Hex had freed himself from Farah's interrogation. The destruction of his bone hadn't been Leviathan throwing a tantrum over a missed opportunity, it had been for no other purpose than to ensure Hex was cornered between Abaddon, Zoe, and his bones. He'd needed to make sure Hex was threatened on all fronts and at his complete mercy. *Motherfucker.*

Hex was still stewing when he arrived back at the NOLA Public Library. But the moment he saw his beautiful girl perk up and glance around the room, his foul mood didn't stand a chance. Obviously, his powers had emerged first, searching for a new victim and allowing her to hear the whispers no one else in the universe could hear. She was getting more accurate at pinpointing his location when it happened, so he decided to appear right behind her and wrap his arms around her tiny waist.

His naughty intentions were dashed all to hell the second he saw the photo in the book she was reading. It looked like someone had thrown a handful of barnyard animals into a blender with a pissed off god.

"Unholy mother of creation, who the hell is that?" he balked.

"Albert Einstein," she answered with excitement.

"No, pretty sure he was both human and a scientist."

"Mary Poppins," Zoe pointed at the photo, as if that might help his brain work out its issues.

"Fictional British nanny."

"Archie Bunker."

"I have no clue who that is, but I'm going to guess that's not right, either." Hex sighed.

Zoe growled in frustration, but turned in his arms with a determined look. "You can't hear it right, but trust me, it's right," she vowed. "I have a hundred books telling me it's right." She gestured to the assortment spread all over the nearest table.

"I mean, this guy's more famous than Satan," she added.

"No such thing as Satan," he muttered, still eyeing the books. "You read all of these already?"

"Not cover to cover, just skimmed through them for

the most pertinent details," she answered. "You were gone a lot longer than I expected, I needed to keep my mind busy."

"Sorry, I had to go to Greece."

"Back up. What do you mean there's no such thing as Satan, and how the fuck do you get off going to Greece without me? That is *so* uncool."

Hex couldn't stop himself from laughing, just as mesmerized by the way her mind worked now, as he'd always been. The way it could run at top speeds, continuously jumping tracks, yet never missing a thing captivated him completely. He plucked the book from her hand and tossed it on the table with the others, then picked her up and set her atop a bookcase that only came to his waist, so he could kiss her between answers. Because he wanted to, and he could.

"Mistranslation," he began after the first kiss.

"Another one?"

"Mm-hmm."

"From what?"

"Ha-satan," he answered. "Hebrew for The Adversary or The Accuser."

"Right, I've seen that before, just didn't realize it wasn't a name." She sighed, then kissed him back. "Okay, next."

"Greece is Leviathan's home territory."

Zoe's face scrunched in distaste. "Explains the accent, but totally marking that off my list of places to visit before I die."

Panic seized Hex, as if she'd started doing just that on the spot. "You and die—never in the same sentence," he growled, crashing his mouth against hers.

As always, he could feel her struggle against yielding completely. Could feel her desire to cave growing stronger each time they kissed, but in the end, she still managed to pull back.

"Look, Hex, as much as I like this new kiss-and-tell tradeoff, I want to hear what happened with Leviathan," she said.

He tried not to scowl, because he was still unbelievably irked over being played and disappointed in himself for allowing it to happen. Yet, he couldn't deny that it had turned out better than he'd expected, so decided to only highlight the good notes.

"He's buying us two more days."

"What does that mean? On day three he's running off to Abaddon?"

"No. No, he isn't going to be running to Abaddon for any reason, ever," he promised.

"How can you be so sure?"

"Mostly, because he harbors something worse than hatred for Abaddon. If he could, he'd wipe every Angel, and especially God, from existence, but more importantly," he explained, pulling the jewelry box from his pocket. "Because of this."

"What is it?" Zoe asked.

"I have no clue." He shrugged. "But he needs it delivered in exactly two days, so he's going to make sure I'm available to do that."

"I see," she said. "May I, or is there some rule against it?"

Hex handed her the box and they both peered inside

when she opened it.

Her gasp was almost inaudible. "It's surprisingly beautiful."

He wasn't sure how to judge such things, but Hex was surprised by the subtle elegance of it. A bracelet of spun gold with delicate pink pearls and real, tiny seashells. Given all he knew about Envy, he would say it was shockingly subdued.

He watched Zoe come close to touching it, but she thought better of it and closed the lid. "Okay, that explains our two-day pass, but how can we really trust that he's not going to betray you the second this is delivered, despite his fantasies of conducting mass genocide on an entire pantheon?"

"Because where I'm supposed to deliver this, he can't go. That's why he needed me to do it for him."

"There's a place Devils can't go?" she asked, before her entire face paled. "Oh God, Hex, do you have to go to Heaven?"

The absurdity of her question got him right in the chest, causing him to burst into laughter. "No, even I can't traverse that realm," he answered. "Fuck, Zoe, you make me laugh."

"Hey, that was an extremely reasonable conclu—"

"No, baby," he cut her off, his tone sincere, before he captured her soft, delicious lips once again. "I mean, you make me laugh in a happy way. In a way that feels good. I can't even explain how significant that is."

Her eyes widened slightly, and her mouth worked soundlessly for a second. It was one of the rare times he'd ever seen her at a loss for words. "Yeah? Well, I mean, I did tell you I was fucking awesome."

Hex just chuckled again and caught her hand, brought it to his mouth so he could kiss her fingers. "Neither Leviathan nor his Legion can travel too far away from a body of saltwater," he explained. "The delivery location he gave me is the most landlocked region of the continental U.S., which means he'd have no way to get there to protect her if he went back on our deal."

"Her who?" Zoe asked, examining the box again.

"His mate," he answered. "It was only a suspicion, but he pretty much confirmed it."

"That doesn't make any sense. Why would she be somewhere he can't go, rather than with him?"

"That's the part I don't know, and was hoping you could help me figure out," Hex admitted. When her brows rose in surprise, he elaborated. "I was in the Abyss for a long time, so I've lost touch with all that's been happening both in Hell and on Earth. It feels like I've missed something crucial. Like Greed suddenly having a mate and now, the idea of Leviathan—of all creatures—finding his."

"Ooh, that's it! No wait, hold that thought, why do you say it that way, 'of all creatures'?"

Hex studied her for a moment, then gestured to her pile of books. "You're better off finding the answer in one of your books. I already know I'm not going to be able to satisfy the extent of your curiosity on the topic."

"Try me," she prompted.

Hex wasn't going to go over Leviathan's long, drawn out history with her so he just went straight for the biggest point. "Do you really think the earth can handle two sea monsters?"

Zoe paled and then looked at the box again. "Do you really think that's what his mate will turn out to be?"

Hex opened his mouth to reply, then narrowed his eyes at her, as her choice words caught in his brain and jammed the gears. "What do you mean, turn out to be?"

She met his gaze again and took a deep breath. "Well, see, while you were in the Abyss . . ."

Hex listened intently, while Zoe filled him in on all the events that had been unfolding on earth since his imprisonment. Like high-ranking demons rising from Hell to do their part in further messing up the world, only to fornicate with a bunch of human women in the process and produce an untold amount of half-demon offspring.

"Fuck me flying," Hex said, running a rough hand through his hair. When he caught Zoe squinting up at the ceiling, he didn't know whether to laugh or groan. "Are you actually trying to picture that?"

"You're the one who suggested it," she pointed out with a saucy grin.

He felt her grin all the way to his cock. "Yeah, well for the record, I can't actually fly. At least not in the material world," he reciprocated. "So, you're telling me that ever since this so-called World Changing Summit took place twenty-five years ago, a bunch of demon-hybrid orphans have been popping up all over the place, and your friend was one of them and she just happened to be Greed's mate and now you think that might be the case for Leviathan?"

"It would make sense, especially since we know she's beyond his reach," Zoe answered. "She hasn't woken up yet, her demon is still dormant. Right now, she'd be under the full assumption that she's a hundred-percent human. Probably a really fucked up one, but you know, those are real."

Hex chuckled again, but he wasn't sure it felt completely humorous or good.

"And there's a lot," she continued. "In fact, your buddy, pretend-Lucifer, has some kind of underwater resort-prison thingy where he's been keeping them all—"

"Wait, what?" Hex jerked back. "Beliel is on earth?"

"Technically, he's underwater," she said. "Actually, right here in the Gulf of Mexico. You know, his name just isn't doing anything for me. I mean Beliel doesn't strike immediate fear into my heart and mind the way Lucifer does . . ."

Zoe's words faded from Hex's ears, as everything inside of him froze and revolted simultaneously, because the name Beliel *did* strike immediate fear into him, as it did all demons. He was instantly put off by the idea of being so uncomfortably close to the Devil of all Devils. Worse, the thought of what might happen if Beliel decided to take Leviathan's mate into his underwater prison. Just as quickly, he dismissed that concern. The woman would be completely safe, because Leviathan would detect her the moment she entered his realm and he'd undoubtedly make Beliel regret ever stepping foot inside it.

"Hex, you're kind of freaking me out here," Zoe said, drawing him out of his thoughts.

"I'm trying to make sense of all this new information," he said. "It's a lot to take in. So much has happened that I wasn't even aware of, and with Beliel so close . . . To be honest, I almost wish we didn't have to stay here two more days."

"Well, I for one am glad we have the extra time. Now, I can get back to researching my new project: how to kill Hex."

He didn't even blink when she kissed him soundly on the mouth, then used his body to swing herself back to the floor so she could saunter her sassy ass over to her books. The layers of her that he could usually read and hear clearly sometimes got muffled and murky. Now was one of those times.

"Again, I can't tell if you're joking," he grumbled. "I don't like it."

"No one really jokes about murder, Hex," she deadpanned. On the other side of the long table, she sifted through the books, until locating the one she wanted and dropping it on top of the others. Then she slapped her hands on the open pages and looked him dead in the eye. "If they mention it, they've considered it, and I will figure out how it can be done, because I think it's the only thing that can save us."

CHAPTER 8

MY SIN

Okay, fine, so Zoe got a sick little thrill out of messing with Hex's head. Who was judging? But she knew better than to push it toward actual distrust. She reclaimed the chair she'd been occupying for the better part of the morning and gave him a tilted grin. When that didn't wipe the look of concern off his face, she rolled her eyes.

"Come on, Hex, I'd never really try to kill you. I was the one who dug a glowing, disgusting knot out of your arm last night to save your life," she reminded him. "But I'm also not kidding about figuring out how it can be done. Or rather, how it *was* done, when you were murdered. I think your death is the key to solving our dilemma."

Hex relaxed and drew closer to the table. "How could my death help us now? It happened eons ago."

"I don't know, that's the frustrating part," she said. "But you're something more than just a temptation demon or Veil Strider, Hex. You were created for some other purpose."

"Yes, to curse people." He nodded. "Which I'm still doing."

She blinked. "Come again?"

"For humans it's a curse to get everything you want and nothing you need," he explained. "All the superficial desires people beg me for never bring them an ounce of true satisfaction or fulfillment. They still spend their lives searching for the elusive cure to their misery, without ever realizing it's because they asked for the wrong things. And, of course, they blame me. I must have tricked them somehow."

"Well, do you?" she asked, extremely curious about him and his demonic powers.

Hex shook his head and pulled up another chair, turning it so he could face her rather than the table. "For thousands of years, I have been doing this and do you know the one thing a human has never asked me for?"

A hundred sarcastic answers popped into Zoe's mind —like genital herpes—but she didn't want to ruin the precious details he was finally giving her about himself. All the answers he'd been evading since they met.

"No, what?"

"To be happy," he answered, leaning forward to rest his arms on his thighs so he could play with the tips of her fingers. "They ask for all the things they think will make them happy, but not a single person has ever just asked to be happy. It's so simple, but no one thinks they can achieve happiness without things, power, position, or money. They can't comprehend that it works the other way around. That they have to be happy first in order to find fulfillment in the rest of it."

Zoe's mind unraveled a little at that insight, which was far more profound than she'd been expecting. He was absolutely right, though. It was human nature to believe that it took achieving some kind of goal in order to find happiness. Hell, they were basically taught that from birth. How many times had she heard someone say that if they could only land a job, a husband, or lose ten pounds, then they'd be happy? To the human brain, happiness was only a perceived outcome, if one could just alter their situation in some way. But by setting happiness away from themselves, keeping it at arm's length in the future and on the other side of unaccomplished goals, they were guaranteeing life would always get in the way of it. Setting themselves up for failure, without even realizing they were the cause of their own dissatisfaction.

"You're already happy with who you are and where you're going in life, that's why temptation has no effect on you," he added, bringing her back to the moment.

His powers were exactly the topic she needed to stay focused on, Zoe reminded herself. It was both the nexus and the crux of the project she was trying to piece together to expedite their survival and her ability to return to the land of Wi-Fi and espresso machines.

"Yeah, well you wanna know what would make me happy right now?" she asked.

His expression turned grim. "More coffee?"

Zoe snorted out a laugh. "That's a given," she replied. "But no, I need you to get naked."

Hex's pale eyes widened before narrowing to slits. "Will you also be getting naked?"

"Why would I do that?" she countered. Again, it was such a thrill to mess with him. "I don't have any magical tattoos."

He glanced down at his hands, which were still playing with hers. "What do you plan to do with my tattoos?"

Lick them? "Uh, try to find them in one of these books," she answered. "I'm just not sure if they're words, sigils, or both."

"They're bindings," he supplied.

"I gathered," she said, and then asked what she wasn't sure she wanted to know, but couldn't stand wondering about any longer. "Is it like a seam? Does each one represent one of your bones and does that mean there's a knot under each one?"

Zoe's heart filled with disappointment when his expression became passive, as it did every time he evaded one of her questions. So, when he actually started talking, she was stunned and captivated all at once.

"In my earliest memories, I was nothing more than a spirit bound to do the bidding of my murderers. *Come forth and hex*, they'd say, *we call on the hex, obey our command, Hex*. I honestly can't recall my death, but I've always known that being a living curse had been the purpose of it. They killed me to make me into this," he said. "As time passed, the more people I hexed for them, the more powerful they became, somehow linked to my actions and siphoning the magic of it for their own purpose. But I also became more powerful and when that happened, they started creating newer, stronger binds to keep control of me. Everything you see before you is a physical manifestation of those bindings. My skin, my bones, blood, all of it."

Zoe's heart thudded hard in her chest and something twisted up in her gut, before releasing. "I'm sorry, you're saying that this"—she gestured to his body—"isn't real? I mean, they didn't take your soul and cram it into someone else's corpse, it's just magic?"

"Yes," he answered. "And the knot you cut out of me, that was Farah's magic. She had to turn the magical link to my bone into something physical that you could sever, so she could sever it magically at the same time. She couldn't do it herself, because she can't be here all the way. In order to keep the door to this demimonde open, she has to keep one foot in the land of the living at all times. So, to answer your question, no. There isn't a knot under each tattoo nor do they each represent a bone. I don't have that many that still exist."

"What?" she gasped, recalling Farah's words of how he would be just fine, because he still had over two hundred bones left. "But, how?"

"I didn't realize until they were already gone, that my murderers had been using my bones to control me the whole time. It's what allowed them to summon me from the Veil," he explained. "I don't know whatever came of them. I floated in the Veil, alone and silent for an immeasurable amount of time, before wondering why my murderers hadn't called on me to curse anyone in so long. When I tried to feel for them, their presence that I'd always been able to detect, all I found were what was left of my bones. I always assumed that whoever had attempted to destroy them, had inadvertently freed me from my murderer's control and perhaps killed them, as well."

"So, then you took the rest and hid them around the world to keep them safe," Zoe deduced, because that's exactly what she would've done.

"Yes," he confirmed. "But it came with the unexpected benefit of being able to remain in the presence of one of my bones, in the living world, for however long I wished. I can't really say if it was the new taste of freedom from my murderers, or my curiosity of the material world, but I ordered the Veil to leave me completely and suddenly, I was wrapped in this physical body you see before you. I've been this way ever since, never returning to my spirit form."

Still stunned, Zoe shook her head slowly, trying to dislodge the questions she wanted answered first from the tumble of the rest. "How many bones do you have left?"

That was a primary concern.

"Eleven now," he answered.

"Eleven!" She balked, whirling in her seat to face him fully. "Hex!"

"What?"

"How are you even walking?" she demanded. "You almost died after losing just one!"

"Little doe, I cannot die," he said, giving her a small smile. "Yes, the bones can be used against me, but they can only weaken me for a short period of time. Even before the new religion rendered me an immortal demon, the Veil sustained me. The best I can deduce, is that when I was murdered to be turned into a living hex, my soul fused with the Veil, rather than just becoming one of its many specters. That's what these tattoos represent—my connection to the Veil. As long as it exists, I cannot be killed."

"Well, that would've been nice to know before I got my hands all bloody!" she erupted, even as his words relieved her on so many levels. "All this time, you've let me believe you were capable of dying? That's a dick move!"

"I didn't know you actually believed it was possible," he said. "I thought you were just being human."

"And what is *that* supposed to mean, exactly?" she seethed.

"Confusing and overly dramatic with your choice of words." He sighed. "I'm not apologizing for mankind's bad habits. Do you know how many times humans say they've been given a heart attack or have been killed by something in their lifetime, when all they've gotten is a little scare or a good laugh?"

Zoe popped her jaw sideways and sneered at him, because she couldn't even argue that point.

"Then why the hell did you freak out yesterday when I mentioned Saphiel tearing the world apart to find you?" she asked.

"I was never worried he'd kill me, I was worried he'd join forces with Abaddon to track me down and send me back to the Abyss," he answered. "I still am."

"And you should be, because he probably is," she cried out. "And now I'm yelling, because I think I'm angry, even though I'm also happy!"

"I'm sorry, baby." He chuckled, reaching for both her

hands this time, but she pulled away, crossing her arms over her chest and turned to face the table. "I never meant for you to worry about my life, I've only been concerned with saving yours."

"Well, shit doesn't work that way, Hex. You don't get to be the only one to worry and plan exit strategies that keeps everyone alive and whole. I told you I wasn't going to just sit by quietly while you play whatever the demon version of a white knight is, and I meant it. Don't you dare say dark knight," she added, pointing a finger at him. "You don't get to ruin Batman for me."

"I have no idea what a batman is," he said grimly.

Zoe gawked at him in utter disbelief. "Are you sure you can't be damned more than once? Because I'm fairly certain your lack of pop-culture knowledge is a fucking sin."

"Little doe," he said. "Once we get out of this mess, you can cram as much pop-culture down my throat as you want. Now, are we still getting naked?"

"I swear every word you just said has actually been used as a pick-up line before, in that exact context," she decided. "And no, now that you've already solved the mystery of your tattoos, you can keep your damn clothes on."

Hex frowned, which made her feel a little better. Her mind was running in circles again, chasing possible answers in the hopes of finding one that was really spectacular. The one that would solve all their problems and save all their lives. Hex believed he'd been human once, a very, *very* long time ago, and she couldn't help but agree since he did have bones. And at death he'd started off as nothing more than a ghost that was somehow able to be conjured by the ones who'd killed him.

"Shit. Byron!" Zoe blurted, jumping up from her chair and going straight for the library's card catalog. "It was murder, of course! A residual haunting, that's how they were able to do it. Something so violent at the time of death that it leaves a powerful energy signature behind."

She knew she was rambling, but it made sense to her, as all the information Byron had given her fell into place in her mind.

"What happened?" Hex asked in confusion.

"We were talking about the different kinds of ghosts and hauntings," she explained, as she flipped through the old index cards still filed according to the Dewey Decimal system, since apparently the computers in a demimonde were just for decoration. "And Byron said that the most powerful ones he'd ever come across weren't poltergeists, they were residual hauntings from extremely violent deaths, like murders. Man, he is never going to let me live any of this shit down when he finds out."

The sound of a chair scraping back and clattering to the floor had Zoe whipping her attention toward Hex in a heartbeat. She found him glowering at her, his expression dark, a shadow hovering in his pale eyes.

"You won't be telling anyone anything, Zoe," he stated firmly. "Nothing you know about us or these various realms are for humans to find out. You wouldn't even be here if it weren't for Greed's new queen telling you more than she ever should have!"

"Whoa, chill," she said, her tone just as firm, though his severe reaction confused her. "First off, Saphiel's the one who told Kami to tell me, so you can back off my best friend. Secondly, I only meant about the fact that ghosts are real. It's been a long-standing debate between Byron and me. And I didn't mean that I planned to rush right back home to deliver the news to him. I don't make it my first priority to announce when I'm wrong."

She watched the muscles work at the back of his jaw. "You don't tell him even that much," he said. "He can find out on his own, when it's his time to join them."

"Fine, Hex, Jesus. I won't say a word," she conceded, because in truth, she wouldn't even know how to explain it to Byron without revealing too much. "Can we drop the hostility now? I think I'm onto something here."

He bent and grabbed the chair he'd knocked over, then set it back where it had been. Then, he just stood there, staring at the table.

"Who is this Byron?" he demanded. "That's a very human boy name."

Realization smacked Zoe right upside the head and she had to fight the urge to grin. *Holy shit, he's jealous!* His dark hostility had never been just about her revealing supernatural secrets. He'd been reacting to her talking about another guy. Oh, it was so hard not to pounce all over that! She was so tempted, but judging by his mood, it had the potential of going sideways real fast.

"A friend," she answered. When he lifted his head to meet her gaze, she added, "About yea tall and maybe as big around as your leg."

Hex's entire demeanor relaxed, pride straightening his shoulders and glinting in his eyes. "Puny, you mean," he stated.

"Very," she confirmed. "Not that it matters, right? I mean, no matter how big he is, he's still only human."

She watched his eyes narrow on hers, his mouth dipping toward a frown. "Now, you're just patronizing me."

"I wouldn't," she said. "Just stating the facts, once again."

He frowned completely. "You think I'm an ass."

Zoe contemplated that for a moment. "I think you're a sweet ass," she decided.

"We've kissed," he said darkly, pointing at her. "Repeatedly."

"Exactly," she replied. "And that's the only reason why you're an ass. Not because you asked about my connection to Byron, but because you think I'd actually kiss you when I'm already involved with someone else."

"You would," he countered without hesitation. "Because you're m–... attracted to me."

Zoe opened her mouth to respond, then quickly remembered she was talking to a demon, not a human. With a sigh, she abandoned the index cards and approached him. When she was in front of him again, she arched a brow and gestured to his chair.

"Sit down."

"Why?" he asked warily.

That made her preen even more, the fact that she could make this big, bad demon leery of what she might do next. By now, he should know better than to give her so much power.

"Because I'm short and I want to talk to your face, not your abs." She gestured. Which was exactly the truth and exactly a lie all at the same time.

Mark another one off the bucket list!

As soon as Hex sank into the chair, Zoe sat herself across his lap and felt his entire body turn to stone. He even stopped breathing for a full two seconds before he grabbed her and pulled her even closer. She instantly felt a small tinge of regret for her choice, as his arms and hands engulfed her, his body heat warming every inch of her, even the parts left untouched. Her sex perked right up, excited over the position. Zoe nearly groaned in misery at herself for such a stupid move.

"If you told me this was going to happen, I never would've questioned sitting down," Hex complained.

"I know, but that's not as fun," she said, draping her arms over his shoulders and tilting her head, as she studied him. "I'm not involved with anyone else, human or demon."

"How many more demons do you know?"

Zoe shrugged. "Saph has a lot of Legion on staff."

His body and expression relaxed again. "Those don't count. They don't even have genders."

She smiled, unable to fight it any longer and gave him a small laugh. Her fingers curled, desiring to plunge into his thick, black hair. The way it was so much longer on top than the sides caused it to always fall over his forehead in that sexy, careless kind of way.

"See? I knew you were patronizing me."

"I'm not, honest. I just don't know how else to react to you behaving so human, Hex."

He grimaced, but it didn't stay. His expression was shadowed, but not dark with jealousy anymore. "That makes two of us," he muttered, before lifting his hand to trace his finger over her jaw to her chin. "You do this to me."

His words, just as much as his touch, shivered all the way to her core. "You shouldn't give your enemies so much ammunition," she advised.

Hex watched his fingers as they slid over the side of her face toward her hair and around to the back of her head. He laid his other hand on her cheek and leaned in, brushing his forehead against hers, the tip of his nose over her cheek. Then, he softy traced the contours of her cheek bones, nose, eyes and mouth with the tips of his fingers. It was the most seductive thing, yet Zoe had never once thought to fantasize about it. It was the way his eyes tracked his own exploration, flicking to hers every so often as he continued taking in her features so intimately, capturing the reactions she was unable to hide from him. Stealing them for his own pleasure.

"You're not my enemy, Zoe," he rasped. "You're *my* temptation. My sin turned against me. Don't you see? You're my greatest desire and I want—"

When he took her mouth, it was slow, devastatingly reverent, and Zoe thought it might be the final death of her remaining brain cells. His breath seduced her, ever as much as the soft friction of his lips and teasing licks of his tongue. Hex's fingers played through her hair, the firmness of their kneading increasing with the pressure of his kisses.

There was no protest left inside of her. Nothing niggling in the back of her brain to slow down or stop, to wait. Maybe it was because she'd already decided to sleep with him. Maybe it was because she was tired of fighting her own desires to know what it would be like, what kind of pleasure she might find with him. Whatever the reason, Zoe surrendered to the riot of sensations without pause, allowing them to both smother and fuel her. Erotic energy zipped through her veins, even as Hex's overwhelming attentions melted her bones. He seemed to feel her yield to the pleasure, because he groaned in a way that sounded like a growl, yet felt like a purr vibrating through her. His mouth abandoned hers to taste down the side of her neck, the very weakness she'd revealed to him the night before last, and then they were flying.

Zoe's eyes popped open on a surprised gasp as she saw the blackness of the Veil all around them beginning to fade, and the familiar bedroom in Farah's apartment coming into view.

"No, not here," she said, every inch of her detesting the idea.

Hex never stopped nuzzling at the side of her neck, sending wave after wave of shivering lust straight to her toes. There was no stopping the giddiness in her chest when the shadows consumed them, false wind rushing over her skin as the Veil moved them to a different location. Zoe landed with a bounce on a large bed in some posh hotel room and laughed as her mind went into overdrive with wicked fantasies.

"What is it that my little doe finds so funny?" Hex asked, lifting his head from her neck far enough to grin at her.

She chuckled. "I was just thinking that with your abilities, we could defile every inch of this city in one go."

She felt his reciprocating laughter against the front of her throat where he'd decided to plunder next. "If that's what you want, just say the word," he replied. "Your wish is my command."

"Aww, and here I thought you weren't a genie," she teased, but her laughter ended on a breathless moan when Hex cupped her breast through her shirt and squeezed softly, leaving her yearning for something harder.

Without warning, he grabbed the hem of her shirt and yanked it over her head. It made her mind spin slightly because she hadn't even lifted herself from the mattress to help, he was simply that strong or talented—one of the two. His eyes were hungry as they peered down at her in just a bra, and in a flash he flicked open the front clasp.

Zoe wasn't sure why it affected her so much when he peeled each cup away slowly, exposing her naked breasts like they were presents under tissue paper. A breath escaped his parted lips, and his eyes widened slightly in a way that confirmed his previous claims of never spying on her in the shower. There was no way he could fake the reaction he was having to seeing her breasts for the first time. His touch was too soft, taunting her shoulders off the mattress as her body arched in search for more. He traced the curve of her breasts, then grazed the pad of his thumb over her nipple.

"Hex," she moaned.

His only response was to duck his head to her right breast and repeat the tease with his tongue instead.

"Oh God, more, please," she whimpered, her hands diving into his hair to urge him on.

Her head pressed back into the mattress as he finally pulled her nipple into his mouth and sucked. The pleasure shot straight to her clit and tightened the cord between each point, making sure she felt the full effect of his assault through her whole body.

"Doe," Hex breathed against her, into her, his mouth and hands growing more aggressive.

"Yes," Zoe hissed in approval, then exhaled with pleasure as he started moving lower.

She never let go of his hair, keeping his head in her grasp as he laved his tongue down her torso, around her navel and over the flat of her lower stomach. Fire licked at her muscles, making them dance. Heat centered in her sex, liquifying her insides with desire and anticipation as he got closer and closer to the center of her pleasure.

Her body was already raring to go by the time he unfastened her shorts and began tugging them off her, along with her panties. He didn't stand, merely leaned to the side so he could pull the material free from her legs. She lifted her bottom from the mattress to make it easier, running on base need and instinct. Not a single shred of her felt awkward or exposed—she gloried in being naked, because that meant they were getting closer to the best parts. And Zoe desperately wanted to feel the best parts. She'd never been so turned on in her life. Hex's tastings and caresses were the perfect combination of tease and deliver, bringing her blood from simmer to sizzle in no time.

"Fuck, Zoe," he groaned, staring at her pussy. He traced his finger over the bare skin alongside the neatly groomed strip of dark curls and groaned. "This is fantastic. You're so tempting, I don't even know where to start. I want it all."

She let out something between a groan and a chuckle, because she could sympathize. She felt the exact same way when it came to his body. Also, because she wanted to feel it all, every little thing she knew he could give her. There was a limit to how much pleasure the human body could take before passing out, and she both feared and reveled in the fact that he was more than likely capable of going well beyond that point.

"Where you're at is an awesome place to start, Hex," she encouraged. "Just—"

Taking her direction, he dipped his head and ran his tongue over the same bare skin his finger had traced, stealing the rest of her words and breath at once.

"Oh God, yeah," she moaned. "Exactly that."

Zoe got lost in the sensations as he maneuvered between her legs, spreading them by placing open mouth kisses and nibbles along her inner thighs. She was deaf to her own noises, blood rushing in her ears as heated pleasure rippled right up the surface of her skin to harden her nipples further.

When his mouth finally made contact with her pussy, his tongue lapping and lips suckling, she cried out. Her hips bucked off the mattress and Hex took advantage of the movement to slide his hands under her ass and curl his fingers over her hips, pinning her to the spot.

"Hex!" she choked out on a moan.

He tormented her with the same slow licks and brushes of his lips he'd used on the rest of her body, followed by a complete devouring, only to start the pattern all over again. Slow and soft to hard and hungry. The mounting pressure of an orgasm swelled, filling her with the promise of explosive pleasure. Her inner muscles locked and released with need, urging the climax on, wanting to feel it more than anything in the world. And then Hex growled right into her clit—what may have been a command for her to come—and it shot her right over the peak. The climax struck lightning fast, pulling the most intense concentration of pure bliss right out of her core, and wracking her muscles with pulsing pleasure she could hardly believe.

"Yes," he snarled. "I want more of that!"

"Ooh," she whimpered and felt the burn in her muscles, as if she'd just done a hundred crunches at the gym.

Her eyes cracked open, when he slipped away from her, rising from where he'd been kneeling on the floor beside the bed and wrecking her with his oral skills. She watched the shadows wash over him for just a moment, taking his clothing with them as they disappeared again, and her mouth dropped open.

"That's cheating," she croaked out, but the offense was already forgotten as her eyes drank in the sight of him completely naked. "Jesus."

His muscles were lean and roped, giving him the

appearance of a warrior that could both rip heads off and win any race. He was incredibly proportioned—his cock the perfect length and thickness for his body type. The lines of his tattoos really did look like seams, now that she could view them without any obstructions. But after learning they belonged to the Veil, she could perceive them as symbols of his powers and abilities, rather than marks left behind by dark magic. By the evil that had been done to him.

"You will not call me Jesus," he reprimanded, his voice thick with unspent arousal.

Approaching the bed again, he bent down and picked her up off the mattress, then in the next second Zoe found herself on her knees, straddling his jutting cock. Without even making an appearance this time, the Veil had answered his whim and transported them both to the head of the bed where Hex sat with his back against the headboard, holding Zoe by her waist.

"You may call me God, as I'm sure you won't be able to help yourself," he continued.

Torn between wanting to snort over his cockiness and wanting to laugh at his continued use of the Veil to maneuver them, she emitted a mixture of both and shook her head at him. "I don't know whether you're just showing off or really that anxious to fuck me."

His eyelids became hooded with arousal as he licked his lips. "You keep that filthy mouth up and you'll learn exactly what I'm all about."

"Prove it," she dared, reaching between her legs to wrap her hand around his cock.

He sucked in a surprised breath that emerged on a

devastated moan. "Fuck, Zoe, don't push me too fast."

The concern in his voice gave her pause as the wildest thought clunked her in the head. "Hex, you have done this before, haven't you?"

His laughter eased her worry. "Yes, little doe. I may not be as promiscuous as the human boys you're used to dealing with, but I have been alive for a very long time, I know what I'm doing," he reassured her, before giving her a soberer expression. "It's just—don't get angry—but your body is very small. I don't want to hurt you."

His worry touched her in a bigger way than she would've expected, melting her insides with something deeper than just desire. "You're not going to hurt me, Hex," she promised. "You know me, if something starts hurting, you'll hear about it immediately. One way or another."

He grinned at that, then captured her lips in a soft, passionate kiss. He tasted like her and yet still managed to give her another one of her favorite flavors, as usual. It was never the same flavor twice in a row, so as their tongues dueled and her body began heating again, she reveled in the mild hints of cinnamon and icing.

"Mmm, I could dine on all your flavors for eternity," he moaned.

"Funny," Zoe said breathlessly. "I was thinking the same thing. One thing, um . . . I'm on birth control, but I've never . . . I don't how this works with—"

Another kiss from him cut her off, before he pulled back enough to look her in the eye. "I can't get you pregnant or give you any diseases, Zoe, this body is a magical manifestation, remember?"

"Oh, right," she said. "Hard to remember that when it looks and feels so real."

He just grinned brighter. "You haven't felt anything yet."

A shiver worked through her, but his goading only spurred on her sass. "Waiting on you, big guy."

Hex groaned, and he gave her a wicked look as he slid his hands up her sides to lift her arms. Zoe placed her palms flat on the wall above his head as he wanted, then gasped in pleasant surprise, when he proceeded to suck on her nipples in that soft, taunting way. His hands smoothed over her back, pressing her breasts closer to his face, before sliding further down to cup her ass. He squeezed and massaged, his fingers plying with more and more aggression, just like his mouth.

"Tell me what you want, Zoe," he rasped.

"I want your cock inside me, Hex," she answered, as if that should be obvious.

"Mmm, that gives me a few options, can you be more specific?"

Heat flared right down her center and she laughed on a moan. "You want dirty talk, huh?"

"You've been talking dirty to me ever since we met, why stop now?"

She both preened and chuckled at that, then ducked her head toward his. "Put your cock in my pussy right now, Hex."

His groan had a bite to it as he grabbed his cock and positioned it against her opening. The feel of it there shot more heat through Zoe's body as her pussy grew wetter and needier. Fuck, she felt so needy.

"Hex, please!" she prompted when he continued to tease her, rubbing the head of his cock all over her sex, smearing her cream and driving her crazy.

Her next inhale lodged in her throat as he fulfilled her wish, lining his cock up with her entrance once again and pushing upward, gripping her hips to lower her at the same time. Zoe swore she was going to come the second he started stretching her, it felt so fucking good. Everywhere he wasn't came alive with need and envy, so when he paused after just getting her over the crown, she growled.

"Don't stop," she said. "All of it, give me all of it!"

"Fuck, yes," he growled under his breath and kept going.

It was tortuously slow, which was insanely pleasurable and frustrating all at the same time. Zoe wanted to scream and moan, gritting her teeth against both, until she felt the head of his cock fill her so deep. The moan won, long and breathless and ripe with how much she needed more.

"More," she demanded on a hungry breath. "Fuck me, Hex, or move your hands, so I can do it myself."

When he lifted his hands from her hips and gave her a wicked grin, she was mildly surprised. "Do it," he challenged.

Power and lust were like twin fireballs through her core as Zoe happily took his dare and started rocking her hips against him. Her hands slid from the wall to the top of his head to use as leverage, then she began rising and falling, chasing her own orgasm. Hex struggled to hold still. She could feel his muscles growing tight, his body shaking with the desire to join in, but the sounds he made were pure pleasure. He was loving it just as much as she was and damn if that didn't just make her hotter, wetter and more determined to come.

"Do it, doe," he encouraged through his teeth, as if he'd read her thoughts. "I want to feel you make yourself come on my cock. I want to see what you look like when you take your pleasure from me."

His words spurred her desire higher, her fingers digging into his scalp, as she rode him harder and faster. Zoe adjusted slightly, spreading her knees out a little farther so she could lean back. With one hand twined in Hex's hair, she stuck her fingers in her mouth first, then started rubbing tight little circles against her clit. The look of pure hunger that overcame his face and blazed in his pale eyes thrilled her.

"No," she rushed out when his hands lifted from the mattress.

His lips peeled back in a silent snarl from the denial, but his hands dropped back onto the bed. His fixation gave her such a rush of empowerment and pride, knowing how much pleasure she was bringing him with the show —as much as her own pussy. As soon as her orgasm took hold, Zoe's movements grew wilder, her outcries louder, and Hex was audibly seething with his restraint.

"That's it, baby, take it," he rooted her on. "Take your pleasure and come on my cock."

The pleasure was so ripe, she lost all control over her own muscles, falling into Hex and not even caring when his arms wrapped around her. At first it was all she could do to hug her arms around his head and ride out the beginning of the storm. Then, she was leaning away from him with the final force of it, her head falling back as Hex supported her with his hands and praised her with words she couldn't even hear.

Zoe was barely aware that they were moving again as she fell from the blissful high. She landed the moment she felt the bed under her back, and peered through heavy eyelids at the beautiful demon positioning himself between her thighs.

"Now, you're mine, Zoe," he promised, his voice at the brink of control. "All fucking mine."

The warm and serene afterglow she'd been floating in was quickly chased away as Hex pulled her legs up over his waist, gripped her hips, and pushed his cock into her again and again. Though it didn't start as slow and gentle as his foreplay, there was still a build-up.

"Yes, God, yes. More!" Zoe couldn't believe that was her own voice.

She had no idea how she was still coherent enough to feel the pleasure, the pressure gathering once again in her womb. Hex managed to find a way to plunge deeper, harder and faster, pulling erotic cries from her very soul. She'd already been covered in perspiration from her solo act, but his unbelievable stamina drenched her. Her back arched off the bed, shoving her breasts into his hands. He covered them and squeezed, pinching and rolling her nipples between his thumb and fingers, changing the octave of her screams to a soprano.

"Fuck, Zoe, fuck!" Hex seethed through his clenched teeth and then lost all control.

Zoe came a third time as he slammed into her like a

wild animal for a full ten seconds, before going completely still. His hands squeezed her breasts hard enough to rob her of breath and bring tears to her eyes, then his head fell back, and his cock pumped hot cum deep inside her.

Half brain-dead from sheer exhaustion and her bones liquified with pleasure, Zoe relaxed deeper into the mattress when his grip on her breasts loosened. She hummed in complete satisfaction and her eyelids drooped closed, unable to be opened again anytime soon.

"Like I said," she slurred. "Very real for being magic."

It was the second time since they'd met that Hex's seductive laughter followed her into sleep.

CHAPTER 9

COMMUNICATION IS KEY

Zoe's scent surrounded Hex as he wrapped his arms around her from behind and pulled her ass right into his hardening cock. He wanted her again already and it was bad. All the intense satisfaction he'd felt the moment he came deep in her hot, clenching pussy had turned into a craving burning in his veins. Ancient didn't even begin to cover his age, yet in all that time, he'd never felt as human as he did now. At the moment, he understood perfectly why they were so driven by their sexual appetites, and that was an uncomfortable feeling. How was he supposed to function at a normal level when his cock refused to remain satisfied?

He hadn't been exaggerating when he'd told her that she was his sin turned against him. Nothing had ever tempted Temptation before, and Hex didn't know what to do with that, because it wasn't going away. He'd given in to it, yet there it remained. Just like all the humans he inflicted, he'd revealed his greatest desire, and now he would spend eternity chasing after it time and again. Never satisfied, always wanting more.

Well, that was only partially true. He definitely wanted more, yet he'd also found immense satisfaction. Hex just hadn't realized it would be so fleeting. That he could actually want her more now than he had before ever having her. It was maddening.

When Zoe moaned and stirred beside him, more blood rushed to his cock. Hex buried his face in her hair, inhaling her perfume, and tried to will his erection away. His body was a magical manifestation, damn it, controlling it really shouldn't be so difficult!

"What time is it?" Zoe asked, the huskiness of her sleepy voice ruining all his efforts.

"Just after three-thirty," he answered. "You should really wake up so you can eat something. It's been hours since you had breakfast."

"I can tell," she replied. "I'm starving and I'm never that hungry."

Hex couldn't help but feel a bit smug over that. "That's because you don't usually exercise so vigorously through lunch," he pointed out. "But now that I've found the way to get you to eat better, we just need to work on the timing."

Her laughter was quiet, muffled by the sheets and pillow her face was mostly buried into.

"Is that the timer I feel against my ass, then?" she asked.

Her acknowledgment seemed to make his cock think that was approval, as it jerked against the plump flesh of her butt cheek and made him ache.

"No, that's a nuisance that can't seem to be controlled," he grumbled.

Zoe rolled over to face him, giving him a full view of her naked breasts tipped with dark rose nipples. Instantly, his mouth watered. His fingers curled into his palm and the throbbing in his cock increased as every instinct in his body yelled at him to touch, taste, and claim.

"I think I can help with that." She smiled slyly, unaware of the damage she was already inflicting.

When she lifted her chin to press her lips to his, Hex backed his head away. "Don't, Zoe," he warned. "You need to eat, and if you start, I don't know if I'll be able to stop."

With a heavy sigh, she glanced down at her hand resting on the sheet between them, then looked at him again. "I have an idea," she said, brushing the sheet off of both of them. "Come on, get up."

Hex rolled away from her, as he sat up and then stood, so she could also slide off the bed.

"Oh." She winced, as soon as she straightened. "Yeah, my idea is definitely going to be our only option at the moment."

"You're hurt," he noted, darkness rising to edge his neediness.

"Hex, look at me," she commanded, gesturing to her petite frame. "Now, look at you. Of course, I'm going to be sore, there is absolutely no physical way to stop that from happening, unless you never want to have sex with me again."

The very idea had his entire body balking in denial. "Oh, we're having sex again," he promised. "But you said you wouldn't get hurt."

"I'm fine, it will work itself out in like an hour." She

dismissed his concern with a wave of her hand. "Just because I have a pussy doesn't mean I am one."

Hex groaned miserably and pinched the bridge of his nose. "No more dirty talk."

Zoe chuckled and disappeared into the en-suite bath. "You coming?"

"I wish," he muttered, then slowly made his way to her, a little leery of what she had in store with her idea. He could only hope it wouldn't be more reasons for his cock to ache with need. "What are we doing in here, little doe?"

"We both need to shower," she said. "And you need some relief that, unfortunately, I can't help you with in the traditional way at the moment."

Hex tilted his head, brows furrowed in puzzlement. "Why do humans talk in circles, rather than just getting straight to the point?"

Zoe arched a dangerous brow at him. "Why do demons question everything humans do?"

"Easy, they're confusing and waste ridiculous amounts of what little time they have with indecision, lying, denying themselves, and talking in circles," he replied without hesitation.

With an unimpressed look on her face, she raised her right hand. "I'm going to use this," she pointed to it. "To jerk you off in the shower, so you'll stop being a cranky dick. Is that direct enough for you?"

Desire surged through his body and his cock hardened even more. "Absolutely," he answered, stalking right past her to get that shower started.

"It's abso-fucking-lutely," she corrected him.

Hex smiled, as he set the taps and reminded himself that her flesh wouldn't be able to handle any extreme temperatures. "You're the boss."

"No shit."

On a laugh, he turned and wrapped an arm around her waist to haul her into the shower with him. With the promise of release, he had no qualms further tormenting himself, by giving into his desire to capture her lips and plunder. Her flavors were so addicting. Her mouth tasted like the most refreshing, thirst-quenching spring, and her pussy tasted like honeysuckle. Just the memory of it had him moaning into the liquid heat of her mouth before he let her slide down his body to stand. Framing her face in his hands, he tilted her head back into the spray of warm water.

"I thought I was supposed to be helping you?" she questioned, her eyes closing on reflex.

"We'll get to it, don't worry," he said as he used his hands to thoroughly saturate her dark curls. He glanced at the selections of soaps on the shelves; tiny bottles provided by the hotel. "Which of these is for your hair?"

Zoe gave him a strange look as she rubbed water from her eyes. "What?"

He shrugged. "This is my first time taking a shower. The Veil keeps me clean all the time. Either that, or my body's just incapable of getting dirty."

Her mouth opened on an incredulous look. "Are you shitting me?"

"No."

"Do you know how much time I'd save if I never had to shower? Man, you demons have it so easy," she griped.

"It's the shampoo first."

Hex grabbed the bottle and popped it open, took a sniff. "It doesn't smell like your hair," he frowned.

"That's because there are different brands and scents —"

"I know that much," he cut her off with a laugh. "It was just an observation. I like the way your hair smells, but I guess this will have to do for now."

After he rinsed all the suds away, Zoe pointed to another bottle. "You have to apply conditioner now," she instructed. "And since that has to set for a couple of minutes, hand me the bodywash."

He grabbed the bottle she indicated, which looked just like the others since they were all sporting the colors and logo of the hotel. Before he could open it to smell it, she took it from him and did just that.

"Oh, you're lucky." She grinned. "It's Irish Spring. I thought I'd get to make you smell like a girl."

Hex gave her a wicked smirk. "I already smell like the girl who came all over my cock," he pointed out.

When she laughed so hard she snorted, he couldn't help but join in. Her sense of humor was just one of the many extraordinary things about her, setting her apart from the majority of her fellow humans. She never blushed, either, didn't have a damn shy bone in her body, and while that wouldn't be a turn off, Hex found he preferred her infallible confidence so much more. It suited her and made sparring with her the best fucking foreplay he'd ever had. For it to carry through in sex had simply blown his mind. He could watch her touch herself while riding his cock every minute of every day for the rest of the earth's existence and never be less turned on by it.

"Well, I guess it's time to change that," she finally managed, the humor still dancing in her eyes.

"What?"

He didn't want to stop smelling like her. He was reveling in it, because he knew it would fade all too soon. He hadn't lied—either the Veil or the magic of his own body kept him very clean. The next time he called the shadows to him, he would lose all traces their hot-as-hell sex had left behind on his skin.

"Zoe, wait—"

Her hand wrapped around his aching cock and all his muscles tensed, as pleasure rippled through his system. She didn't move, only stood there holding him and looking at him expectantly. A quick debate flashed through his mind and Hex decided fuck it, he could always get her honeysuckle sweetness all over his cock again later.

"Never mind," he said, his jaw tight.

She chuckled. "That's what I thought."

And then she showed him exactly why, as her small hands started smearing the slippery soap all over his cock, racking his body with erotic sensations he'd never experienced before. Never, in his long existence had a female ever taken him in hand in such a way. And when she sandwiched his cock between the flat of her palms, gliding from crown to root and back up again, Hex couldn't hold in the moan it dragged out of his chest. Tingling pleasure awakened in every nerve ending, all the way up to his shoulders. It was fucking amazing.

"Little doe," he encouraged, getting lost in the sight of it, ever as much as the feel. "So fucking good."

She didn't leave a single inch untouched, swirling her fingers just under the crown and over, teasing the thick vein underneath. Sliding her palms down to the base again, she wrapped one hand there and squeezed, the other slicking between his legs and cupped his balls.

"Fuck yes," he moaned, leaning back against the shower wall when she massaged him gently. "Harder, baby, squeeze harder."

She tried, but apparently she was afraid of hurting him. "Like this," he showed her, placing his hand over hers and guiding it up and down his shaft. "That's how tight your pussy squeezes me when you come."

Zoe stroked him, before switching it up to trailing her fingertips lightly up and down all sides, then back to stroking. The combination was driving him wild. Watching her do it while drinking in her naked body was the best goddamn thing he could remember in forever. She released one hand and quickly stuck it under the spray of water, before returning it to his cock. The water made the soap even slicker, which felt twice as good as before.

Hex was panting, the pleasure beginning to center at the base of his spine as his balls drew up tighter and tighter.

"I don't think I can take much more, Zoe," he warned. "I need you to go faster now, fast and just a little harder like I showed you."

Her immediate compliance had his eyes practically rolling into the back of his head as all the pleasure she'd been bringing him before multiplied, intensified, but he didn't want to miss it. He forced his eyes to remain open as she double-fisted him, stroking up and down with a steady increase in speed that left him perched right on the edge of heaven for what seemed like an eternity. Unable to take the torment any longer, he wrapped his hand around both of hers and forced her to increase the speed.

"Against the wall," he directed.

She shifted slightly to her right and backed up the one step to the wall, with him turning to face her simultaneously, because they were both still stroking his cock. Hex braced an arm against the wall above her head and drooled over her delicious, naked body as they brought him to the brink of ecstasy together. The thought of losing his load all over her naked tits shot him even higher.

"Yes, Zoe!" he hissed through his teeth just before his climax took hold. "Fuck, I'm gonna come all over you."

He kept his promise when the orgasm struck, and he stilled Zoe's hands on his cock so he could aim ropes of cum all over her breasts, nipples, and down her stomach. The sight of it increased all the pleasure to a point beyond reason. It was just one more piece of evidence that Hex grabbed on to, proof that Zoe was indeed his mate, for it was the only way she could bring him to such heightened levels of ecstasy.

He took a moment to revel in the lingering pleasure, using his thumb to smear the cum over her nipple and watch the effects of that cross her features. Watched the arousal give her cheeks a rosy glow and the fantasies spark to life in her eyes.

"So fucking dirty," he praised on a growl of approval. He straightened so he could use his free hand to grip her hair and slid his other down her torso, smearing more of his cum along the way. He found her clit and started rubbing loose circles against it to get her warmed up. He played around with the speed and pressure, until he had her gasping and gripping his arm tight.

"There, right there," she cried. "Don't move."

"Mmm, are you're going to come all over my hand, dirty girl?" he taunted, brushing his lips over her temple.

Her nails dug into his flesh when he added a bit more pressure and Hex grinned like a lunatic.

"Move again, and I'll fucking kill you," she snarled.

"That's what I like to hear," he approved with a thick laugh. "Come on, baby, you know how to take what you want."

Zoe used her hold on his arm to grind her pussy against his fingers and Hex felt his blood starting to stir again. Damn, so much for getting his release. If they didn't hurry this along, they'd be facing the same problem they'd just relieved.

She sucked in a sharp breath and her legs started quivering, just before she moaned nice and loud. Her body bowed off the wall, so Hex cupped her pussy, rubbing the heel of his palm into her clit to draw her pleasure out.

"So fucking hot," he moaned, capturing her mouth while she was still writhing and swaying on his hand. "You're going to give me another one."

She whimpered and tried to shake her head, but he'd

already plunged back into her mouth. He kissed her deep, using her own delicious juices to work her clit over again. He was rougher and faster, sending her flying right over the peak a second time while she cried her pleasure into his mouth.

And he was fucking hard again.
Fuck.

****

Following their very dirty shower, Hex wrapped them both in the hotel's complimentary robes and whisked them to the nearest department store for fresh clothes. It had been like something out of a teenager's wildest fantasy for Zoe, grabbing anything she wanted without having to worry about paying for it. She'd settled on a light cotton summer dress in white with strings fed through the material up the sides of the front piece, which tied around the back of her neck. It left her entire back bare and the skirt was loose enough to be comfortable, landing about mid-thigh. Then, Hex had used his special skills to get them some food, and much to her surprise, a soda for her. She'd noted that despite not even touching his breakfast earlier, Hex ate very little of their late lunch. She figured it must be another demon thing.

Now, they were back at the NOLA Public Library to pick up where they'd left off in their attempt to formulate the best survival plan. Zoe lounged on a long sofa across from the research table still covered in all the books she'd skimmed through that morning. She was relaxed, her belly was full, she still miraculously had 20/20 vision and her sexual needs were momentarily satisfied. She couldn't say the same for her poor demon. He kept looking at her with a combination of hunger and hope in his eyes before forcing himself to refocus on whatever it was he was working on.

"What are you working on?" she asked, following that thought.

He sat in her abandoned chair on the other side of the table. Whatever book he'd been reading, he closed and tucked under one of the other stacks.

"Nothing, just passing the time," he said. "Have you found anything?"

Zoe had been making notes about the information she'd found on Asmodeus, Demon of Lust, that seemed the most likely to help them in some way. Hex had told her the older the source, the better, because all of the newer versions would be nothing but a mixture of compounded theories and old wives tales. That had taken a little more digging, but what she'd turned up was a bit unbelievable, making her doubt his advice.

"Nothing concrete, since I can't ask you if it's true." She sighed, then had a thought. "If we can get this sin's name to Farah, do you think she could find a way to contact him without alerting Abaddon or even Saphiel?"

"No, there's no guarantee of that, or that anyone will respond. I have to be honest, that route may be fruitless. We should probably focus on something with better chances of success."

"Like what?" she asked, then shook her head. "Hex, there's a reason the name of this Devil was taken from you, so I have to ask, do you think he'd be on our side?"

"I want to say yes, Zoe, honest, but it's unclear." He sighed in frustration. "Breakers never coagulate outside spectrum minors—"

She cut him off with a frustrated growl and slapped her hand on the open book in her lap. "Someone really wanted to make sure you couldn't talk about this fucker!"

"What did I say?"

"Just a bunch of nonsense," she answered, then swung her feet to the floor so she could face him straight on, because she needed to somehow confirm the information she'd found. "Hex, I don't think this Devil is like anything else in existence. Well, not anymore anyway."

"What do you mean?"

"If the oldest stories about him are true," she replied, keeping her words paced and watching his face for signs of confusion. "He may very well be the last living Nephilim."

When Hex's brows furrowed, she felt the disappointment sharper than before. It was just cutting deeper each time, and she wasn't sure if that was due to the frustrating communication obstacles or the anger she felt toward whoever had damaged Hex's brain. Her number one suspect was Abaddon, of course. Who else would have the motive to cripple Hex in some way, or the ability to somehow magically remove just one thing from his brain?

Zoe's eyes widened, an epiphany striking her at the same exact moment Hex's face lit up. Before she could follow her mind's route to the connection it had just made, he rose from his chair and launched over the table toward her.

"Zoe, that's brilliant!" he exclaimed.

"Duh." It was a knee-jerk response whenever someone was wise enough to point out that most obvious trait of hers. "But why am I so brilliant this time?"

He grinned even brighter, but there was a whole lot of unmistakable hunger in his eyes. She could practically hear the naughty thoughts running through his mind and it triggered her own.

"Mmm, I'm almost tempted to barter answers for clothing," he replied. "What do you say, doe? Should we see just how far that phenomenal confidence of yours really goes? It's been well over an hour."

"You really need to learn how to focus on one thing at a time," she grumbled, because her body had begun heating with his invitation. Again. Honestly, one would think five orgasms in one day would be enough, but her libido was turning her into a greedy little nympho. "Back to my brilliance."

His expression deflated, but he didn't argue. "Write everything you found on a piece of paper. I'll take it to Farah."

"I thought you said that might be pointless?"

Hex shook his head. "That was before you reminded me of his origins."

Zoe glanced down at the pages of the book. "I don't follow. How could him being a Nephilim keep Abaddon or Saph from finding out?"

"Because the Nephilim are half human," he answered. "Farah can track that side, rather than his Angel side, which means the other Seven might not ever detect it. Just one human contacting another."

Zoe's mouth opened on a slow grin. "She can do that?" she questioned, then shook her head and waved her hand. "Never mind, of course she can, she's like a super Voodoo goddess."

Hex chuckled and waited for her to scribble out the name and pertinent details about Lust onto a scrap of paper.

"Here," she said, handing it to him. "Can you also find out when she plans on coming back?"

"She was planning to?"

Zoe nodded. "She mentioned it after we cut the knot out of your arm. I could use her help with something."

His eyes narrowed on her, but before he could ask, she set her book and notes aside, then stood up on the sofa to drape her arms over his shoulders.

"I'll try to explain when you get back, I promise," she vowed. "I'm just not sure your brain will let you hear me."

Though he grimaced, he nodded in acceptance. "All right, baby. I'll be right back."

"Kiss me first."

That perked him up, and he wrapped his arms around her and dove in for a sultry promise—a kiss filled with the hints of something fantastic yet to come. Zoe moaned in protest when he backed away first, which just had the demon grinning all smug like.

"Oh, how the tables turn," he teased.

"Zip it," she snapped, but there wasn't enough fire in it to convince her own ears, let alone his.

Which was why Hex was still giving her a smug

smirk when the shadows took him away.

Curious and unsure of how much time she'd have, Zoe hurried around the long table and searched for the book Hex had been reading. When she pulled it out from under the stack and read the title, everything inside of her melted like a nauseating Hallmark movie. *Pop Culture of the Twentieth Century.* That he had taken her love for the topic seriously enough to actually try to catch up on it was better than any present any man had ever tried to give her. It filled her heart with more sentiment than flowers, chocolates, or even coffee—and that should be impossible!

Zoe was still standing there, thumbing through the book like a sap, when Hex reappeared. Her first reaction was to jump into his arms and place a heartfelt kiss right on his mouth. He didn't hesitate to reciprocate, his arms banding around her to hold her to him. Before it could turn into something deeper, Zoe's eyes flew open at the sound of a woman clearing her throat.

Caught in the act, she saw Farah standing just off to the side looking nice and comfy in her hunter-green summer dress and hair scarf, despite the solid white eyes. Zoe pulled away and frowned at Hex.

"We need an inter-dimensional doorbell," she stated.

He merely smiled, completely content with the idea of having witnesses to their displays of affection, it seemed.

"Your demon is speaking in tongues," Farah announced, before handing Zoe the scrap of paper she'd written on. "And brought me this, which I can't make out."

"What?" Zoe took the paper from her and gasped at it in disbelief. It was still in her handwriting, but all of the words had changed into gibberish. "How is that even possible? I'm the one who wrote this, not him."

"Apparently, someone doesn't like your demon talking about things he shouldn't," Farah deduced. "In any medium."

"Well, there goes my theory," Zoe exhaled, lifting a hand and letting it drop again.

"What theory?" Hex asked.

She gave him a hesitant look, then turned him by the arm to face Farah and brushed the hair from his forehead. "See that?" she asked, pointing to the dark strawberry-red scar.

Farah moved closer, her eyes narrowing in scrutiny.

"I think his brain has been magically lobotomized," Zoe stated.

"What is it?" Hex asked. "What's on my head?"

Farah and Zoe both peered around the library, before the former simply disappeared. She returned in a blink with a mirror in hand, which she gave to Hex. He peered into it, his eyes wide with surprise.

"What is that?" he asked, startled.

"I should have guessed you wouldn't already know about it." Zoe sighed. "I've never once seen you look into a mirror."

"I have no need," he began, before scowling at his reflection. "Obviously, I had a need, but I don't recall ever getting this, so didn't know to look for it."

"May I?" Farah interrupted.

When Hex lowered the mirror, Farah held her hand

up to the mark, her palm about three inches from it and closed her eyes. She started whispering under her breath, but it didn't sound like the chanting Zoe had heard her use the night before. It sounded more like she was reciting a spell than performing a ritual. Several moments ticked by, but neither Zoe nor Hex were willing to break Farah's concentration.

Eventually, she lowered her hand and shook her head. "It wasn't magic," she revealed. "It was organic, whatever it was."

"Like a turnip?" Zoe blurted.

Farah chuckled. "No child, something living."

Zoe gasped and looked at the mark again. "Ew, like invasion of the body snatchers?"

"My guess would be something less alien," Farah replied with amusement.

Hex made a frustrated sound. "You two have lost my understanding," he complained.

"He doesn't get pop-culture references," Zoe explained to Farah, before giving him a sly look. "Yet."

That improved his mood again, and he gave her a sexy smirk.

"Change of plans, I need you to get half naked, after all," she said clapping her hands. "Off with the shirt."

Though he didn't hesitate to start peeling the material over his head, he gave her a puzzled look. "I already explained my tattoos to you."

"Yes, these," she agreed, running her fingers over the black marks on his arm. "But not the ones on your back."

"I have tattoos on my back?"

Zoe shot a concerned look at Farah. "Shouldn't he

know that?"

"I told you last night. Evil has been done to your demon."

"I am right here," Hex complained mildly, before smiling slightly. "But I am also her demon and I like that you keep acknowledging it."

"Focus," Zoe snapped her fingers.

Hex grinned at her as he turned, so she flipped him off and stepped around to his backside to see what Farah could make of the colorful tattoos down his spine. Despite appearing circular, each one had an open space cutting through it, which was filled with a strange pattern and never facing the same direction as any of the others. Where one open space might be completely vertical, another was horizontal, then the next diagonal, and so on. The half-circles on either side were made up of two parts, an outer ring filled with ancient letters and what looked like a celestial symbol in the larger section. Each individual tattoo was a different color of the rainbow and there were seven in all.

"Any thoughts?" she prompted, when the woman remained silent.

"The first thing that comes to mind are the chakras," Farah said. "Only they're the wrong colors."

"You mean the things hippies use to keep themselves spiritually centered?" Zoe asked.

"Hippies aren't the only ones who take care of their spiritual health, Zoe," Farah chastised.

"It was the first reference to pop into my mind, just tell me I'm right," she returned, not in the mood for some lesson in spiritual anything, unless it had to do with what was wrong with Hex.

"You're right," Farah conceded on a sigh. "But these are not."

"What are they?" Hex asked.

"If I had my phone I could take a picture and show you," Zoe sang.

"I wasn't asking you, sassy girl."

"I need to consult with my spirits," Farah replied. "I'm not familiar with these symbols or the magic that was used to create these marks. I will return once I have an answer."

"Oh, wait," Zoe said before she could disappear, rushing back to her notebook on the sofa. After she rewrote the same message she'd sent Hex with before, she handed it to Farah. "If there's any way you can reach out to him, or at least the side of him that was once human, I think he might be our only chance of getting out of this the way we want to."

Farah read over the information. "Another Devil?"

Zoe nodded. "The one bio-leeched from Hex's brain."

The woman's eyes widened, and she nodded firmly. "I'll see what I can do."

After she disappeared, fading out a lot faster than she had the night before, Zoe turned her attention back to Hex. He was brooding again, and it made her heart ache with empathy. She could only imagine what it must be like to learn things had been done to him that he couldn't remember, his memory obviously wiped clean of the crimes committed against him. If she were in his place, she'd feel angry, frustrated, and helpless, which would trigger more anger. Zoe had no way of helping him, but perhaps there was a way she could take his mind off of things until Farah returned.

"Hex, can I ask you a favor?"

He turned to her and she watched him struggle to fight back his foul mood, giving her a somewhat smoky expression that made her blood tingle. It only stirred her admiration for him that much more.

"Does it involve me removing the rest of my clothes?" he asked.

Zoe couldn't help but smile, though she shook her head and approached him. "We have time before Farah comes back, and I've done about all the research I can. I was wondering if you could use your super demon powers to take me around to some of the places here in New Orleans that I've always wanted to see? I don't know if I'll ever get the chance to see them in the living world."

He put his shirt back on, then wrapped his arms around her, lifting her from the floor so he could touch the tip of her nose with his own. "Where should we go first?"

Though Zoe had thought of the plan as a way to distract Hex from his troubles, she couldn't deny the excitement that bubbled up inside of her. Wrapping her arms around his neck, she smiled and placed a sound kiss on his mouth.

"Let's go visit the dead."

CHAPTER 10

BONE COLLECTOR

As Hex accommodated Zoe's wildest dreams by taking her to places like the Lafayette Cemetery and The Hotel Royal, she filled him in on the supernatural pop culture associated with each location. On the steps of the St. Louis Cathedral, she asked if he was going to burst into flames when they entered and he laughed so hard, she was still grinning ten minutes later when they exited again—both of them still whole and in one piece with no crucifixes harmed in the process.

"So, am I to understand that most of your life you've been this enthralled with the idea that vampires, witches, and werewolves might actually exist?" Hex asked as they stood on the grounds of the Destrehan Plantation and studied the architecture of the house.

They'd just arrived there after Zoe had 'oohed' and 'aahed' over the interior of Boutique du Vampyre, playing around with the most realistic fake fangs she'd ever seen before.

She shrugged. "I don't think it's so much the specific types of supernatural beings, I've just always been open-minded to the possibility of *any* supernatural beings existing," she answered the best she could. "I've always had this feeling that what we see and know is only the surface, and that there's more underneath. A hidden world coexisting alongside ours."

"Like us. Demons and Angels."

"Exactly." She smiled.

They studied the house a moment more. "Do you want to go inside?"

"Not this one," she decided. "Brevard House."

Zoe liked the feeling of being wrapped in Hex's arms a little too much. Especially, when his warm hands splayed over her bare back in a way that felt just as possessive as it was reverent. It was a heady combination she could get used to real fast.

The moment they were standing on the path leading to the front door of one of the most iconic houses in the entire city, though, Zoe was so starstruck she could only stare at it and drink in every little detail.

"This one we're going into?" Hex asked for confirmation.

She thought she would want to. Zoe had imagined herself bursting right through the door and exploring each and every room, but she shook her head.

"No," she answered. "I don't want to change the way it looks in my mind."

"Was this not from one of your vampire movies?" he asked.

"Not this one," she replied, taking in the black shutters and wrought-iron balustrades across the second story gallery. "I've only ever seen it as it was written in a book about a family of witches and their heirloom spirit."

"Yet, you don't believe in ghosts," he mused, teasing her.

Zoe gave him a smirk, but it wasn't too hostile. "I didn't think they were really sticking around causing trouble, no," she corrected. "Their reported behavior just didn't make enough sense for me to be convinced of that."

Hex moved away from her, going to the wrought-iron gate and looking out at the rest of the lower Garden District.

"This city is very haunted. It could convince the most skeptical of humans if they spent enough time here. The entire culture is centered around the dead and their continued presence, the very air breathes with it. I think that's why I've always been so drawn to this place. We're accepted here, celebrated."

Zoe's brows creased, and it pained her to hear him talk about being accepted. The thought of him spending thousands of years alone with nothing but the darkness and the dead to keep him company pierced her with immense sadness. Desperate humans begging for new faces or fatter bank accounts had been his only interaction with the living. Was it any wonder he'd ever deigned to barter her best friend's freedom rather than return to the Abyss where he couldn't even have that much contact? Swallowing through the thick knot of understanding and heartache in her throat, Zoe realized she forgave him. Perhaps she'd already forgiven him, but if there had been any lingering doubts, they were gone now.

"But, Hex, you're not a ghost."

"Aren't I?" he asked. "Isn't that what all dead humans are, no matter how long ago their deaths?"

"Perhaps you were once," she conceded. "But you said yourself that the new religion rewrote your destiny, immortalized you as a demon instead."

He released a long breath that wasn't quite a sigh and turned to wrap his arm around her, pulling her close to his side. She wrapped her arms around his waist in turn.

"I'm sorry, little doe," he murmured into the top of her head, brushing a kiss over her hair. "I didn't mean to ruin your tour of the city."

"You didn't," she reassured him. "I've seen everything I've ever wanted to see that we can get to. Still wish we could make it to Shreveport, but I'm over it."

He gave her a small smile, then turned his attention back to the scenery. "I guess I just can't stop thinking about these marks on my body that I never even knew about. It has me questioning if I've ever really known the truth about myself at all. If I really am what I've always thought I was."

"Well, you can still travel through the Veil, obviously," she pointed out. "Which means you're still the only Veil Strider."

"True."

"And you can still tempt humans, right?"

He was quiet, but she felt his muscles relax. "I see what you're getting at, baby."

"I have an idea," she said, chewing on her bottom lip. "Let's go rob a candy store, get a massive sugar rush, then fuck like rabbits."

Zoe never even felt her feet leave the ground, causing her to laugh all the way through the darkness of the Veil, until they reemerged in a child's dream come true—a little shop filled to the brim with every type of candy one could imagine. With a clap of her hands, she darted to the large pastry display shelves at the front counter, only to find them empty.

"Aww." She deflated. "I guess all the cooked food has to be taken from the living world."

"Why, what did my sassy girl have her heart set on?" Hex asked, leaning over her shoulder.

"Cinnamon rolls." She smiled at him, batting her lashes. "Be my genie?"

He laughed and kissed her square on the mouth. The heat was still there when he disappeared, seeping in and adding to the warmth of her desire, which had already begun stirring for him the moment she'd suggested their evening activity. Hell, if she were honest, it had never really left. Just looking at him brought all the memories of their afternoon pleasure to the forefront of her mind, a live porno she got to watch over and over again until she was ready to burst.

Hex reappeared, instantly filling her senses with the delicious aromas of fresh cinnamon rolls and Zoe's stomach growled. Her mouth watered, but when he looped an arm around her waist and hefted her onto the counter, it was his mouth she went after rather than the dessert. She wrapped her arms around his neck and pulled him in tight, her sole objective to kiss the breath right out of him. He quickly ditched the box of rolls atop the display glass and returned her affections with equal fervor.

It was madness, pure and simple, how badly Zoe wanted him right then and there. She didn't want to wait a second longer and it wasn't like they were going to get caught by the shop owner. That thought had her grinning against Hex's mouth, and she started pulling the hem of his shirt up. He didn't put up a single protest, but then, Zoe had a feeling her demon would fuck her right on the counter in the living world with everyone watching and not even think twice about it.

God, that made her so hot.

"Now," she demanded, attacking the button and zipper of his jeans. "Fuck me right now, Hex."

"I'm fucking going to," he growled, taking over for her and shoving his jeans down his legs before he slid his hands slid right under her skirt, gripped her panties, and yanked on them. Zoe propped herself on the counter enough to lift her ass so he could remove them, then yelped when he scooted her closer to the edge. "You're a fucking goddess, Zoe, you know that?"

"I did, do, I mean . . . God, please just do it," she stammered. For the first time in her life, despite the naughty circumstances, his tone had been so sincere it tripped her up and she wasn't used to that.

She'd much rather focus on the desire, so reached behind her own neck to untie the top of her dress and pull the material down to expose her naked breasts. Hex's nostrils flared and his eyes burned with hunger. He quickly shoved the material of her skirt out of his way and yanked her ass off the edge, guiding his cock to her pussy. She was already nice and wet for him, she knew. She'd felt herself growing more and more aroused since he'd first returned with her cinnamon rolls. As soon as he thrust into her, Zoe felt the aching need begin to subside, replaced with pure pleasure. She wrapped her legs around his waist as he plunged deeper and deeper. One hand supported her ass while the other covered her breast and squeezed so perfectly right.

"Yes," she mewled. "Mouth. Use your mouth, Hex, suck on my nipple."

"Fuck yeah," he snarled, her words causing him to thrust harder as he ducked his head down to her other breast and complied.

The heat of his wet mouth covering her nipple had Zoe's body arching into his face. Her thighs tightened around his thrusting hips, her hands gripping his thick hair to keep him right where she wanted. It was hot and deliciously erotic. Ecstasy filled her entire body. The feel of his cock sliding so hard and fast against her inner walls, the fullness of his girth stretching her, it was just sheer bliss. She couldn't get enough. Even as she felt the swell of an impending orgasm beginning deep in her pussy, she didn't want it to end. So, when Hex's hand abandoned her breast in search of her clit, Zoe shook her head and grabbed at his arm to bring it back.

"No, not yet," she panted. "I just want to feel you fuck me, Hex. Just fuck me until I come and then—"

The rest of her words were lost as he made a sound of excited approval that seemed to heat his very skin. His mouth made quick work of both her nipples, before sliding up to nuzzle the side of her neck and drive her even crazier. He gripped her hair and the hand supporting her ass lifted her from the counter higher so he could roll into her harder and deeper, but not faster. His pace slowed, but the effects had Zoe gasping every time he slammed home again. It almost hurt, it felt so fucking good. She'd never felt pleasure so concentrated that it could be painful, and yet that was exactly what he was giving her. All she could do was hold on to him and gasp for breath.

It was too much, too intense. Just when she thought she couldn't take it anymore, her climax struck. It started off as part of the pain, then spiraled outward, swelling into the pleasure until that was all she could feel. It stole the air from her lungs, stole the beat from her heart. Her only outward response was the tightening of her thighs around Hex's waist and the nails she dug into his scalp. Finally, when she reached the peak and started coming back down, her body convulsed from the sensitivity and she was able to make short bursts of outcries with every exhale.

"Unholy Hellfires, baby, that's it," Hex encouraged, riding out the remaining contractions of her muscles. When they all but relaxed again, he straightened and peered down at her, running his hand down her throat to her breasts. "Fuck, you're going to come like that again. It's going to be the only way you come from now on."

Zoe didn't even want to argue, but she doubted her body would obey his attempts a second time around. Once had already zapped a lot of her energy, and it was all she could do to cling to his arms when he shoved both hands under her skirt to grip her hips and step up the pace again. His gaze kept flicking between where his cock thrust into her pussy and the way her breasts moved as he fucked her.

"Play with your nipples, doe," he said. "Give me another show."

Heat flashed through her again, and she moaned, covering her breasts with her hands and kneading them. The more she rolled her nipples between her fingers and thumbs, the more arousal washed over Hex's features. When she pinched her nipples and pulled them upward, she thought he was going to choke on his own breath.

"Oh, hell yes," he moaned, then took her by surprise when he shoved her legs up onto his shoulders and bent over her, gripping the back of the counter for leverage. "I'm going to make you come again, and this time, you better scream my fucking name."

Wildfire scorched over her, the command of his tone ten times stronger than his usual bouts of bossiness, and it reawakened all the energy she'd thought depleted. The new position had his cock piercing her at depths she never thought possible, bringing about the same painful pleasure she'd felt before a hell of a lot faster. Zoe was a symphony of panting moans and short shrieks as her muscles tried to absorb the impossible amount of pleasure he was bringing her. The biggest shock came when the orgasm's first bite registered and the strength of it made tears slip from her eyes.

"Oh, that's it, baby, grab onto that," Hex praised in the most erotic voice she'd ever heard—it was pure seduction with the amount of desire, admiration and pride laced through it. "Give me your pleasure, Zoe, come on."

She wanted to, wanted to feel it, despite how damaging it might be. With another growl, Hex rose just a little higher and drove himself into her faster, but always with a steady, hard finish that had her toes curling behind his head and her lower back lifting from the counter.

"Hex, Hex!" She smacked his arms, then dug her fingers into them. "HEX!"

The climax was so powerful her breath vanished, and her body wanted to stretch all the way out with it. Hex had to pin her against himself to keep from losing her off the other edge of the counter. He let her legs drop back to his waist and took his pleasure from her at the same wild speeds he'd managed earlier. His pace lessened and he tried to still as he choked her name out into the center of her chest, but he just kept coming.

"FUCK!" he roared with a final jerk of his hips, and she could feel more hot cum spurting inside her.

His breath was ragged, but he remained sheathed deep inside her, his head resting on her breasts. Zoe giggled to herself and played with the silky strands of his hair. Unlike her hair, his never grew damp with sweat.

"Awfully winded for a demon," she teased.

His laugh was broken by that very fact. He lifted his head to rest his chin on the back of his hand. For the longest time, he merely stared at her, his pale gaze penetrating all the way to her damn soul. Zoe wasn't one to squirm under a spotlight, but something about the way he was looking at her made her feel antsy.

"You're unbelievable, Zoe," he finally spoke, and again, it was too sincere, making her want to choke up like a damn sissy. "I don't even know how to describe how riveting you are. Everything about you is just mind-blowing."

This is the part where you say "Duh" and move on to the next subject, lady. What are you waiting for? But she couldn't. The usual snark that never failed her was nowhere to be found. Her armor was gone, leaving her feeling a little vulnerable.

"And I'm not saying that because I just came harder than I've ever fucking come in my existence, but because you spent all evening trying to keep my mind off my memory issues while showing me how much a city I love means to you," he continued. "Because you shared that part of yourself with me in a way I know you've never shared with anyone else–"

Unable to take any more, Zoe gripped his face in her hands and brought his lips to hers, so she could kiss him. And with the kiss, she hoped he could feel how much his words meant to her, because she wasn't sure how to say it. Her life revolved around blunt comebacks, brutal truths and witty remarks. The only person she'd ever been able to let her guard down with was her best friend, whom she loved dearly, but this was different. This felt life-altering and frightening and too important to risk saying the wrong thing. So, she said nothing, merely poured it all into her kiss.

And once again, her demon proved that she didn't need words, that he could see and hear every layer of her, when he gasped and pulled back just enough to peer into her eyes.

"My little doe." He melted back into their kiss,

stroking his hand over her hair softly. His voice was a gentle purr filled with understanding. "It's okay, baby, I hear you."

****

Hex didn't sleep. He had no need of it, but he enjoyed lying in the center of the bed with his beautiful girl sleeping naked beside him. She was too small to drape herself over him, but that didn't keep her from trying, which was just as amusing as it was heartwarming.

And that was his newest addiction.

His body still burned for her, yes, but Hex craved a whole other part of her now. He didn't just want all the physical pleasure she brought him, he wanted her fucking heart. More, he wanted her to accept his in return, because it already belonged to her. There wasn't a single doubt in his mind, and surprisingly, it had nothing to do with already knowing she was his mate. That had been mostly physical—a connection felt in the blood and sparked in the brain. It had been spending all this time with her, learning her, hearing her and getting to see her in all her various wonders that had awoken that connection in his heart—the last piece of the whole, and he wanted the whole of her just the same.

He'd gotten close to getting her heart in those precious moments the night before, when he'd still been buried to the hilt inside her body and she'd poured her feelings out in a kiss. He'd felt it all, heard all the words she hadn't been able to say. And somehow, knowing that she'd been aware he could feel and hear them, made it all the more significant. But it hadn't been a complete surrender, and that was his new goal.

As he felt the sun rising, Hex peered down at her mostly hidden profile. The curve of her cheek, the way her dark lashes cast a slight shadow on it, the slope of her nose and the small glimpse of her lips. Her curls were spread against the arm he used to keep her cradled to his side, her hand resting on his chest with delicate fingers and a tiny wrist he could snap like a twig, yet he'd never once doubted her when she'd threatened to throat-punch him, and that just made him grin.

He'd spoken nothing but truth, when he'd told her that she was utterly unbelievable. A marvel of a human being he had more fun trying to wrap his head around than any mystery he'd ever come across throughout history. Which is why he knew what he had to do. Zoe had tried to warn him, had spent a lot of time trying to convince him, but Hex simply hadn't been able to believe it before. Now, he understood that if Greed felt in any way for his new queen the way Hex felt for Zoe, then he was super fucking fucked. Because if anyone ever tried to do to Zoe what Hex had planned on doing with Pheldra, he would kill them without a second thought. Saphiel couldn't kill him, but he could damn well make Hex wish he wasn't immortal. He needed to figure out a way to keep that from happening, because he had a lot more to lose now than just his freedom.

His only hope slept right beside him. His only link to the reasonable part of the merciless Greed. He needed Zoe's help to figure out how to right the wrong, and pray that for once in his miserable existence, Avarice wasn't the same unforgiving bastard he'd always been.

Forcing those grim thoughts away, Hex carefully untangled himself from Zoe's warm, sexy body and slipped out of bed. Not that he wouldn't love to stay right there, but he wanted to surprise her. After their hot-as-fuck defilement of the candy store the night before, she'd been too drained to do anything other than curl up in his arms and let him carry her back to the hotel room, tuck her into bed and hold her. So, she hadn't gotten her treats and he wanted to give her something to smile about when she woke up, rather than see any kind of worry or regret in her eyes. Hex wouldn't be able to handle it if she regretted what had transpired.

Without the need for clothes, he called on the Veil to transport him back to the candy shop. Inside, the pink box filled with her cinnamon rolls still sat atop the glass display case, but that wasn't all. With a wicked grin, he bent and picked up Zoe's discarded panties. He brought them to his nose, inhaled her honey-sweet scent and dealt with the backlash. His cock swelled, spurred on by her delectable scent just as much as the hot memories of what they'd done right on the counter in front of him. Fuck, it had been phenomenal. Her need had been so strong, her desire blazing like a homing beacon to his own. It was a little surprising they hadn't spontaneously combusted.

With a groan, Hex grabbed the pastry box and left before he could make his condition worse. He was in the process of picking out new clothes for the both of them at their favorite department store, when he felt Farah's presence loud and clear.

"Shit."

He'd planned to return to the hotel naked, just in case his little doe felt frisky, but now he dressed right there in the store so he could see what Farah had discovered. He followed her presence to the replica of her own shop, where Zoe had cut the physical tie to his destroyed bone in the apartment above. Remembering to stuff her sexy panties into his jeans pocket first, he stepped out of the shadows in front of the counter Farah was leaning over, scanning a row of documents. The parchment was so old and thick, it almost resembled skin or animal hide.

She looked up at him. "Ooh, cinnamon rolls?"

He tucked the box closer to his side. "They're Zoe's."

Her mouth quirked up in an amused smirk. "Your human seems to be adapting to her new world of Devils and sea monsters rather well."

"She was already fully aware of it," he muttered. "What have your spirits discovered?"

With something close to a sigh, she straightened and rubbed her palms together. "They want your bones."

Hex stilled. "Why?"

"You walk with spirits, you tell me why." She spread her hands. "All they kept saying was that the answers lie in your bones."

Nothing about that felt good. Uneasiness swirled inside him. "All of them, or just a few of them?"

Farah arched a brow. "You think we mean to control you, the way your murderers did." It wasn't a question, because she was right, and she knew it. "I have no need of your abilities, demon. You are not of my faith. I answer to my spirits and they speak on your behalf, otherwise we wouldn't even be having this conversation."

There was a pause, then she lifted a finger. "That and I like your human," she added. "She's sharp and she's got fire. Little thing tried to attack me when she thought I meant to take your shadows from you."

What? Hex's mind spun with that news. It wasn't that he couldn't picture Zoe ever doing that, because he could, it was that she'd done it out of fear for him. To try to protect him, when he'd been unable to protect himself. He already knew Farah hadn't tried to steal his shadows, nor would she ever be capable of it, but he could imagine it must have looked that way to Zoe when they'd emerged out of reflex to help shield and heal him.

The new insight settled inside him, mixing with all the other feelings Zoe stirred up that were constantly evolving and growing stronger.

"If you want answers to your mystery, gathering your bones in one place again is the risk you're going to have to take," Farah concluded.

Hex didn't like it. The risk was tremendous. But he also understood that was his price. Everything had a price, especially when it came to those ancient spirits and their help. His only other choice was to continue on, not knowing what had been done to him, questioning his purpose and origins. How could he hope to win Zoe's heart when he didn't even know the whole truth of who or what he was anymore?

"I'll have them here before sundown."

Farah studied him for another moment and then nodded in acceptance. "I will prepare, then."

Her ancient parchments disappeared with her, leaving Hex to contemplate how badly Zoe was going to react to the news. She'd undoubtedly try to convince him to take her with him, which couldn't happen. Outside the demimonde, the chance that she'd be detected immediately was too great—even in the Shallows, and he couldn't take her any deeper into the Veil than that. No, she was going to have to stay behind again. He already knew she was not going to be happy about that at all.

Glancing down at the pastry box in his hands, he felt the sharp edge of disappointment that his morning surprise for her was essentially ruined. With a heavy sigh, he made a quick stop back at the department store for her clothes, then finally returned to the hotel room. The bed was empty, but he didn't panic, because he could hear the shower running. And her singing.

All other thoughts forgotten, his mouth curved into a smile as he followed the sounds into the bathroom. He propped a shoulder against the wall and watched her shaking her sexy little ass through the steam-fogged glass, singing off key in a way that was more adorable than painful. Hex was so amused and unsurprisingly turned on, that he forgot how bad it was to sneak up on her.

She spun while singing and then screamed with fright to find him standing there, her hand instantly going to her chest above her heaving, naked breast.

A look of pure murder came over her face.

Ah, shit. So much for making her smile first thing.

"What is wrong with you?" she demanded.

"I was enjoying the show."

"I swear to fucking God, Hex, I'm going to kill you before you can kill me!"

Hex lifted the pink pastry box and gave her his most charming smile. "But I brought cinnamon rolls."

"You brought . . . " Her words trailed off, and for a moment she just stared, before she started laughing.

She laughed so hard, she fell back onto the little built-in seat in the shower. And it had every muscle in Hex's body going stiff with worry, because there was nothing humorous in the sound of it. Tossing the box on the counter, he immediately went to the shower, opened the door and shut the water off.

He crouched in the doorway, pulling her hands away from her face.

"What are you so afraid of?" he asked, because he would kill it, whatever it was. Anything to remove the fear from the layers of her laughter.

"You," she answered. "This. You, me . . . us."

It felt like she'd punched him in the chest, but the pain wasn't sharp, it was deep and heavy.

"I don't know how to go back to my life the way it was," she whispered. "I can't picture it anymore."

And she grieved for that, he could hear it. The pain in his chest twisted. His mind circled, wondering where everything had jumped track, going the wrong way. Inciting fear and sorrow, instead of what had just been there. He'd almost had her heart, now it was gone.

"It's all changed," she added, her eyes distant, as if she were still trying to picture her old life.

That's when it hit him. Change. Hex had changed her life when he'd entered it. When he'd decided to risk it all to save her from Abaddon's Legion. She'd been happy with her life the way it had been, and he knew that beyond a doubt, because it was the entire reason why his temptation didn't work on her. He'd taken that happiness from her and now she was afraid she'd never get it back, because he didn't make her happy enough to replace it. Looking back on their time together, all he could see were the multiple accounts of when he'd angered her, insulted her friend, offended her with the thoughtless way he spoke truths. He'd been so ignorant to think that her physical affections meant he actually made her happy. He was a fucking demon, for Hell's sake. He'd never made anyone truly happy, it had always been artificial and temporary. A curse. He cursed humans, and Zoe was no exception to that, if that alone.

At a loss, Hex rose and peered around the room, but saw nothing of it. He couldn't look her in the eye. He didn't want to see the truth of all her regret there. It was already killing him.

"I have to go," he announced. "Gather my bones. Farah said the spirits need my bones. I don't know when I'll be back."

The Veil responded to his immense desire to be taken away quickly, but he caught her expression of surprise and her attempt to stop him when she leaped off the shower seat, her hand reaching for him.

"Hex! Wait!"

He fled into the deepest, coldest depths of the Veil where he couldn't hear or smell her anymore. There, he roared long and loud, expelling the hurt until it turned into something else. Anger at himself for ever being so *human.* Despite his own warning to her, he'd allowed her to humanize him over some foolish notion that she would just leap happily into his arms because they were destined to be. Because she'd accepted him as a demon, embraced his demonic ways without qualm. But Zoe wasn't one of the half-demon orphans she'd told him about, so why had he managed to convince himself that being mated to a human was rational? Her differences had merely enraptured him, that's all. His inability to tempt her had captivated and marveled him, making him believe it meant something more, when it obviously didn't. It was over now. Mystery solved. She couldn't be tempted, because she was already happy and content with her life.

The life without him in it.

Hex came to the first location of one his bones on auto-pilot, remaining hidden just inside the Shallows, despite the darkness of night. Though not nearly as large as Moscow, Omsk was a major Siberian city with over a million citizens. The large, gold dome of the Uspensky Cathedral before him glimmered with the specifically placed lights giving the main structure a blue glow. More ground lights kept the surrounding area of the manicured and treed square lit up, but Hex wasn't worried. What he needed was far beneath the ground, where no one would see him retrieving it.

There was nothing profound or spiritually meaningful about where he'd chosen to bury his bones. He'd simply picked places least likely to ever see an excavator. With the Veil, he didn't have to dig. There was nothing solid he couldn't pass through, including layers of earth. It felt strange to have one of his bones in hand again. He inspected it in the Shallows, the ancient symbols his murderers had carved into it, allowing them to call on him for their evil plots against others. He wondered if it matched the symbols marked into the skin of his back. The tattoos had to be more magical renderings, just like the ones lining his sides, since his flesh had never been known to those who'd killed him.

Hex left Siberia and went on to his next bone. Sometimes he specifically chose isolated locations as places of refuge, just like his island in Papua New Guinea. Other times, like in Omsk and Cape Town, South Africa, he chose populated locations so he could walk among the people, learn how to blend in with them and stay caught up on current events, modern technology and other advancements. It was vital to be up on the times, so he knew how to tempt his victims with their version of what was deemed beautiful, powerful, and enviable. The sins may never change, but the perceptions of them did. In ancient times, when a woman wanted to be beautiful, she desired to be a little plump with a healthy glow to show men how fertile her body was. Now, when women wanted to be beautiful, it was to look like what had been deemed frail and sickly in ancient times, so Hex had to stay current with his victim's perceptions.

That was the majority of it. The other part was loneliness. Something he'd never acknowledged before finding Zoe. The idea of going back to his previous existence, even free from the Abyss, suddenly felt horribly and miserably lonely.

The pain spread through his chest, and Hex dug the heel of his free hand into it, as if that could help. It was just the death of hope. That's all it could be. He'd been wrong to think Zoe would accept him as her mate. Now that he'd taken the human-hued glasses off and looked at it with the dark realism of his true nature, he could see that. They weren't even from the same realm. She had everything she needed and wanted already. And just as everything in the living world eventually did, the pain would come to pass and grow into a distant memory from which he could detach himself.

From the shores of Loch Ewe in the Scottish Highlands to Vienna, Austria, Hex collected his ninth and tenth bones. His last stop was Bleaker Island in the Falklands off the coast of South America, then he would return to the New Orleans demimonde and get some answers. Regardless of what had happened between him and Zoe, Hex still wanted to know the truth about himself, and he was more determined than ever before to never see the Abyss again. So, he had no other choice than to cooperate with Farah and her spirits. He also needed to ensure Zoe's safety from Abaddon, though he pretty much knew how to make that happen. The same way he'd been too prideful to consider at the start, which was to allow Greed to keep her safe in his stead. Provide for her what Hex could not.

When the Shallows spread thin enough for him to see through without being detected, Hex was momentarily confused to find himself not in the Falkland Islands, but the Greek ones. Then, he knew exactly why he was there, and felt the rage boil through his veins.

"Leviathan!" he roared.

CHAPTER 11

DUMBASS

Zoe was stunned speechless when Hex straight up disappeared after announcing his bone-gathering news, but once her mind jolted back into working order, she knew exactly who to target first.

She quickly dried off and got dressed in the clean clothes Hex had brought her, which he'd apparently picked up along with her forgotten cinnamon rolls. When she'd woken to find him gone, Zoe hadn't known where he might have vanished to or why, but she'd been okay with it. The time alone had given her a chance to think, to start sorting out everything he'd revealed to her the night before and how she felt about it. To examine how much it all affected her in ways she'd never experienced with any of her previous relationships. Which was funny, because she could've sworn she'd been in love before. Wasn't that how all relationships felt at some point? Especially as a teenager, when your hormones were in chaos and everything felt a hundred times more extreme than it really was?

Now, she knew there was no way her heart had ever

fallen before, because it felt completely different with Hex. And no matter how irrational it was or how recklessly fast it was happening, Zoe was definitely falling for him in a big way. So, yes, the change to her life scared the shit out of her, but most of that was due to their unusual circumstances. For so long, her business had been her sole focus and she dedicated all of her time to it, but now she had another priority. Plus, she had no idea how her and Hex's relationship was going to affect the relationships she already had with her friends and employees; all the secrets she'd have to keep and lies she'd have to tell now. Those people were very important to her. She had the right to worry about them and her business, damn it! How dare he bail on her when she needed to talk to him!

Zoe grabbed the box of cinnamon rolls and set out on foot from the hotel. The heat of the morning didn't help dry her hair any faster, because it was too humid. She'd gotten a little spoiled by Hex's ability to zip her around the city in a flash, so it seemed to take forever to reach her destination. At last, she was pushing the door open to a musical clash of windchimes and inhaling a full meadow's worth of natural herbs.

"Farah!"

She wasn't sure which realm the woman would be in or if she'd even be able to hear Zoe. Hex might be the only one who could draw her attention, but Zoe had to try. When nothing happened after several moments, she headed up the stairs to the woman's apartment.

"Farah, I really need to talk to you!" she shouted. Another minute ticked by. "Far–!"

"I'm here, girl, what is all the noise?"

Zoe whipped around to find the woman sitting on the long sofa, going over some ancient-looking documents spread across the surface of the coffee table.

"Why the hell is Hex out there digging up his bones?"

Farah looked up from the table with a frown. "Did he not tell you?"

"No, he dropped the bomb, then took off before I could even get a word out."

"My spirits need his bones," Farah explained. "They claim the answer to his riddle lies within them. Perhaps your demon thought you'd try to talk him out of it, who am I to say? I don't speak for demons."

Zoe snorted and gestured to the documents. "No, but you'll spread yourself between two realms trying to help them."

"I don't. Usually." Farah sighed, then narrowed in on Zoe's inability to remain still or calm. "I have the feeling your demon's sudden disappearance isn't the only source of your agitation, young Zoe."

"That's none of your business," she snapped.

"Ah, so a lover's quarrel, then."

"It wasn't a quarrel, it was just . . ." Zoe lifted a hand as if she could pluck the right word out the air. "Feelings, you know? But just like before, if it's something he's not comfortable with hearing, poof!"

"Sounds like a typical male reaction to feelings," Farah commented.

"Exactly!" Zoe said. "But when he was pouring his heart out to me last night, did I just up and poof? No! I let him say his piece, for the most part, but I confess one little thing this morning and he's gone."

When Farah didn't say anything, Zoe stopped pacing and turned to see the woman just watching her with a perplexed expression. "Sorry, you lost me at a demon pouring his heart out."

"Ugh! This is why I need Kami," she complained. "No offense, you're powerful and know things, but you're not a half-demon eternally mated to a King of Hell."

Farah's eyes widened, and Zoe wondered if she'd just made a mistake. She already knew better than to reveal any secrets about the real existence of Angels and demons, but Farah had seemed safe to discuss those things with, since she obviously already knew Hex and Leviathan, at least.

"That explains what your demon meant about you already being fully aware when I mentioned you processing your new world fairly well," Farah finally remarked, easing Zoe's concerns.

"Yeah, don't worry about me," she said, giving her a small smile of appreciation for the concern. "I'm already fully processed."

With a heavy sigh, she felt a little calmer now that she'd vented somewhat. Which allowed her to remember the real reason why she'd called Farah there in the first place.

"So, what exactly do your spirits plan to do with Hex's bones?"

"Won't know that until he brings them back," she answered, skimming over the documents again. "Your next question is why am I scouring over these old documents then, and the answer to that has more to do with how we're going to track down your Lust Devil."

"We?"

"Mm-hmm." Farah nodded in confirmation. "If he is half human, I may be able to scry his closest location, a place he would leave protected for himself on earth. Your demon is connected to him somehow, we believe, and you are connected to your demon while also remaining completely earthbound, so with the right scrying spell," she tapped her finger on the documents, "we should be able to do this without alerting any non-earthbound demons."

"Good, because I think they're all on earth at this point," Zoe said.

"Yes and no," Farah said. "Like me, they have to keep a part of themselves in their natural realm in order to visit the other."

"No, they really don't," Zoe corrected her. "That's what they have familiars for."

Farah looked at her with mild surprise, then considered her words for a moment. "Do you happen to know what this Devil's familiar is?"

Zoe shook her head. "No, I couldn't find any references to one. The only thing—"

Her mind spun as she recalled reading the oldest tales and what Lust seemed to have a knack for always finding. For being the only one in existence able to find it.

"The only thing, what?"

"I need to go back to the library," she blurted.

Farah waved her hands over the documents and they disappeared, then she stood from the sofa and approached Zoe, rubbing her palms together.

"All right, this might take some effort," she said, taking Zoe's free hand in hers. "Just repeat after me."

Zoe would be lying if she said the idea of partaking in a real life spell didn't excite some part of her, but fangirl geekdom aside, it also gave her anxiety. The last thing she needed was to get spliced up in some inter-dimensional transport gone wrong just because she mispronounced a word.

"I can walk," she said.

"You, Zoe, are not a coward," Farah stated, tightening her grip and beginning to chant.

"It's like less than a mile," she continued to protest.

When Farah simply chanted louder, Zoe quickly switched her focus and started repeating the words, lest she really did cause her own destruction. It was a hundred times different than when Hex moved her from place to place through the Veil. With Farah's abilities, Zoe wasn't sure if she was fading out of the apartment, or if the apartment was fading away and being just as slowly replaced by the interior of the library.

Once the library completely surrounded them and was solid, Farah stopped chanting.

"Not bad for your first time," Farah said, giving her an amused, but impressed look.

"Last time," Zoe had no qualms correcting her, which only caused the woman to chuckle. "Now, where was that book?"

Still on the sofa with her notepad, right where she'd

left it. Great thing about demimondes, you didn't have to clean up after yourself. Zoe set the pastry box aside and started flipping through the pages. The book was filled with enough information to make your brain bleed, yet never clear or definitive enough to claim anything as factual. Perhaps that's why she hadn't connected the dots sooner. Just like with Asmodeus, the thing she searched for had too many variations, had been called too many things to draw any kind of concrete conclusions.

"Here," she said, when she finally found it. She carried the book over to the table where Farah had taken a seat. "In one story it's called a stone, in another it's a powder, but in this one, it's known as the Shamir worm."

She set the book in front of Farah. "According to one tale, only Ashmodai, or Asmodeus, knew its whereabouts, so King Solomon had him captured and brought back to him so he could use the Shamir to build his temple."

"You think this worm might be the Devil's familiar?" Farah asked.

"If he's storing some of his power in it, wouldn't he always know where it's at?" Zoe answered. "But this gets better—or worse, rather. Hex's mark on his forehead . . . You said it was made by something living. Doesn't the smallest inner circle look like tiny little teeth marks to you?"

Farah sat up with a start, her eyes and mouth going round.

"I know," Zoe nodded. "I threw up in my mouth a little when I put the two together. And you dismissed my alien body snatching idea so quickly, too."

Farah exhaled on a stuttered laugh and shook her

head. "What if it has?" she asked. "Burrowed itself inside your demon's brain?"

"No, ew, please no." Zoe whimpered, feeling sick to her stomach just thinking about it. "Look, no matter which variation, the Shamir is always able to cut precisely what it's shown without damaging anything else. So, what if it was used merely to cut away the names of Lust from Hex's brain for whatever reason?"

Farah wagged her finger. "I like that theory a lot better."

"Me, too," Zoe admitted. "But that poses a bigger problem now, because I sincerely believed it had been Abaddon who'd removed Lust's names from Hex's mind, but if the Shamir is Asmodeus's familiar–"

"Then perhaps you've been accusing the wrong demon," Farah finished for her. "Which means, contacting him might not be a wise decision."

"Exactly." Zoe scowled, frustrated because it left them back at square one with no Hellish allies. "I guess I just thought it meant something with Hex being a temptation demon, that he would have some kind of connection to Lust."

"That's a reasonable conclusion, but humans are tempted by much more than just lust," Farah pointed out. "They're tempted by power and what they covet of others, money and vanity, pride and all the things deemed sins, so with that line of thinking, he could very well be connected to any of your Devils."

"Then why was Lust the only one removed from his brain?" Zoe questioned, not Farah directly, but just tossing it out into the universe with the hope that someone might have the answer. "And why only the names? Why not take away any memory of him altogether, so Hex would never know something was missing?"

"Perhaps, they couldn't," Farah reasoned, spreading her hands. "Perhaps his memory is too long."

That was a valid possibility. Deflated, Zoe plopped into a chair beside her and peered around the library, spotting the empty and abandoned silver carafe atop one of the shorter bookcases from the day before.

"You know what else is too long?" she complained. "The hours between my caffeine intakes. Did Hex happen to mention how long this chore was going to take him?"

"He said he'd have all his bones returned before sundown."

"Oh, hell no, I am not waiting that long to get some coffee into my system," Zoe stated, rising from the table.

"Where are we going now?"

"You can go wherever you want," she waved over her head. "I'm gonna go rob the closest convenience store of all their frappuccinos, then finally enjoy my damn cinnamon rolls."

****

Hex found himself in the center of the same office he'd visited before, seething at the smug Leviathan comfortably seated behind his desk. He turned Hex's last bone over and over in his hands.

"Missing something?" The Hellmouth asked, before holding the radius between his index fingers so Hex could see the carved symbols. "Now, this is a language I haven't seen in a very long time."

"What game are you playing at, Envy?"

"Oh, we're still on the same topic as before and it is far from being a game," Leviathan answered soberly. "I need you to deliver that package tomorrow as promised, so I can't have you distracted with your puzzle box just yet. Once you deliver, I will give you your final bone and you can solve the mystery of your making until your little black heart is content."

"I made a deal, I will not back out on it," Hex stated. "That has nothing to do with my answers or my bones."

Leviathan laughed. "You say that now, because you're this." He gestured to Hex's body with the bone. "There is a very slim chance that will be the case when you're not any longer."

"You're speaking in riddles that make no sense!" Hex raged. "This is all there is, all there's ever been."

Again the beast roared with laughter and it was the most infuriating sound he'd ever heard. Hex was bulging with the desire to whip across the room and rip the fucker's vocal cords right out of his throat.

"I wouldn't do that if I were you." Leviathan grinned darkly. "Whatever damage you wish you could inflict upon me, I promise it will only end terribly for you. I have no qualms teaching you a lesson in real power. You may be very old to this world, but you are a mere toddler to me, running around bumping into things and toppling over, drooling on yourself and forgetting your own name."

"If you know me so well, then tell me," Hex

challenged, because he didn't believe a word the beast said.

Angels were incapable of lying, and thus the Fallen carried the same fate. The rest of the demons simply didn't grasp the concept, it wasn't natural for them and at any rate—they liked it better when their truths made humans squirm uncomfortably in their skins. Leviathan was a total mystery when it came to his ability or belief in lying. He was primordial in origin, the oldest creature on earth that Hex knew of.

"No, I think I'll let that remain a mystery," he answered. "Until after you deliver the package."

"Yeah," Hex scoffed. "Thought as much. You don't know anything, because if you did, you'd know that you and I? We're not that different. We're both fighting against the same Angels and Devils to save our mates."

Leviathan was before him impressively fast, almost as if he'd moved with a mere thought.

"Would you like to add me to that list, Strider?" he warned, all humor completely gone. Again, he emphasized the title, as if it held some other kind of meaning. "Because, you see, while I expect and want you to deliver that package as promised, I don't actually need you to do it. You're simply my most expedient route, but I do have other options. You, on the other hand, have nothing but a lot to lose, so tread very carefully, before I decide to go with plan B by destroying every single one of your remaining bones, your witch, and your mate, just for trying my patience."

Hex was livid, fuming and once again perplexed by the cryptic messages, but he also wouldn't risk Zoe's life on the off chance that Leviathan was bluffing about any of it. That didn't mean he was just going to stand there and take a blatant threat on her life to his face as if it didn't matter. Envy wasn't the only one with lines that shouldn't be crossed.

"Tomorrow, at dusk," he ground out through his teeth. "You will hand over my bone and if you try to go back on your end of the deal, you will be the one adding me to the list of all the creatures you despise so much, and I won't even have to kill your mate the way they did. All I have to do is give her the one thing she desires most, then her soul is mine."

Hex was gone before the beast could respond, his anger so thorough and ripe he didn't even care if he lost the bone Leviathan was holding as leverage. In fact, he was more than a little surprised when he made it all the way back to the NOLA Public Library without feeling its destruction. Perhaps the Devil had taken his word for the promise it was. If Envy came anywhere near Zoe, Hex would take his mate's soul for all eternity.

Out of habit, Zoe's presence had drawn him right to the library, as did the full release of the Veil, because she preferred it that way. A matter that struck him full on, when the cinnamon roll hit him square in the chest with a dull thud, smearing icing all down the front of his shirt on its way to the floor.

"That's for your second dick move," she fumed, marching right toward him. "Or did you think I'd be okay with you dropping a bomb on me like that and then bailing?"

It hurt to see and hear her, so he attempted to block

it. To think of her not as his mate, but just a human he needed to protect. She wasn't the woman that made him laugh, made him happy, and turned him on with her sexy body, just as much as her quick and clever mind. He didn't admire her confidence, courage or her sharp tongue. He didn't feel anything at all. That was his new goal, just to turn it all off until he couldn't feel the loss anymore.

"I wasn't aware that I needed your approval to do anything," he countered as he bent down and picked the pastry up off the floor.

Zoe's gasp was quiet, but she recovered quickly, the shock on her face returning to anger in a split-second. Hex caught her arm when she attempted to sock him in the gut and then moved just in time to evade her kick to his shin, but the shadows emerged.

"Stop," he stated firmly. "You cannot hit me and remain intact. If the Veil even lets you make contact, you will break your bones."

"Aghhh!" she raged, but stopped trying to attack him. "You're an asshole! I open up to you about *one*— just one—of the many things I'm feeling and thinking, and you decide you can't handle it, so you fucking run?"

"I had to collect my bones," he reminded her.

"Oh, that's bullshit," she snapped. "You obviously had all damn day to do that, since it only took you like three hours. You bailed, because you didn't like what I was saying—yet again—and I'm getting real tired of being the only nonpartisan member in this relationship, Hex!"

Emotions leaked through the cracks of his newly

placed armor, trying to confuse him, but the only thing he seemed able to focus on was her use of the word *relationship*. The very thing he could have sworn she didn't want any part of, was too afraid of to even consider.

"You made your feelings clear this morning, Zoe," he stated, trying to ignore the hurt as it continued to mock his weak attempts at blocking it out. "In every way. I could hear the truth of it in your voice when you said that this scares you, could hear the grief when you said that you can't picture your life anymore—"

"Yeah, because I'm human, Hex," she cut him off. "Look at me. I'm human, and humans are afraid of change, and they grieve over change. But that doesn't mean that they—that I—don't want the change or know that the change is going to be so much better than anything before it. It's just a natural reaction that I have to go through first. That I have the *right* to go through. I've never once held your demony-demonness against you, so how dare you hold my humanity against me. You either accept me for who and what I am, or you can really just fuck off!"

Utterly stunned, Hex couldn't even move when she stormed out of the library. His chest and mind felt pressurized with clashing emotions, the extremes rising and falling, as another one took its place. Surprise, regret, happiness, guilt, hope, shame. He hadn't been aware that he'd been holding her humanity against her, really. It wasn't anything he'd been doing on purpose. Humans were normally just targets to him. On top of that, he was used to relying on the things he heard in people's voices or saw in the layers of their expressions they thought they were keeping hidden. That had always been his most trusted source of information, because humans were liars and deceivers, to themselves just as much as to others. No, his mistake hadn't been holding Zoe's humanity against her, it had been forgetting, in that moment of hurt, that she wasn't like any other human in existence.

The sound of stoneware coming together, cup to saucer, brought Hex out of his thoughts. He sent a grim look at Farah still sitting at the long table where she'd witnessed the entire argument. A full coffee tray and snacks set amongst the books. No doubt Zoe's idea.

"Hmm-mm, don't look at me, this is like getting free pay-per-view," Farah said. "But you might wanna go put that fire out, before it burns this entire demimonde to the ground."

With another grimace, Hex left the library the conventional way, knowing his little doe couldn't have gotten far on foot. He was surprised that she'd already made it halfway down the next block, her little legs carrying her on a mission. To what, he could only imagine the worst. The demimonde carried everything the real New Orleans did, including weapons. She slowed to a stop, and he had to wonder if it was because she could feel him behind her, even though she didn't turn to face him.

Hex ran a hand over his hair and face, the clash of emotions swirling in his chest. He'd give anything to go back to the night before when she was giving him all her thoughts and feelings in a kiss. The fear was ripe, because what if he'd already ruined his chances by taking off?

"It dawned on me that you were happy before. You know, the whole reason why temptation never worked on you was because you were already completely happy with your life the way it was," he began, as soon as he was close enough to speak without shouting. "So yes, I took off, because I couldn't handle hearing how much I'd changed that, how much less happy your life has been with me in it."

When she didn't respond, Hex felt the fear rise and his hopes begin to crash. He managed to hold both at bay. Until he could hear her voice and see her face, he wouldn't know for sure what she felt about it and he didn't want to make the same mistake twice by coming to the wrong conclusion again.

"Zoe, just—"

She turned slowly, awkwardly. "Hex?" she whispered. "I don't feel so good."

His blood turned to ice the second she reached for him with a hand that was literally fading out of sight, just like her other one, and it was spreading.

"Fuck!" His immediate reaction was to grab her up into his arms, and instantly, he could feel an immense power trying to pull her away from him.

He called the shadows around them and it cut that power off abruptly. A few seconds passed and he panted with relief to see Zoe's corporeality returning.

"Oh, I think I'm going to be sick," she said weakly. "It feels like I just rode the scrambler a hundred times in a row."

He had no idea what that was, but it sounded self-explanatory enough to get the gist.

"Hold on, baby, I've got you," he reassured her. "We'll fix this."

He was back in the library in an instant, but he didn't dare take Zoe out of the Shallows. Rather, he merely thinned them as much as he could to be completely visible.

"Farah, Zoe's being attacked."

"What?" Farah leaped out of her chair and approached them.

"Something powerful is trying to pull her from this world," he explained quickly. "The Veil stops it, but I can't keep her in here for too long. The land of the dead will start having its own negative effects on her."

"I know you're not going to like this, but I need to feel the power that's attacking her."

She was right, he detested the idea.

"It's making her fade the way you do when you leave here. She said she feels extremely sick."

"That's not enough." Farah shook her head once. "I know you're worried, demon, but I have to figure out what the threat is, if I hope to stop it."

Hex ground his molars, peering down at Zoe's pale face.

"Little doe?"

"I'm okay," she said. "Just keeping my eyes closed until the spinning stops. Let her check, Hex."

He hated it. Every fiber of his being protested, but he released the shadows. Farah placed her hands on Zoe, closed her eyes, and started invoking her magic. Ten seconds passed and Zoe jerked in his arms, her eyes flying open.

"It's happening again," she choked out, her eyes filled with panic.

"Farah," Hex growled, but the woman continued her hushed words, some kind of incantation.

Another handful of seconds passed, before Farah finally lifted her hands and opened her eyes. "Take her back in!"

Hex didn't hesitate and neither did the Veil, enveloping them at once.

"They have a dozen priests and priestesses working on this, demon," Farah revealed, her tone heavy with concern. "They'll take her and possibly rip this place apart. We have to act now."

"How could they know?" he demanded.

She shook her head. "They don't. At least not entirely, or they would have attacked me by now, but they must have things that belong to Zoe. Personal items. If they're powerful enough to pull her from a demimonde, they may already have her location just from the short amount of time they were able to grab hold of her. It won't be long now before they either find me or start tearing the walls down from around us."

Hex roared in frustration. He should have foreseen it. Saphiel's security on Zoe's apartment had only been to protect her, not her belongings. Abaddon's Legion could have easily walked in and taken everything she owned. Greed would've been none the wiser. And that was assuming he hadn't taken the items, himself, which was also likely.

"Where are your bones?" Farah asked.

"Leviathan is holding the last one ransom until I

deliver a package for him tomorrow," he answered.

"But you have the others?" she asked.

With just a thought, his shadows spread to the closest empty table and deposited all the bones he'd collected. Farah approached after his shadows receded from the area.

"This is it?" she asked, confused and even more worried. "Ten bones?"

"I only ever found fourteen to begin with," he confirmed. "I lost two over the centuries to unforeseen events. The first one when an underground magma flow changed course and the second in a very large underground bombing during the Battle of Messines."

"Then your sea monster just destroyed a third and is holding a fourth," Farah concluded.

"Seven. The halves," Zoe muttered in his arms.

Confused, Hex glanced down at her, but Farah gasped, regaining his attention.

"Oh, she's right, demon," Farah said, picking up one of the bones to examine the carvings. "The markings on your back, seven circles made of fourteen halves."

Hex was struck by that, his memory trying to make clearer pictures out of his murky history.

"So you're saying, maybe fourteen bones are all there ever was?" he asked.

"Perhaps that was all they needed for their purpose," she replied. "If you don't mind, I'd like to see if these carvings match the symbols on your back."

He wished his shirt away, and the Veil made it so. Then he turned his back on Farah and called the Shallows forward just enough to clear his back, while making sure all of Zoe remained inside it. Her hand lifted, palm to his chest and she willed her eyelids open.

"Do they match?" she asked Farah.

"Yes," Farah answered after a moment. "Only the outer rings, though."

"Why—" Zoe began, then cleared her throat. Hex could hear her determination to regain her strength in that simple sound and it filled him with even more admiration for her. "Why was the knot in his arm, then?"

"Doe," Hex hissed firmly, when she tried to sit up in his arms. "You cannot be outside the Veil."

"Just hold me up a little higher, I want to see," she said.

He adjusted his hold on her, pleased when she tucked her arms and hands against his chest between them. "You can peek over my shoulder, but do not let a single hair outside the Shallows."

"Trust me, I won't," she said, keeping her face deeper inside the Veil than his own as she peered over his shoulder at Farah. "Well?"

"I need to get these to my spirits," Farah replied. "Perhaps, even without the final one, they can still reveal whatever answers they were alluding to. How much longer can you keep her in the Veil?"

"I'm fine," Zoe claimed.

"Minutes at the most," Hex corrected.

"I will return that quickly either way, but without their assistance, I'm not sure what else we can do," Farah said.

"Just hurry," he replied.

He gave the shadows their full reign over his entire

body again and turned to see Farah gather his bones, then disappear. Without the threat of being anywhere outside the Veil, Zoe laid her head on his shoulder, so he adjusted her again to the more comfortable position of having her legs wrapped around his waist.

"Are you still feeling sick?" he asked.

"No, just zapped." She sighed. "Like I have no energy to even hold my head up."

"Most likely it was your energy they grabbed hold of the longest to try to pull you from the demimonde."

"Makes sense," she said. "The first thing I felt was lightheaded and then I felt strangely like the sidewalk was turning into mud that was getting deeper and thicker, then the ability to take another step forward became impossible. That's when the sickness started."

"And the fading," Hex said through clenched teeth.

"I don't remember that part," she said. "I remember hearing your voice getting closer, but it still sounded too far away, until you said my name and then I could tell you were there, but everything had already started going hazy."

Hex tightened his hold on her out of reflex, as if reliving that awful moment from her point of view had the power to make it happen all over again. "I'm sorry, doe," he said. "I'm so sorry for everything you've been put through because of me. As soon as Farah returns, we'll find a way to get you safely back to your friend and under Avarice's protection."

Zoe lifted her head and slid her arms over his shoulders to help hold herself up. "It's a little late for that, don't you think?"

He shook his head. "No, it never should've been this way," he said, scowling with the anger he felt toward himself. "I was so determined to keep you safe myself, to prove that I had just as much ability to do so as any Devil, that I didn't keep you safe at all. I left you alone to be attacked by Leviathan, which put you in the position of trying to save me from my destroyed bone and now these fuckers, whoever they are—"

"Hex—"

"You're mine, Zoe," he blurted. All the feelings that had been twisting up inside his chest all damn day finally swelled over, unable to be contained anymore. "*My* mate. That's why I bothered to care about a human I didn't know, why I couldn't just hand you over to Avarice without some kind of guarantee that he wouldn't sacrifice you to save his own mate. That's why I risked everything to save you, why I would never trade you for my freedom and that still stands now, even knowing—"

"Knowing what?" she whispered, her eyes searching his.

The hurt was still there, but he found it a little easier to say everything now that he'd already said it once before, even though she hadn't heard him. "How much better your life was before I came into it. Before I changed it and made you miss the way it had been without me."

"Is that what you think?" she asked, her expression both sincere and devastated, just like her voice. "You left this morning because you thought I meant my life was better without you in it?"

"It made sense," he said. "The proof has always been

there in the way my temptation never worked on you, because you were already completely happy with your life the way it was. And I couldn't help but look back at all the times I made you angry or upset, or offended and frustrated you."

"Oh, I see. The evidence was stacked against you," she said. Her tone gave him pause, as the feeling of trepidation crept in—impending doom just on the other side of a tripwire. "I mean how could I ever possibly be happy with a demon that's saved my life at least twice, steals coffee and cinnamon rolls for me, takes me on geeked-out tours after just getting some messed-up shit dumped on his own plate and has never once fucking lied to me? You know, for someone so ancient and clever, you sure are a dumbass."

Stunned, yet again, Hex didn't even know what to say. It was more than just her words, it was the genuine feelings behind them.

"Zo—"

"No, you listen. Just because I don't dwell on things missing from my life hard enough to be a target for temptation, doesn't mean I don't want them. Yes, I love my life. I love my business, my employees and my friends, but I was also lonely, Hex. Before you came into my life, I'd never known what it was like to have a partner who not only gets my sense of humor, but makes me laugh with his own, or who thinks my threats of physical violence is some sort of foreplay, and who fights with me—not just to be a jerk, but because he has the confidence, self-respect, and intelligence to do so. A demon who claims to be no kind of good, yet is always so conscientious of my comfort, my pain levels, my pleasure, in ways plenty of males never have the decency to worry about, no matter their species. And can we talk about the flavor thing?"

His head was spinning, her words causing his chest to puff up with unexpected pride, immense relief and happiness that she felt and thought those things about him.

"Flavor thing?" he asked.

"Yes, watch," she said, then kissed him.

Liquid heat rose through his veins to fill his muscles. He lifted his hand to cradle the side of her face and took the kiss deeper. All the regrets and hurtful thoughts he'd believed to be true since that morning were washed away not only by her words, but the way she kissed him with all her feelings, just like the night before. Only this time, she'd given him her words first and the combination was a hundred times better than just one or the other, making him feel exactly like the dumbass she'd called him for ever doubting the connection they shared. That electric storm that had been there from the start, drawing them closer and growing bigger with every moment they spent together.

"Mmm, God, see? You taste like chocolate oranges," she moaned, breaking from the kiss for just a moment, before diving back in.

He did?

"Ahem." Farah cleared her throat.

Zoe smiled against Hex's mouth. "And cue the Voodoo Queen," she said. "This is how all Hallmark movies should end."

He had no idea what she was talking about, but her smile triggered his own. Factually, it had only been a handful of hours, but it felt like it had been too long since the last time he'd seen that gorgeous mouth of hers spread with sincere amusement.

"I'd love to share in your humor, but I'm afraid my news is rather unsettling," Farah interrupted. "First, though, I have something that might keep our Miss Zoe protected outside of the Veil for a while."

"What is it?" Hex asked, because that would be another relief.

"My spirits have blessed this talisman, which has already been warded for physical protection," she answered, lifting a handmade necklace of bones, raw stones, sinew knots and feathers. "Their blessings added protection for the spirit."

He accepted the necklace, and then helped Zoe place it over her head. "Tuck it into your shirt," he advised. "It will work better against your skin."

After she pulled her hair free from it, she shook her shirt to get the necklace settled underneath and Hex felt a shiver run through her whole body. "Kinky. The feathers tickle," she said, giving him a naughty little smirk.

He wasn't stupid—he filed that insight away for later use, even as he released the shadows. He continued to hold her, just in case the talisman failed. The three of them remained silent, waiting for a full minute, before beginning to relax.

"Either they've stopped their attempts, or this thing packs a powerful punch." Zoe said in relief.

"We can always hope for both," Farah stated. "Now,

demon, about your bones."

The grimness of her tone had no place for the renewed happiness Hex was feeling, but it captured both his and Zoe's attention right away. He let his beautiful girl slide back to her feet, but he refused to let her out of reach, capturing her hand in his and holding tight.

"Your spirits gave you answers," he presumed.

"Yes," Farah said, as she lay the bones back on the table. "I don't know how else to say this but straight out, so here goes. These bones, they're each from a different person."

"What?" Zoe and Hex asked in unison.

"Not a single one belongs to the same skeleton," Farah repeated. "And my spirits are quite adamant that none of the people they came from was ever you."

"Hold on, what?" Zoe balked. "Why in the hell would he be linked to bones that never even belonged to him? Who would they belong to, then?"

Hex had gone completely still with the news, unable to react at all, yet he knew the answer deep in his gut. Not from the memories which still evaded him, but from his long knowledge of ancient magical practices, rituals and rites.

"Sacrifices," he said, before Farah could.

Zoe gasped, her face whipping back to his. "What? What!"

"That was the message of my spirits," Farah confirmed. "Fourteen people were sacrificed to create this version of you. The purpose behind that is what's unclear, even for my spirits. They aren't sure if you were meant to be a weapon or just—"

"Just what?" he hazarded.

"Contained."

Hex's mind circled out, encompassing everything he remembered of his own existence, being called upon to curse people for centuries, generations of humans passing his bones down to be used, and then it abruptly stopped and there had been nothing. He thought of the cryptic ways Leviathan alluded to him being something else, as well, and if anyone knew the truth, it would be the oldest creature on earth.

"Leviathan," Zoe whispered, jerking him out of his thoughts as if she'd heard them loud and clear. "On the island, he said something about how you hadn't revealed your true self to me, yet. What if that's because they wiped your memory of who you'd been before, after changing you?"

It was a damn good theory, but there was still one thing that bothered him about the whole thing. "This is who I am," he said. "I don't care how many humans were sacrificed, you can't change the core purpose of one of us. I'll go out right now and kill twice as many humans and perform the same ritual on Abaddon and he'd still be the demon of Wrath. Saphiel would still be the demon of Greed, Leviathan would still be Envy. These things were set in motion by the new religion and unless that religion dies out completely, they cannot be changed."

"No, you're right, not changed," Zoe said. "Harnessed into a smaller vessel that could be used as a weapon. Farah, you said that temptation could be connected to any of the sins. What if he'd been connected to all of them?"

Hex watched Farah's expression turn grim, as she looked at him. "Assuming a demon gains its power from its sin—"

"We do," he inserted, his mind grabbing onto the line Zoe had just laid before them.

"Then I can't even begin to fathom how powerful that would make you," Farah concluded.

"Too powerful," Zoe said quietly. "That's why they did it."

"But," Farah said, still appearing worried and uncertain. "Who are *they*?"

That was the answer Hex wanted.

CHAPTER 12

THE GANG'S ALL HERE

Hex's fingers tightened around hers when Zoe tried to pull away. She gave him an exasperated, but adoring look, though she didn't attempt to free herself from his hold again. She understood his need for reassurance. Not only because of the attack on her, but their emotional morning that wasn't getting much better after Farah's revelations.

"I'm fine, Hex," she assured him. "I just want to get a better look at this puzzle."

Though he finally let her hand go, he held her gaze, his expression dark. Undoubtedly, because he'd heard the worry in her voice. If he only knew the reason behind it was completely selfish. That in connecting the dots behind the mystery of his origins, his lack of memory and the markings on his skin, she'd essentially discovered that the demon she was falling in love with wasn't even real. That freeing him, which is what she was determined to do, might change him into something beyond her reach. Beyond her heart. That it might turn him into something that couldn't love her the way she felt and knew on some level, he loved her now.

You're mine, Zoe. My mate. Would that be strong enough to withstand the reversing of a spell that had taken fourteen human sacrifices to create?

"Can you turn around, please?" she asked him, since he'd yet to replace the shirt that had simply vanished upon Farah's previous request.

"Do not move out of my reach, doe," he said firmly.

"What's beyond your reach, Hex?" she teased, trying to lighten the mood. "Besides Heaven?"

The fact that he understood her attempt, giving her a head shake along with another firm look before turning around, only made her heart hurt more. She forced herself to focus on his marks as Farah stepped up beside her.

"I still don't get these symbols here," Zoe said, pointing to the celestial type markings in the large spaces of the half-circles. "They almost look like they belong on a zodiac chart, but these aren't the usual zodiac signs."

"No, they're not any kind of zodiac, but I do think you're right about them being astrological in nature," Farah agreed. "There are probably half a dozen books here with our answers, but I fear we don't have the time for any more research."

Zoe knew she was right and that just ticked her off. What they were attempting to do, shouldn't be done so haphazardly and without any kind of inclination of what the end result might be. Yet, the idea of Abaddon or Saphiel finding them with their small band of witches before they could free Hex from his prison felt like an even worse outcome.

"These things are driving me nuts," she complained,

lifting her hand to gesture to the circles. "I'm not usually one to nitpick, but don't those look like pressure locks to you? I just want to grab those dividing patterns and turn them until—"

"Until they all line up." Farah finished for her, as if the light bulb had gone off for both of them. "Zoe, I think that might be it."

"Really?" she asked, unable to keep the skepticism from her voice. "I mean, unusual OCD feelings aside, I just think that's too simple. Why would all the other markings be there?"

"Well, we can't know for sure unless we try," Farah said. "Perhaps once they are lined up, the other markings will reveal a more recognizable pattern."

She couldn't really argue that idea. "How are we supposed to change the direction of tattoos, though?"

"They're not really tattoos," Hex intervened. "They are magically rendered, just as the ones on my sides, by things I am linked to."

"Oh yeah, so that brings me back to my previous question," Zoe said. "Why was the link to the bone Leviathan destroyed in his arm, when these tattoos are clearly marked with the same carvings made in each bone?"

Farah gave a small sigh. "Well, I could attempt to assign some logical reason to it, or I could give you what my gut says."

"I'll take gut answers for three hundred, Alex," Zoe said without hesitation.

Farah gave her an amused smirk as she went to the table and collected all the bones again. "He had fourteen bones, right?" she said as she assembled them on the floor behind Hex into what looked like a stick man. "Two for the head, two across for the shoulders, two for the torso and two for each limb."

"Why two for everything?" Zoe asked.

"One for each half of the circle," Farah answered, gesturing to Hex's back. "Which could represent a number of things—the dual astrological symbols, or the duality of the human body and the two sides of the brain, both of which are necessary for the motor and cognitive skills of the whole."

"But Hex didn't even have a body for a long time," Zoe pointed out. "Wouldn't he have been given one right away if this ritual had been designed to basically trap him in it?"

"I can almost guarantee you the ritual had been designed to do just that."

"I believe she's right, Zoe," Hex said. "The ritual created the links to the bones, but there was no reason for the links to become manifest while I was still in the Veil."

"Because the Veil isn't of the material world," Zoe sighed. "Okay, I got it. So, how are we supposed to do this?"

"With a lot of magic," Farah sighed. "And even more luck."

"Zoe," Hex called her to him.

She stepped around his side to stand before him and he didn't hesitate to pull her into his arms. With a hand in her hair, he tilted her head back and captured her mouth. His heat seeped into her instantly, spreading to fan the flames that no longer belonged to only her lust, but her heart. That just made it all the more powerful.

"Whatever happens, just remember that you are mine, Zoe," he whispered. "Nothing can change that."

She smiled against his mouth when he kissed her again. "As if you could forget being mated to someone as awesome as me," she said. "Besides, you still owe me a phone."

He laughed at that, kissed her again and brushed a thumb over her cheek, staring deep into her eyes. Zoe didn't acknowledge the concern she saw in his any more than he acknowledged what he saw in hers.

"This may take some trial and error," Farah said grimly when Zoe rejoined her.

"What can I do to help?"

"I'm not sure yet," Farah answered. "I first need to make an attempt before I can know for sure."

"Well, there's already one set vertically," Zoe pointed out. "Which of the bones match it? Perhaps there's some marking on it that will explain why it's facing the way it is."

"That's my brilliant girl," Hex said.

"Must I really repeat myself?" Zoe asked.

He smirked at her over his shoulder. "I know; duh."

She beamed at him and then got to work with Farah, trying to match the bones to the one vertical circle. In just a matter of moments, they realized none of them matched at all.

"It belongs to two of the bones already destroyed," Farah stated the only conclusion.

"Shit," Zoe exhaled. "What if that's the only way to turn the others?"

Farah started sorting through the bones again, holding them up to Hex's back to find its match and finally settled on one. Then she settled on another.

"Here and here," she pointed to the top circle and the fourth one down. "Both of these circles are also missing their match. We know a third bone was destroyed and also that Leviathan is holding another."

The top circle's middle pattern was exactly horizontal, but the fourth circle's middle pattern was at a diagonal slant. "I say we try the fourth one down first, since it's already almost vertical."

"I agree," Farah nodded. "By destroying its match, we should be able to prove your theory beyond any doubt."

"Whoa, wait," Zoe blanched, remembering too vividly what had happened the last time one of Hex's bones had been destroyed. "We can't just destroy the bone, it hurts him physically."

Farah looked at her. "Sorry, I meant destroy the link, not the bone," she amended.

Zoe's stomach turned, and she gave the woman a disgusted scowl. "I don't want to cut anymore knots out of his skin, either."

"We won't have to," Farah smiled. "The need to do so before was only because the bone wasn't here and already in the process of being destroyed. Now that we have the bones, I can use them to draw out the magical link and sever it."

"Except, we're still missing one of them," Zoe deflated. "Leviathan knew exactly what he was doing by holding that last one hostage."

"One is better than all," Farah said. "To free your demon and save yourself from an army of priests and priestesses, can you cut out one more knot?"

Zoe didn't like it, but when the woman put it that way, how could she possibly refuse? "Yes."

"Then let's hurry, I don't think we have much time," Farah said as she faded out of view.

"Um."

"Where did she—"

Before Hex could finish his question, Farah returned with the same knife that Zoe had used once before.

"Oh," Zoe made a face. "Right."

Hex didn't look any more pleased than she felt about it, but Farah ordered him to turn around again and he did so without any protest. There was nothing for Zoe to do while Farah held the bone of the fourth circle down and began chanting. She watched both the process and Hex, ready to put a stop to the whole thing at the first sign of trouble for either of them.

After a moment of chanting, Farah appeared to be jerked toward Hex's body. Zoe watched as she allowed the bone to lead her, still chanting, until she was kneeling at his left side. There were no visible signs of what might be pulling the bone, but Zoe recalled the way the woman had strained as she'd pulled on some invisible force the night they'd cut the first knot out of Hex's arm, so she had no doubt Farah could feel it.

With her curiosity stoked, Zoe put herself in a position where she could watch the tattoo on Hex's back and Farah's work at the same time. Just like before, Farah's words grew in volume and she began making a cutting gesture with her free hand. The shadows started emerging from Hex, but it appeared he was holding them back the best he could. Farah's cutting gesture and voice grew faster and more aggressive, until finally something in the air snapped and the hand that had been pulling on the bone flew to the ground as it was obviously freed from the link.

Zoe's lips parted when she saw the circle on Hex's back fade and then reappear in a heartbeat, the middle section now completely vertical like the other one.

"It worked." She exhaled.

"You sound surprised," Farah mused.

"I guess I am," Zoe admitted. "It just seems too easy, considering what it took to put them there in the first place."

"More often than not, it's easier to unravel a spell than it is to successfully cast it," Farah informed her. She peered up at Hex next. "You're not going to cause me trouble if I continue, are you, demon?"

"I cannot predict that," he answered. "It might be better to cut the link to my missing bone before going any further."

"I agree," Farah said.

"Ugh, I don't," Zoe griped, even though she really did. "Let's just hope Leviathan doesn't notice before we finish the rest of them."

"We'll work quickly," Farah said. "First, we'll locate the others, so we have a better idea of where the knot will form, that will cut our time in half."

"Process of elimination is our favorite technique, isn't it, Hexy?" Zoe asked.

He gave her an exasperated, yet appreciative look over his shoulder. "It is."

One by one, Farah was able to find the links for the remaining bones. Then, she narrowed that down even more by circling Hex's body while chanting the same words at each of the four areas that hadn't linked to any of the bones.

"Here," she announced, stopping in front of Hex, her hand facing the right side of his rib cage. "I can feel the link buried in there."

Zoe made a face, but in truth, after Farah had linked a bone with the left side of Hex's head, she'd been so worried she might have to dig into his scalp. To know it was the ribcage relieved her tremendously. Apparently the bone that had linked to the right side of his head had already been destroyed.

"Ready when you are," she exhaled, gripping the handle of the dagger tighter.

"Try to keep your shadows in check, demon," Farah said to Hex.

"Or don't," Zoe butted in. "Honestly, if they block my line of sight, I'm okay with it."

Farah gave her an amused look. "For such a brave young woman, you're awfully squeamish."

"Only when it's real," she replied, not even trying to deny it.

"It's not real," Hex interjected. "It's only magic."

"You're sweet, but that doesn't help," she said. "I can see it and feel it, that's real enough for my stomach."

"The last time, I had to locate the link first," Farah said. "So the ritual won't take nearly as long this time, I need only pull it to the surface. Remember, we must cut at the same time."

"Trust me, I haven't forgotten."

"I could do it," Hex said.

Farah and Zoe looked at him, but then Farah shook her head. "No, Zoe is earthbound," she said. "It's easier for me to link with her on this."

"Says the Queen of Spirits," Zoe remarked.

Farah merely shook her head, apparently unwilling to explain her reasoning. "Get ready."

Before anyone could say anything further, she began her chanting and gathering, her hands moving in the same fashion as before. It wasn't long before she was grabbing the invisible power and pulling on it, so Zoe watched Hex's flesh for any sign of glowing. The shadows were fainter than the night Hex had been unconscious, and she figured it was because he was holding them back, as Farah had asked.

Much to her disgust, Zoe actually saw something moving below the surface of Hex's skin just before the blue glow started, dim and then growing brighter the closer it got.

"Blade," Farah order between chants.

Zoe held it up, and Farrah caught it between her hands just like when Zoe had attempted to cut through her power that night. She whispered her magic into the silver for a few seconds, and then her eyes opened.

"Now," she said. "Cut together."

With a steadying breath, she watched Farah's hands. When they came together in that slicing motion, Zoe cut into Hex's skin above the glowing knot.

He grunted as the blood ran out of the wound and down his abs. She glanced up at him with an apologetic look.

"I'm sorry," she whispered.

"You're fine," he said. "It's the magic that hurts, not the blade."

"Focus, Zoe," Farah commanded.

"Shit." Guiltily, she quickly looked back to Farah and watched her closely.

With Hex's help, it didn't take nearly as long to cut the knot out of his ribs as it had to cut it out of his arm. Unfortunately, the downside to that was her ability to see more of the disgusting gore she caused in the process, but the pain-filled grunts and hisses Hex continued to make distracted her from the nausea. She just wanted it over for his sake. Once she cut the final side free completely, she threw it on the ground and started stomping on it, roaring out her anger over the entire situation.

"Baby, come here." Hex's voice was remorseful as he gathered her up in his arms. He pulled the dagger from her hand and tossed it on the floor, then brushed the hair back from her face so he could kiss her mouth. They were momentarily distracted when Farah didn't hesitate to issue a single magical word and the knot caught flame, but then Hex leaned his forehead against hers and peered deep into her eyes. "You don't like it, doe, but it's helping. I can feel a part of myself waking up with urgency. I'm growing anxious with an inexplicable desire to be free."

"Then let's not waste more time," Farah said. "I don't know how much longer that talisman is going to work for Zoe."

"I wish I had the magic to help both of you," Zoe confessed.

"You help your way, I help mine," Farah smiled. "You can gather the bones and hand them to me after I break each link."

"That works." Zoe sighed, then leaned forward and pressed another kiss to Hex's mouth, just to feel the warm texture of his lips again.

Farah took the first bone while Zoe gathered the rest. It was a much faster and bloodless process, thank God. But the farther along they got, the less Hex's shadows played nice. He seemed incapable of holding them back. They swirled madly, creating a false breeze to lift Zoe's hair and rustle Farah's dress. When Farah lifted the seventh bone to begin her chanting anew, the shadows actually solidified and shoved her backward.

"The Veil is fighting against us," Hex hissed through clenched teeth. "I can't stop it."

"Oh, hell no," Zoe spat, dropping the remaining bones at her feet and bracing Farah from behind. "I've got you!"

Farah began chanting again, her voice stronger and louder. Despite the Veil's attempts, it couldn't move both of them. Farah's voice echoed and increased, becoming a chorus. A chill ran right through Zoe's shoulders and down her arms toward Farah's back. Startled, she looked up and gasped to see ghosts. Dozens of them circled all around them and chanted the same words as Farah. They had to be the spirits Farah was always referring to.

"Okay, well shit," Zoe said, her voice a little shaky to

see their hands on her—the cause of the chills in her shoulders. "We've got help."

That didn't seem to surprise Farah. Zoe kept trying to catch a glimpse of Hex's face through the swirling black clouds. He just appeared to be staring unblinkingly into the Veil.

"AH!" Farah fell back into Zoe after cutting through the link. "It's getting harder to get through each one, something is fighting to keep him trapped."

"Can we do it?" Zoe asked, peering around at all the spirits again as she bent to pick up the next bone. "There's only three left."

Farah nodded, accepting the bone and starting again. She wasn't joking. It not only took her longer to even get the bone to link to Hex's body, but to cut through it. The spirits never backed down, appearing more determined to aid their queen than anything else. The Veil never backed down, either. It continued to attempt to push at them and solidify in their way.

"Let me out!" Hex started roaring. "Let me out, let me out!"

Zoe's heart broke at the sheer desperation in his voice. To know that some dormant part of him had always been aware of being imprisoned gutted her. For him to have spent so many centuries locked in a cage of magical rendering, unable to escape, unable to remember how it had happened or even what he'd been before, was unimaginably cruel. She wanted to track down those responsible and bloody them until she couldn't scream or move anymore.

When Farah accepted the final bone from Zoe, half

her spirits began a different kind of chant that seemed to be aimed directly at the Veil, because it started thinning, yet swirling faster as if it knew it was under attack. The library was all but invisible to the naked eye now, the shadows moving like a funnel cloud around them, thought it didn't cause much more wind than before.

Zoe's eyes narrowed on Hex's back, as she followed Farah to his right side. She wanted to see the pattern all but completely aligned down his spinal cord, but the continuous momentum of black clouds shielded most of it from her view. What she managed to glimpse almost appeared to be a river that curved, rather than running straight, as the outer lines would suggest.

When they made it to his right arm, Hex looked at her with such a painful and desperate expression, it broke her heart all over again.

"Out?" he keened.

"Last one, then you're free," she promised.

Farah and her spirits had to really fight to get the final link severed. Zoe couldn't do anything except keep her gaze locked on Hex's and brace Farah's shoulders as much as possible. They were moved, but not dislodged. The spirits were doing their damage on the Veil's attempts, thwarting its desire to solidify time and again. Farah's chanting grew hoarse but louder than Zoe had heard it before, as it seemed to take more of her power and effort to finalize the ruination of the ancient spell.

At last, the link broke and she stumbled back into Zoe. The spirits faded from sight, and Zoe gasped as she watched Hex's pale blue eyes turn reptilian, just before he thrust his arms out. His head fell back on a loud roar, and all the swirling shadows of the Veil rushed into his body through the tattoos down his sides.

"Oh no, what have we done?" Farah gasped, her tone filled with fearful concern.

Zoe followed her gaze and her eyes widened to see that the pattern curving all the way up Hex's spine wasn't a river at all. It was a snake. When it started moving, Farah yelped and grabbed Zoe's hand.

"We have to go," she said.

"What? No, we can't just leave him!"

In the next breath, Hex's body burst apart like a confetti bomb of flesh-colored ash that just floated in the air. Pure darkness rose up toward the ceiling in a serpentine fashion, knocking tiles loose and causing light fixtures to sway dangerously as it turned to head back toward the floor and them. It was the snake. Hex was just a giant fucking snake made out of black shadows. His nearly white eyes locked right onto her and Farah upon his descent.

"Now!" Farah yelled.

Zoe didn't fight as Farah hauled her toward the exit. Hex's ginormous slithering body demolished the interior of the library, smashing tables, chairs, and bookcases as it moved. When they made it outside, running as fast as they could, Hex smashed through the windows to follow. Glass shards and bits of metal exploded outward and the building groaned in complaint from the force of it. Zoe couldn't run fast enough to keep up with Farah, her legs were much too short, yet the woman never let go of her hand.

"We need to get out and close the door," Farah called

over her shoulder. "We can't let him loose in the living world!"

"You want to trap him again when we just freed him?" Zoe balked, halting.

Farah whirled, her expression horrified. "Don't stop—"

"He's not going to hurt us," Zoe cut her off, the surety of that filling her so completely there was no room for doubt.

"But—"" Farah's gaze flicked to the giant serpent quickly bearing down on them.

Zoe grabbed her other hand, pulling Farah around to face her completely. "Trust me," she said. "Your spirits wouldn't have helped us if he was dangerous, right?"

She saw a flicker of doubt in the woman's expression before it calmed. "No, they wouldn't have," she answered. Hex reached them, his large body coiling around them. Farah clamped her eyes closed, squeezing the life out of Zoe's hands. "Oh, I hope you're right!"

Zoe barely heard her over the rush of power that flowed all around and through them. She could feel Hex in every particle of her body, heating her blood and filling her heart. Her very soul felt lighter, happier, as if she were experiencing his joy over being freed. It made her want to laugh and cry all at once. Even Farah's eyes and mouth opened with surprise, apparently feeling the same happiness. Then her mouth curved into a bright smile, confirming it.

She exhaled a rush of pent up breath that held a hint of laughter and her muscles visibly relaxed, before she gave Zoe's hands a different kind of squeeze. "Thank you, Zoe," she called over the loud wind, for Hex's body of smoke was ever moving, never stopping. "It's been an honor getting to know you and your demon. I hope we'll meet again someday in the living world."

They embraced and then Farah faded from the demimonde altogether. Just as the last of her outline faded, gravity failed and Zoe's feet lifted off the ground, her body tipping until she was floating on her back in and among all the coiling darkness.

"Hex?"

She didn't get a verbal response, only the feeling of traveling quickly the same as she'd always felt whenever he moved them through the Veil to a new location. It lasted for a good five minutes or so, before a sense of familiarity came over her. The sensation of moving began to subside and she somehow knew they had reached their destination. Like gentle hands, the shadows lifted her back into an upright position, and gravity took hold once more, her feet landing on solid ground.

As the fog began to thin into the hazy veil she'd gotten so used to, Zoe gasped to see the English pub inside Saphiel and Kami's house, the bar just to her right.

"Kami?" she called, as she stepped out of the shadows completely.

There was a sudden burst of movement to her left, and she turned toward it to find the lounge area quite full. Kami and Saph were both staring at her over the back of a long sofa, while three other Devils sat in armchairs angled around every other side of the coffee table. Each one had a small band of Legion gathered behind them for added protection and they'd all gone on alert with her sudden appearance. It looked like a damn mob meeting. Zoe only recognized one of the three Devils, her eyes narrowing in on Leviathan with utter disdain. The other two were tall, dark, and handsome, yet otherwise completely different. Where one had short espresso hair that waved away from his face, the other's was black and fell pin-straight to his shoulders, tucked behind one ear. The former had eyes like burnished gold and features that could cause a woman's panties to spontaneously combust, whereas the latter's eyes glinted like a silver blade and boasted a face that was entirely way too beautiful.

"Zoe?" Kami leaped to her feet and gaped at her, before the shock broke. "Zoe!"

"Kam!"

They started toward each other, Kami's heels clicking wherever a priceless Turkish rug didn't cover the hardwood floors. Suddenly, black shadows wrapped around Zoe from behind, stopping her. Kami followed suit, her eyes and mouth widening as she backed up a step from the surprise.

"Kameo!" Saphiel barked, just as Wolfe lunged over the closest armchair, growling and snapping at the shadows as he put himself securely in front of Kami.

"Wait, it's okay," Zoe said, even as she glanced over her shoulder to see the black shadows swirling and whipping out, taking on some kind of shape that was like a man only a lot bigger. "He's the one who saved me."

Saphiel wrapped an arm around Kami's waist, lifted her from the floor and set her behind him in one suave move, without even breaking stride. He stared the shadows down over the top of Zoe's head with all the confidence of a Devil who would win any fight. Reaching his hand out, he gestured for Zoe to come to him and his eyes, like Wolfe's, were beginning to turn red. Unfortunately, even if Zoe had wanted to move, the shadows were holding her too firmly.

"So," Hex said, each letter drawn out and spoken with a voice she didn't recognize. It sounded as if it gathered from every point of the Veil, itself, before emerging. "They all band against me once more."

"We only banded together to find the one you abducted," Saphiel countered, his tone the epitome of cold malice. "Now, you will let her go."

"This human freed me."

There was an old wives' tale which claimed that when your ears start ringing, someone somewhere is talking about you. Zoe now knew that wasn't true, as the sharp tones began deep in her eardrums, drowning everything else out. It was the sound of a piece of her soul dying. And the pain, it wasn't crushing or overwhelming, it was so terribly hollow. It emptied her, body and mind. He didn't know who she was. Hex was gone. The thing she'd freed wasn't him, after all. It had never been him.

"Zoe."

Kami's voice penetrated the fog trying to settle over her mind, but everything was blurred by the tears she hadn't noticed forming in her eyes. Before they could completely destroy her, the sound of the front door closing drew everyone's attention, especially when the new arrival began whistling on his way to the pub.

When he finally emerged from the hallway, Zoe

realized no amount of hollowness could have stopped her from taking notice. He was tall, decked in a three-piece suit the color of dried blood with all-black shirt, tie, and accessories, including the pocket watch tucked into his vest. His hair was every shade of blond imaginable, yet still darker than Leviathan's, longer on top than the sides and brushed back in an arrogant style that managed to be neatly untamed.

"So, there I was, minding my own business—" he said in way of greeting. He scanned the room, and his eyes were like frost-covered lakes in the dead of winter—fathomless below the icy surface, the dark blue depths beckoning you to dive in, despite knowing it would be fatal in the most painful of ways.

"Thanking the powers that be that I wasn't invited to this living nightmare," he continued a bit more grimly. "When all the sudden I felt a . . . disturbance in the force, if you will."

Zoe's eyes narrowed not on him, per se, but in wondering why he would choose that particular phrasing. Then he sent her an amused smirk that startled her so much she physically jerked.

"You can stay right the fuck out of my head," she snapped, not even caring who the Devil was.

"But you're so easy to read," he remarked, continuing to appear amused. "And you did free my long-lost friend, so I feel the need to pay homage. Serpent, it's been too long."

The shadows stretched out a large hand and set it over the Devil's entire head for a moment, before it dispersed and reformed where it had been before.

"First Fallen," the shadows responded. "Where are we?"

"New York, twenty-first century, and thanks to you, the earth now hosts two billion descendants of Adam and Eve."

"Why thanks to him?" Zoe asked.

The look he gave her was almost sinister with the way it managed to be both amused and cruel all at once. "Because the apple doesn't fall far from the tree?" he offered. "Because the tree was deliberately put there? Because humans were the world's first spectator sport? Take your pick—pun most definitely intended."

Zoe instantly dismissed the first thing to come to mind. There was no way Hex was . . . The moment she thought it, she realized how very wrong she was. There absolutely was a way, because he wasn't Hex anymore. Whatever she'd freed really could be *that* Temptation. The serpent in the tree, tempting Eve to eat the apple.

When her vision cleared again, she found the Devil studying her intensely.

"Hmm," he remarked. "You tell a human that their very inception was plotted by a bored deity, that the Almighty God who created the heavens and the earth and every microscopic speck of dust in between *chose* to birth Temptation the very second he uttered the words "Thou shall not," forbidding Adam and Eve from eating of the Tree of Knowledge of Good and Evil—a tree he could have planted anywhere on earth or, here's a concept, not at all—yet *chose* to plant it in the Garden of Eden within reach, within temptation, and they usually have some kind of reaction."

"What am I supposed to say?" Zoe countered.

"The usual rhetoric is that God was testing man's obedience, loyalty, and or faith," he supplied.

"Seems to me it doesn't really matter what I think. You obviously have your mind made up already about God's motives and I'm not your damn soapbox."

"Well, defensiveness is right on the nose one way or another," he mused.

Zoe didn't bother pointing out that her defensiveness had absolutely nothing to do with anything he'd said. It was already taking all of her energy just to stand there and not think about how much she was dying inside, knowing that the demon she'd fallen in love with didn't even exist anymore.

"Please do get on with it, Mas," Saph invited. "We've enough to sort out as it is."

Zoe's heart gave a start, recognizing the name from Kami's stories of all she'd gone through to get Saph back from the insane coven of human occultists—including being held as a hostage-guest in the underwater orphanage belonging to Mas, which was just a short name for the Mastema, Beliel's title. The Devil of all Devils. The one humans mistakenly called Lucifer.

"That's why I'm here, brother. Haven't you heard? The Devil's in the details," Beliel replied as he entered the room further, completely at ease in his surroundings. He stopped looking about at all the décor and narrowed in on Zoe's best friend. "Kameo Kross, delighted to see you again, though I must say since your awakening you seem to have lost all that admirable moxie. Such a shame."

When his cold eyes slid to Zoe again, she decided to

take back everything she'd said about his name not doing anything for her.

"I suppose if there's one thing to be said about human ignorance, it's the entertainment of their pointless bravado," he continued. "But you're not ignorant, are you, Zoe Bankes? Why don't you share with the rest of the class exactly how you managed to free an ancient malevolent force from his two-thousand-year-old prison?"

"I severed all the links to his remaining bones," she answered.

"You did? All by your lonesome without a single shred of magical knowledge in your entire tiny little . . . you are a very small human."

"Thank you for your observation," she said dryly.

"You're the size of a child," he continued as if she hadn't spoken. "Yet *you* freed the Serpent alone?"

"Another human helped her." Zoe jumped slightly when the shadows spoke, forgetting for a moment that it was still there and listening to everything they said. "I will show you, First Fallen."

Beliel approached the shadows, and once again a giant hand of black fog settled on his head. Zoe hadn't expected the images to start filling her mind as well, but apparently, since she was still caught up in one of his arms, she got linked into the same feed.

The images came through in flashes, starting from the moment she assumed the Serpent had become fully aware, taking over Hex's consciousness, which was just before he'd started screaming to be let out. It was painful to recall that she'd thought it had been Hex the whole time.

"Stop," Beliel ordered. The image froze for both of them, showing the seven perfectly aligned circles down Hex's back. "Do you see that, Zoe Bankes?"

"Yes, but I can't read it," she admitted.

"Fourteen lambs brought blood to the bones, fourteen stars brought fire to the blades, seven sacred circles cast by the flesh of the earth, and the serpent was trapped by all," he read aloud every symbol Zoe's mental eye passed over. The fourteen celestial symbols in the inner circles lit up when he mentioned the fourteen stars. "Remember your Sunday schooling."

Zoe gasped. "Of course." She exhaled. "Angels are stars in scripture. Angels did this to him?"

"Seven Archangels and Seven Who Fell the Farthest. This sigil here"—Zoe watched one of the two celestial symbols of the third circle down glow gold—"belongs to Raphael, and its counterpart, Azazel."

"If the lambs were the sacrifices, then who were the seven fleshes of the earth?"

"The anointed ones who'd been tasked with performing the ritual and casting the circles for the rites," Beliel answered. "In the centuries that followed, they were hunted down and burned as witches. Perhaps it was decided that they knew too much."

The paused memory faded, and the pub came back into view. Zoe studied Beliel and couldn't find any part of her that doubted him.

"Why would angels sacrifice humans to trap a demon?" she asked. That seemed the most significant answer to get.

He looked thoughtful for a moment, as if trying to find the right words. "What you call sacrifices were more like willing participants," he explained. "They were told they'd be honored in Heaven for their part in stopping the evil of Temptation for all mankind."

"But he wasn't stopped," Zoe pointed out.

Beliel made a gesture that must've been a Devil's equivalent of a shrug. "His powers were severely weakened, as were ours. To the humans of that time, it would have seemed like a great reprieve. You see, Temptation is the root of all sin. Humans cannot sin without first giving into the temptation of it. So you, smallest human on the planet—"

Zoe rolled her eyes at him.

"—have unleashed the greatest power ever created," he concluded. "And inadvertently gave us, the Seven Deadly Sins, a lifetime supply of steroids in the process. I don't know about my kindred, but I haven't felt this powerful since before the flood."

"I like this human," the Serpent stated.

"That's probably a good thing, since I think what my uncle just so eloquently danced around is the fact that she is now at the top of the Grigori's hitlist," the golden-eyed Devil interjected. His voice was like an eargasm, the most precise balance of huskiness and whiskey-smooth timbre she'd ever heard in her entire life. Yet, all it accomplished was to make her ache for Hex's sexy baritone.

Wait, did he say uncle? That wasn't even possible. If Beliel was the Devil everyone mistook for Lucifer, then . . . Oh. It was a little embarrassing that it took her brain longer than it should have to connect the dots, especially when she was the one who'd done all of the fucking research on him.

"Lust," she blurted, pointing at him. "You're Lust."

"What gave me away?" he asked, his smile so ridiculously carnal it could be labeled obscene by the FCC.

Zoe waved it off as an annoyance. "You were erased from his memory," she said. "When he was still trapped, you were the only sin he couldn't speak or hear about. And he had a mark, on his forehead that looked like it might have come from your familiar."

"Asmodeus is Nephilim, he has no need for a familiar," Saphiel intervened.

Shit, why hadn't she thought of that? A Nephilim would already be half earthbound, of course he wouldn't need one. "Well, then whatever that worm thing is, the Shamir," she amended.

Asmodeus turned his head toward the silver-eyed Devil, as did Saphiel and Kami.

"The Shamir was one of the ten miracles God created at the Twilight of Creation," Beliel said as he entered the room further. "A highly coveted weapon, one might say. Who among us would have that trinket handy, I wonder?"

It seemed they were all heading toward the same Devil, except Leviathan and Asmodeus, who remained seated in their armchairs. Zoe's gaze narrowed in on their target sitting all the way to the right end of the coffee table and was dumbfounded to think a being that beautiful could possibly be Wrath. No, it just couldn't be him, that was too absurd.

"You think your spies go unnoticed," Asmodeus said to him. "Yet strangely, they disappeared from my realm when the Hex did. I believed he'd left of his own accord, and your spies followed. I never for a second thought you would actually imprison him in the Abyss, that loathsome place meant only for the ones who Fell the Farthest. What was the Hex's crime to justify his capture and confinement?"

"I need no justification," the silver-eyed Devil spoke, and Zoe knew at once that he truly was Abaddon, Demon of Wrath, for his voice was utterly empty. "All of you act so surprised to learn that I took a weapon for myself after it was abandoned when my motives have remained steadfast since the dawn of our inception."

"The Hex was never mine to abandon," Asmodeus stated, his tone darkening further. "He was a free demon of Lust to come and go as he pleased, not a weapon."

"Perhaps you should have remained in Hell then," Abaddon stated. "Why any of you prefer this realm is beyond comprehension, but it does not matter. Both the Hex and Pheldra belonged to me, and since the Hex has been completely destroyed by that human, I will take my soldier and be on my way back to the Abyss."

Zoe jerked, blanching at his words that cut right into her. She felt sick. She was grateful no one was paying any attention to her. At least, that's what she thought, until she caught Leviathan staring right at her, his aquamarine eyes brewing. Apparently, he wasn't happy to realize that the bone he was holding ransom was now completely worthless, but Zoe couldn't care less.

Beliel's callous laughter thwarted whatever reaction

Saphiel may have had to Abaddon's claims, which was undoubtedly a blessing. Once again, epic hellish battles were not at the top of Zoe's bucket list anymore. Not since she'd realized they were actually possible.

"You really don't get how mates work, do you, brother?" Beliel jabbed. "Pheldra's human soul and demon life now belong to Saphiel for all eternity. You can't bargain, bribe, buy, or steal either one. When she dies, she already has a place in the second plane of Hell, where she will rule as its queen until the earth folds in on itself. You need to take this loss and leave, while you can still do so with your dignity intact."

Abaddon looked beyond Beliel, his lifeless eyes latching onto Zoe. "I demand the human's life in exchange for destroying my weapon."

"That's not going to happen," Saphiel stated when Kami gasped, her face whipping toward Zoe's with fear.

"Pheldra can find another pet. I demand retribution," Abaddon persisted.

When he rose and started forward, Kami stepped right into his path. "She is not a pet and her life is not up for negotiation!"

Though Abaddon's expression never changed, the tension in the room thickened. "You dare speak against your king, demon?"

"No. I would never speak against my king," Kami replied, making a point of it to look at Saphiel when she said as much, before looking back to Abaddon. "And that's Queen Avarice to you, not demon, and certainly not soldier ever again."

"There's that moxie," Beliel delighted. "I tried to

warn you, brother."

Abaddon was staring Kami down with his Legion backing him one second, and in the next, he was right in front of Zoe. In less than a breath, she understood what it meant to be frozen with fear. It was an infinitesimal moment of indisputable reality when you knew something horrible and possibly fatal was going to happen to you, and there was no way on earth to stop or avoid it. She was fairly certain Kami screamed, but Zoe was too caught up in the moment to hear beyond her own panicked heartbeat.

Even as Saphiel and Kami rushed forward to stop Abaddon, a shield of hazy black smoke fell over Zoe's vision and the Serpent struck. It was a coil of solid black, striking at lightning speed right past her face and recoiling just as quickly. Abaddon jolted backward with a hiss and shook his hand where veins of black rapidly spread over his skin. He clutched his arm on an outcry of shock and pain. Zoe's eyes widened to see it branch out of the collar of his shirt and up the side of his neck to cover part of the left side of his face.

"You will not harm this human, Angel of Death, or I will make sure you never walk this earth again."

Zoe wasn't sure what stunned her most—that the Serpent would issue such a threat when he had no idea who she was, or that the damage to Abaddon's flesh wasn't healing. Without another word, he backed away from them, turning only once he reached his Legion, and then they all hurried from the house.

"Does anyone else wish harm upon this human?" the Serpent demanded.

"Absolutely not," Kami answered.

"She's my best friend, they won't hurt me," Zoe said, though her voice didn't carry into the room because she was still behind the screen of shadows.

The Serpent heard her, that was all that mattered. He lifted the protective barrier, though he'd yet to release her completely.

"First Fallen, you will tell me everything that has come to pass."

"I will," Beliel agreed.

"Then let us leave this place."

Though she knew in her mind he was no longer Hex, the idea of him leaving startled Zoe's heart. What if she never saw him again? Never heard of him again? He was all that remained of the demon she'd loved for too short a time. It wasn't fair that they hadn't gotten more time! She had to fight the tears threatening to form in her eyes. There was no way she was going to cry in front of a room full of Devils and Legion.

"Will you hear his version alone, Temptation?" Leviathan spoke up at last, rising from his chair.

There was no response for a moment, and then, "Perhaps not, Ancient One."

"What do you care, Hellmouth?" Beliel questioned, sneering the name as if it were an insult. "He's just another one of God's creations, and you'd rather us all extinct."

"My care is none of your concern, Fallen," Leviathan returned just as snidely. "And the choice is not yours to make."

"It may be wise for both of you not to annoy the

thing capable of permanently damaging the Sparks," Kami pointed out.

Zoe had no idea what a Sparks was, but she couldn't help feeling a rush of pride to see her bestie standing tall in the midst of Hell's most notorious yet again. The way she'd stood up to Abaddon just moments ago deserved a bottle of champagne—if not a full-out party.

"My gratitude for your part in freeing me extends all eternities, human named Zoe," the Serpent said. "Perhaps one day you will share with me your reason for doing so."

Zoe couldn't respond. Her throat had tightened around all the tears she'd been fighting, so she merely nodded. She could feel everyone's eyes on her, but she couldn't bring herself to look at anyone directly. She merely watched as all the shadows gathered around Beliel and Leviathan, leaving her at last. She'd never felt so empty. Much like she'd witnessed Hex do a thousand times, the Serpent took the two Devils and simply disappeared into the Veil.

"I will take my leave as well," Asmodeus said, before any awkward silences could fall over the room. "I do hope you and your exceptional queen will come visit my new club, uncle. If the rumors I hear about her abilities are true, I won't be able to keep Hell's gates closed."

Saphiel gave him a rather smug expression, but didn't confirm the rumors. "If we can get away, perhaps we will come take a look," he answered. "But I won't be accountable for your drop in revenue once Greed has left the building."

Asmodeus laughed. "I'm certain I'll manage," he said with his own confidence. "Greed is not the only sin capable of persuading purses to empty."

"Hm," Saphiel smirked in skepticism.

Half of the remaining Legion moved to follow Asmodeus from the house, but Zoe stepped forward to stop him. He turned, giving her his full attention.

"Do you know where the Shamir is?" she asked.

He studied her for a moment, his golden eyes giving off a welcoming glow. Everything about the Devil was designed to lure you in—from his tall, broad-shouldered build, to the easy way of his appearance; too soft to be polished, despite the expensive suit and accessories. He looked inviting on every level, yet Zoe didn't feel it at all.

Nor did she feel any fear when he moved closer. Unlike Abaddon or even Beliel, Asmodeus didn't strike her as a Devil who looked down on humans as being beneath him. Perhaps it was because his mother had been human.

"When I look at people, I immediately know certain things about their future," he said. "King David's commander was the first one I'd ever looked at who had not a future predestined for me to catch a glimpse of, but for me to participate in and see it come to fruition. I was at this astonishing new crossroads I had never been before, where I literally had the power to change a man's future by either revealing what I saw or by withholding it. Do you know what I did, little one?"

Zoe's mind raced back over the bits of the story she'd read, trying to piece an answer together, but she honestly couldn't even guess.

She shook her head. "No."

"I looked around at all the other people there and could no longer see any certain future for any of them," he answered. "Because I had not yet decided, and my decision would alter all of their futures. I didn't like that, the uncertainty. It was different from what I knew in an uncomfortable way, so I followed the teachings of my divine learning, those Angel instincts, and spoke the truth of the Shamir's location."

She waited for a heartbeat. "What does any of that have to do with what I asked?"

Asmodeus smiled. "Had I not first met Benaiah when Solomon sent him to capture me, I never would have known where the Shamir was. Despite what the tales claim, I'm not capable of finding the Shamir any more than any other demon or Angel. I only knew, because when I first looked at Benaiah, I saw him finding it in his future. You see, I had to know him, and he had to know me, in order for the Shamir to be found at all. To this day, that little divine test has never been presented to me again, but I can't help looking back and wondering what would have happened had I decided in favor of an uncertain future for all. What would the world know of Solomon's temple had I not first met David's commander Benaiah?"

Zoe was still marveling over that when he leaned in close enough to whisper in her ear. "Even if I could find the Shamir, it would only kill you, not take away your memories of the Hex."

He straightened, giving her a look that managed to be sympathetic without offending her, which she attributed to his sin. He backed away from her, then glanced at Saphiel once more.

"Bring the human when you come to visit," he said. "Everyone loves the unexpected. She'll have them all eating out of her hands."

With that, he turned and left the house with his Legion. It wasn't praise, if it was true, but unfortunately, Zoe could no longer feel the confidence of her own awesomeness. She doubted she could consider herself awesome when she was responsible for the annihilation of the one she loved.

"Wolfe," Saphiel commanded quietly.

Zoe glanced over to see him and his familiar leaving the room, along with the handful of Lee's that had been standing guard.

"Zo." Kami opened her arms as she approached.

Struck by the sudden quiet and lack of Devils, Zoe peered around the room, as if reason could be found there, but it couldn't. And the dam broke on everything she'd been holding inside since the moment she'd realized what she'd done. When she recalled how easily and frequently she'd joked about killing Hex, or even used it as a threat when he scared her in the shower. She hadn't meant it. She never should've said it!

"Oh God, I'm going to be sick," she clapped a hand over her mouth and rushed behind the bar, where she retched into the prep sink.

Kami was right there making worried sounds and rubbing her back, which only increased when the sobs broke out, cutting through the remainder of Zoe's dry heaves.

"I killed him," she choked out in between them, grabbing a dish towel to cover her mouth as if she could take it back. But the tears continued to fill her eyes and spill over onto her cheeks. She dropped to the floor. "Oh God, I did. I thought I was freeing him, but it killed him, everything we did completely unraveled him. He just burst apart!"

Kami dropped to the floor right beside her, wrapping her arms around her. "Oh, Zoe, I'm so sorry," she said. "I had no idea you'd grown attached to the Hex."

"Hex," she corrected. "His name was Hex. He wasn't an object or a weapon, damn it. He was a living demon! And I wasn't attached, Kami. I loved him and he loved me. He said we were mated. He said I was his, and then I helped destroy him just like that bastard said. I did that, Kami. I completely wiped him from existence!"

CHAPTER 13

GIVING IN

Zoe hadn't necessarily wanted to stay at Saphiel and Kami's, but by the time she'd finished bawling her sorrows out on her bestie's shoulder, she'd been too drained to argue. Despite the luxury of the guest room she'd found comfortable beyond words the last time she'd stayed there, Zoe had tossed and turned, her dreams a dark and painful replay of her time with Hex. It had been well past midnight when she'd finally given up and wandered into the pub to help herself to as much alcohol as her body could handle. If she couldn't find sleep, then she'd dive headfirst into drunken oblivion.

There had been no surprise when Kami had joined her, and just like old times, they'd curled up on the sofa together. Zoe got drunk, revealing more details about everything that had transpired from the moment she'd first felt Hex's presence in her room until she'd been brought back by the Serpent.

"I know they're all excited to have Temptation freed, but I wish your Hex would've trusted you and just brought you straight to us." Kami had sighed afterward. "Neither Saph nor I would've ever let anything happen to you. Abaddon had no leverage with or without you. He was never going to win."

Zoe thought back on the moment now, when she'd doubted Saphiel's willingness to fight for her in what had seemed an impossible situation. Honestly, there was no way she could have blamed him if he'd been stuck choosing between her or Kami. Yet he'd been the first to speak against Abaddon on her behalf. He'd even tried to get her free of the Serpent before realizing who he was. She no longer doubted that he would've fought to save her, had it been an evil force rather than one determined to protect her.

"We're here, Miss Bankes," Lee said, bringing her out of her thoughts.

In the backseat of one of Saphiel's many town cars, Zoe watched the sunlight dancing off the water through the window. She'd woken two hours prior to something jabbing into her hip only to find her long-lost cell phone and the jewelry box containing someone else's bracelet on the sofa cushion where she'd passed out. Her first reaction had been to search for signs of Hex and that had damn near brought her to tears again. Waking up to the reality of him being gone had hurt a lot worse than trying to sleep without him, but she'd soldiered through it. Not because she was strong, but because she was afraid. She could already feel the urge to lose herself in all the grief and it was so fucking tempting to do so. To stop caring about anything else, until she lost her business, her apartment, friends and employees. Zoe didn't want to become that.

After tracking Saphiel and Kami down, she'd asked if she could borrow Lee for a while and set off on one last mission. She needed to cut the final tie, so she could try to get back to whatever was left of her life. She had no doubt chaos awaited her there in the form of her business, if it was even still thriving.

"I don't know how long I'll be," she said, before climbing out.

"I will wait for you, as I've been ordered," Lee replied.

Zoe knew he wouldn't leave under threat of dismemberment from Avarice. Saphiel didn't trust that his brother had given up all hope of either retrieving a weapon or retribution, one of the two, and she couldn't help agreeing with him. Hex hadn't been exaggerating when he'd said Abaddon was not a Devil to be forsaken —as he'd proven the day before.

Despite normally being a bit of a drive from Greed's estate, Lee had somehow used his powers of demonic persuasion on the other drivers and the traffic lights to get them all the way to Orchard Beach in just a few minutes. Zoe had needed somewhere she could actually step into the water that also had less crowded areas than the other waterfront parks in the city. Had it been winter, there would be no issue, but it was getting close to July and the sun was blazing nice and hot.

Rather than heading toward the crowded beach, Zoe took off from the parking lot toward the Twin Islands shoreline. She made sure she was fairly sheltered by the trees before removing her shoes and stepping into the water.

"Leviathan," she said aloud, though she didn't raise her voice. She had a feeling she wouldn't need to at any rate. "I have something of yours."

She stood there for a few minutes, then returned to the shore to sit by her shoes and wait. Ten minutes slowly bled into thirty, and again into forty. Zoe decided she'd give it a full hour and then she'd have Lee take her home. It wasn't like the sea beast wouldn't be able to find her if he wanted to, New York was completely surrounded by his beloved saltwater kingdom. At the one-hour mark, she stood to brush off her shorts, and caught movement out of the corner of her eye. Leviathan casually strolled toward her from the farthest point of the shore after rounding the treeline, his clothes and hair completely dry. She wondered if he'd arrived by speedboat again, even though she hadn't heard a motor, or if he was simply impervious to his own element.

Once he was close enough, he held his hand out for the jewelry box, but that hadn't been Zoe's intention.

"I'll deliver it," she said. "I just need to know where."

His eyes, which had been nearly as dark as the filthy water surrounding them, took on a light of surprise. "Why would you do that?"

"Because even though you went back on your end of the deal, I know what it's like losing someone you love," she answered.

He gave a short laugh that outdid anything even Beliel was capable of. "Because you've felt that pain for a whole two minutes?"

Zoe swallowed the bile of her anger and grief, hating him even more for pointing out that he'd felt no end to his own suffering. It filled her with despair to know fate might have the same in store for her.

"How did I break our deal?" he demanded, appearing angry for admitting so much to her with that one remark.

"You promised us two days, but in under twenty-four hours an army of witches nearly succeeded in physically pulling me out of the demimonde."

His expression turned grim and he looked toward the trees. "Abaddon," he sneered. "You should have sent the Strider to me, I would've put a stop to it and then neither one of us would be in this situation."

Zoe looked out toward the water. "Maybe you wouldn't have, but I would've ended up here, regardless," she said, meeting his gaze again. "I was never going to let him return to being a prisoner in the Abyss."

"Congratulations. Now he never will," Leviathan said.

She took the sting of his words, clenching her teeth against any retort. She wanted to be done with him and any other demon that wasn't part of her personal circle, so she could figure out how to start moving forward.

"Just give me a location and I'll personally deliver it, then you have nothing left to bitch about," she said.

He held his hand out again. "I don't need you to deliver it, I have other ways," he informed her. "The Strider was simply my fastest and easiest option."

"Fine." She handed it over. "Goodbye, Leviathan. Good luck with your second chance at happiness."

Zoe bent down and picked up her shoes, then started walking away as fast as her legs could carry her. She hated the bitterness festering in her soul, yet couldn't stop it from brewing.

"You do realize you're still mated?" he called after her, causing her steps to falter.

She stopped and turned toward him slowly, fighting against having any kind of reaction to his words. "What?"

"You were never mated to the Hex," he said. "You've always only ever been mated to Temptation. Perhaps you should just give in."

He saluted her with the jewelry box, then turned on his heels and walked back toward the end of the island once more. Zoe's mind tumbled, her heartbeat picking up with the shot of adrenaline hope pushed through her body. Hopping on one foot then the other, she slipped her shoes back on and then booked ass to the parking lot.

"Take me home, Lee," she rushed out as she dove into the back seat.

"Are you all right, Miss Bankes? Do I need to call Queen Pheldra?"

"No, I'm fine. Please just drive," she answered, swallowing air as if the world was running out. "And whatever mojo you can use to get me there faster will put me forever in your debt."

Her fingers twisted in her lap, all rational thoughts defenseless against blind hope. It was too strong. Her heart was already too invested in the possibility, her grief didn't even hesitate to slide into the whirlpool of denial that what she'd shared with Hex wasn't really gone for good. Perhaps she'd been willing to try to live without it, for what else could she have done? But now . . . now, if Leviathan was lying and just being cruel, Zoe didn't know what she'd do. No, Hex had said that demons had no need to lie, and even though Leviathan was different, she still felt that was true. He would rather be cruel with honesty than with lies. Then again, she was best friends with Saphiel's mate, and it was no secret the sea monster despised all of the Angels.

By the time Lee was pulling up outside of her apartment building, Zoe's hope had begun to fade somewhat, and she felt like her insides were twisted up in knots. She was torn between wanting to believe Leviathan and not trusting him at all.

"Lee, can I ask you a question?" she asked after staring out the window for a second.

His silence drew her gaze to his reflection in the rearview mirror and she sighed aloud to see the brackets of concentration on his face.

"I know, that was a question and yes, I'm capable of asking questions. I just want to know, am I mated to Temptation?"

He turned in his seat to look her in the eye. "Sorry, Miss Bankes, I'm just a soldier. I'm not gifted with that kind of divining."

She swallowed the tears that wanted to form in her eyes and nodded. "Thanks, Lee," she whispered. "Let Kami know I made it home safely."

"I should walk you upstairs," he said.

"No, I'll be okay," she said as she got out of the car.

She knew she wouldn't be able to stop him if he really wanted to follow, but he remained in the car, where he'd probably stay until he knew she'd made it inside her apartment safely.

It seemed to take longer than normal for her to climb up the stairs. She paused at the second to the last landing, recalling vividly how Hex had grabbed her right there on that final step and whisked her away to the other side of the world. Halfway down the hallway, her mind replayed the memory of when he'd appeared out of nowhere to stop her from going to Kami's, just about startling her right out of her skin and giving her neighbor a good show.

"Please?" she whispered, her chest and eyes swelling.

She didn't even know who to pray to. God? Why would he care if she found happiness with a demon? And Satan didn't exist, so who was there? Beliel?

Inside, her apartment was exactly the way she'd left it that morning. Her coffee still in its travel mug on the island where she'd abandoned it. The shades still drawn up to allow all the sunlight in—sunlight Hex's shadows could dim into a murky midnight setting in just a matter of seconds. Zoe tossed Kami's set of keys on the counter, since her purse and everything in it was still on a half-destroyed island in Papua New Guinea. She approached the windows. Sure enough, the black sedan was still sitting below along the curb. Zoe waved, and it finally pulled away, disappearing into traffic.

"Serpent," she spoke aloud, then shook her head. "Temptation?"

Who was she supposed to call on?

Leviathan had suggested that she give in and she

knew what he meant, but Hex's powers had never worked on her. How could that be different now? How was she supposed to give in to temptation, when there was nothing she wanted, except Temptation himself?

That was it! She clamped her eyes closed and tried to focus with all her heart and soul. Rather than latching onto the grief of loss and the pain of her memories, she focused on the feelings she wanted back. The laughter and the sense of partnership they'd developed in such a short time. The admiration and respect she'd felt for him. The trust, pleasure, security—all of it—because despite their situation, there had been precious moments of true happiness.

Do you know the one thing no one's ever asked me for?

Zoe's lips parted, her eyes opening to a well of tears as Hex's words floated back to her. "To be happy," she answered aloud, and the desire for it was suddenly so strong, it choked her up. "I want to be happy again. That's my greatest desire!"

She spun back into the room, her watery vision searching for any signs that she'd been heard. "Do you hear me, Temptation? Give me my happiness back! I'm willing to give you anything for it, isn't that what you want?"

She repeated herself, until her voice broke, yet nothing happened. Not a single dust mote stirred, and it crushed her heart all over again. Sinking to the floor, Zoe covered her face with her hands and cried the blood out of her soul. Leviathan was just a cruel fucker after all, but she couldn't spare him any anger. She was already too angry at herself for believing him, and for letting Hex convince her of the power of being mated, then dying. She needed a target, but had too many to choose from and the one she really wanted to scream at no longer existed. The desperate ache in every fiber of her being caused her to lean forward and pound her fists on the floor.

"LIAR!" she screamed. "You said you'd never lie to me!"

Hex. That is the name you will call me, when you're ready to tell me what you want. What you truly desire more than anything else. And then, little doe . . .

"What?" Zoe stammered on a sob, looking up, because the words had seemed to come from more than just her memories.

With an effort, she fought back the anger and tears, trying to calm her sobs as she climbed to her feet again.

"H-Hex?" She hesitated. Part of her was fully aware that it was desperation most likely causing her to go crazy, but once again, she couldn't keep from clinging to any shred of hope there was. "Hex. HEX!"

She spun in slow circles, repeating his name like an insane woman, until the hope started crashing again and the tears threatened to rise in its place.

"Am I not desperate enough?" she demanded. "Is my desire not strong enough? What more do I have to do?!"

She knew her neighbors were probably on the verge of calling 911, because she couldn't stop screaming, her emotions too wired to do anything else, and she didn't care. She was beyond the point of caring, her hopes had been lifted so high that the shattering of them was too painful to describe.

"Doe."

Zoe gasped, choking on her own saliva as she whipped around just in time to see Hex reach her. His hands slid across her cheeks, diving into her hair as his mouth crashed down on hers. It was so jarring, she jerked back, her eyes wildly surveying his face in disbelief.

He looked different, yet exactly the same. His features were even more attractive now, like the rest of the Devils, too handsome to be human. His black hair was brushed back from his forehead, which no longer sported the dark, strawberry-red scar from the Shamir. Yet his eyes were still the same pale, pale blue and his mouth still tasted like her favorite flavors.

"Shh, don't panic, baby, it's really me," he rushed out, holding her more firmly. "Hades' breath, Zoe, forgive me. Please forgive me."

Zoe suddenly felt like a zombie, her brain simply too shocked to comprehend what he was saying. She couldn't understand how he was even there. "How?"

"When you first freed me," he explained, his expression full of so much regret, "I had been trapped for so long, for so many centuries, and only my oldest memories that had been trapped with me were able to come through. I swear, I never would've believed it possible to forget so much of everything, to forget you, us. I just couldn't capture it all at first, nothing of my time since being bound in that ritual. But with Leviathan's help, it all came rushing back. I remembered everything, Zoe, and I couldn't get to you fast enough."

"Leviathan?" she repeated, her brain unable to compute that revelation.

"I just left him," he said. "He called me to him, to remind me of all I'd forgotten."

Zoe stumbled away from him, her emotions caught in some kind of suspended state. Her eyes roamed over him in his all-black suit. Every tattoo she'd memorized was gone, but there was one that had replaced them. A black serpent, its thick coils appearing over the back of his left hand, then again across the front of his throat, only to bend back and around his nape until the head appeared angled across the right side of his neck, it's forked tongue licking his jaw.

"How are you here, in this body? Who are you now?" she croaked, her throat raw from crying and screaming.

"I've been called many things," he answered. "But you're the only one in all my existence who ever asked my name. The truth is, I was never given one until that night. I am Temptation, that is my sin, my purpose. The Devils will all call me the Serpent, for that was the first physical form I ever took after my inception, but you, Zoe . . . you named me Hex. I may have provided the name, but you gave it life and meaning. The name which you've whispered, spoken with laughter dancing in your voice, screamed out of anger and frustration, out of need for my protection, a name you've sassed countless times and moaned with such mesmerizing pleasure. So, if it's all the same to you, I'd rather like to keep it."

Zoe's eyes watered again as reality began breaking through the shock. It was really him. Holy fuck, it was really him!

"I–I thought I'd killed you," she stuttered on a

hiccup. "I just wanted you to be free of Abaddon, of everything . . ."

"I know, baby. Fuck, I know." He reached for her. "Please tell me what I can do to make it up to you. Is there anything?"

Determined, she fought her quivering chin and wiped at her drenched cheeks. When she felt like she could speak again, she nodded.

"What I called you here for," she answered. "I want my happiness."

"You don't know what you're asking–"

"I do."

"Me being here isn't enough?" he asked, but his tone wasn't hurt or angry. It was edged with both longing and warning. When Zoe shook her head, his presence seemed to intensify. "You want me to take it?"

She nodded.

He approached her again, brushing the curls back from her face as he tilted her chin up to peer into her eyes. "That's what you really want, Zoe? Is that your greatest desire, to be happy?"

The heat from his hands and breath fanned over her skin, seeped into her body and filled all the hollowed-out places—the emptiness that only he could make whole again.

"With you," she whispered. "I'll only be happy with you, Hex, forever."

He groaned, a tormented sound that shivered right through her core. "I should resist this, little doe," he said softly. "By your human standards, it's selfish to desire owning your soul for all eternity."

Zoe wasn't about to let him back out now. "Be the demon you're so proud of being, Hex, I'm already damned."

"I should be a better demon and deny your request," he debated further, rubbing his thumb over her lips. "But I'll never be able to let you go. You are my only temptation, Zoe, the only thing worth giving in to."

She wrapped her legs and arms around him when he lifted her from the floor, a grin pinching her cheeks against his devouring mouth. With a hand on his cheek, she looked him right in the eyes.

"Duh."

EPILOGUE

You're never too old to learn new things, that's the general consensus. That didn't mean you had to like it, as Zoe discovered, when rather than the chaos she'd been expecting, she found that her two amazing employees had managed to run her business just fine without her.

"Look at this," she complained, showing the screen of her tablet to Hex, who was still lying in bed even though she sat propped against the wall. "They don't even need me."

He took the tablet, shut it off and tossed it at the end of the bed, making her gasp. She laughed when he rose up and tackled her back under the covers. "That's what you get for being such a boss," he teased, moving her exactly where he wanted her by tucking her halfway under him. "You've led them to greatness by example."

Zoe opened her mouth and then moaned when he nuzzled into the side of her neck. "Are you buttering me up for something?"

"No," he said, his deep baritone vibrating into her skin and inciting goosebumps. His arm banded around her waist and pulled her ass right into his erection. "I speak only truth."

"Hex." She gasped, her entire body responding with a fresh wave of arousal, as if they hadn't already spent most of the night making up for lost time.

Well, that and delivering a bracelet to a small farm in Nowhereville, Kansas. Zoe hadn't been surprised in the least. She'd known Leviathan hadn't helped Hex regain his lost memories out of the kindness of his heart, he always had an ulterior motive.

"I have to work. Those greatness-seeking employees are going to be here soon."

"I need to be inside you again, little doe, I'll make it quick," he promised, sliding his hand between her legs and cupping her pussy. She suppressed the quiver that wanted to course through her body as he started rubbing and kneading her.

Zoe's insides melted, her juices flowing with anticipation and desire, yet she still managed a proper snort of contradiction. "You don't know how to be quick."

Not that she was complaining about that for any goddamn reason, but she really didn't want to greet her employees fresh from another round of sex.

Darkness crept over them, a haze of stagnant shadows stretching their fingers like a canopy until she and Hex were mostly covered. The world seemed to go quiet in that eerie way you never noticed until there was a power outage.

"What are you doing?" she whispered.

"Removing us from time," he answered, his lips brushing over her shoulder and he pointed. "Watch your clock if you'd like, it will not change."

Zoe grinned as she did exactly that. "One of these days, you're going to have to give me the full list of all your abilities, Hex, because there are so many ways I plan to exploit them."

He laughed and nibbled on the curve of her neck to make her do the same. "Use me all you want, baby, because I plan on returning the favor."

She didn't even get a chance to respond before he sank deep inside her nice and slow, his muscles flexing around her.

"So good," he groaned, wrapping his arms tighter around her. "Every time is just so fucking good, Zoe, I can't get enough of you."

She knew what he meant and also knew it wasn't normal, so it had to be a part of the whole being mated thing. Why else would it feel like the first time every fucking time? And it wasn't just the sex, but the arousing anticipation leading up to it. The way Zoe burned and ached and longed to feel him all over was insane. She was addicted to every minute of it.

He wasn't quick, but she'd stopped watching the unmoving clock, swallowed by the pleasure of his deep and deliberate penetrations, by the way his hands slid over her, as if he needed to feel all of her at once. He teased her nipples, then groped and massaged her breasts before stroking down the curve of her side and gripping her there to grind into her a little harder. Hex used his leg to force hers to bend as he arched off the mattress, his thrusts growing faster but remaining relentlessly deep. His cock hit her in all the right places from that angle, causing the pleasure to gather like a storm cloud until she couldn't contain any more bliss and finally burst. Her toes curled, her body straining against his.

"Hex!" she cried out as she flew over the highest peak into pure ecstasy.

"Yes." He exhaled savagely, his hand groping over her almost reverently as he tried to still as much as possible to feel her muscles clenching and releasing around his cock. "Fuck, that's so good."

He didn't last much longer after that, rolling into her faster, his rhythm growing erratic, before he choked out a moan. "Zoe, fuck!" he growled and stilled, spending every last drop of his seed deep inside her for the fourth time since their reunion.

His body was still magic, only now it was a manifestation of his own making, rather than rendered by some ancient ritual. When she'd asked, because hello, she was Zoe Curiosity Bankes, he explained to her that Sparks were also known as Divine Embers—the remnants of an Angel's Grace that burned up when they fell from Heaven. Only the most powerful of Devils were able to use them to forge their bodies of flesh and blood. As the one and only Temptation, Hex was more powerful than any of the Devils, which is how he'd been able to cause permanent damage to the Sparks Abaddon used for his body. It also meant that Hex, himself, could never use the Sparks for his own body, leaving magic as his only option.

Zoe didn't care what his body was made of, as long as it wasn't someone else's corpse or even a stranger's possessed body. What she got off on and loved to drool over was a hundred percent Hex and she wouldn't trade that for anything. She stretched into his hollows, all those places perfectly molded against her curves, and hooked her arm around the back of his neck so she could see what delicious flavor his mouth had in store for her this time.

"Mmm, espresso, my favorite," she hummed, content. "Can you still travel through the Veil as fast as before?"

"Faster," he said, nipping at her lips. "I'm the reason the Veil even exists."

Zoe blinked, wondering how she hadn't connected those dots already. She blamed the demon keeping her naked and too drugged on pleasure to think straight. It was time to change that up.

"Good, then while I take a shower, you can go find my purse which is still somewhere on your deserted island," she said, giving him one last kiss, before quickly climbing out of bed.

She knew if she didn't act fast, he would lure her back into the never-ending foreplay, which would lead right back to another round of sex. She chalked it up to his magic that she still had the ability to walk, because by all-natural laws it shouldn't even be possible at that point.

Since the clock had started counting down the minutes again, Zoe didn't waste any time getting ready for the day. It only took her thirty minutes to emerge from the bathroom, showered, dressed and made up enough for video calls. She made a quick one to Byron while Hex was still gone.

"I feel bad, but I don't think you should give up," she said, after explaining that she'd forgotten to run a regular

EVP recorder at the same time as his beta app. "Obviously, the app picked up something."

He arched a brow. "You're awfully supportive without any evidence," he commented.

She shrugged. "I was in New Orleans for a while. That place has a way of changing your perspective on the paranormal. You should go sometime, I think you'd really like it there."

"Huh, thanks, maybe I will."

"He is definitely puny," Hex remarked, appearing beside her the second she signed off the video chat.

"Jesus, Hex, can I get the whispers?"

He shook his head. "You won't hear them anymore," he explained. "You've given in to Temptation, so there's no need for my powers to assess you as a potential target."

"Fuck, take backs?"

"Never," he stated so severely that Zoe felt a punch of guilt.

"Sorry, that was a bad joke." She kissed him. "But it was just a joke, I promise, I never want to take this back."

"Nor do I," he said, taking the kiss deeper for a moment. "I brought breakfast."

Zoe glanced at the island counter and saw a spread of breakfast foods and fresh coffee. "Hex, I appreciate this, I really do, but we're not in the demimonde anymore, there's no need to steal. I have food here we can cook."

"I didn't steal it," he corrected her. "I had one of my —"

"Personal shoppers?"

"Yes." He grinned. "I had one of my personal

shoppers get it for us."

That explained why it had taken him longer than she'd expected. She noted her missing purse also sitting on the counter and kissed him again in gratitude, then popped up to help herself to coffee. After savoring the first sip, she turned and leaned back against the counter to study him.

"I'm going to need you to lie," she stated.

His eyes narrowed, before he gave her a knowing look. "I won't have to lie."

"What about keeping your existence secret from humans?" she challenged.

"Humans only believe what they want to, and they don't want to believe we're real." When Zoe arched a brow, he grinned. "You're the exception. I will only speak the truth, and I guarantee your friends will take it to mean something else. Something they're more comfortable accepting."

"Was that a wager I just heard?" she perked up.

Hex's eyes grew smoky with wicked thoughts, before he sobered. "I want you to teach me the way of human business."

"Left field, Hex," she griped.

He smirked, then rose and ran a hand through his hair. "I want to provide for you in this realm, the way Saphiel provides for your friend, Kami."

"Oh, honestly, that's unnecessary," she said. "No one really needs to be provided for *that* damn much."

He chuckled, wrapping his arms around her waist and pulling her into him. "I used to think the Devils were masochists for involving themselves in human business, but now I see the importance of it. I want to live here, in your realm with you, Zoe, so I need to follow its rules. Those rules were established by Greed, Lust, and Pride, it's only natural that I partake in them as Temptation."

Shit. He had a really good point there. "Okay, I know where you can start," she said, leading him back into the bedroom.

She found her discarded tablet and pulled up the most basic articles about business, handing it over to him. "Just click on any link that sounds interesting, or try different keywords in the search bar here if you think of a question you want answered."

He smiled. "This is like your research at the library."

"Yeah, only I have a feeling you won't run into any word issues this time."

He sank down onto the bed and started reading, so Zoe went back to her coffee. When Franki arrived just a few minutes later, they curled up on the sofa together and Zoe thanked her for keeping the business going so well in her absence.

"We learned from the best," Franki said.

"Awww, my young padawans are growing up." She feigned a sulk. "Do you know what this means?"

Franki stifled a laugh and shook her head.

"I have no more excuses not to take vacations," she said.

"The hell you don't, I'll give you a new list every week," Franki deadpanned. "Just because we managed, doesn't mean we liked it."

Zoe laughed. "Okay, that makes me feel a little better."

"Especially after this last one, huh? I'm sincerely stunned that you managed to stay out of prison with no phone."

"Honestly, me, too." Zoe laughed again. She'd already half-assed explained her absence as a spontaneous out-of-town trip that had gone awry before getting a little better, blaming the loss of her phone for her radio silence. It was the only story she felt wasn't a complete lie. "But you know, it turned out to be a life-changing experience in a lot of really good ways, too. Now, I'm even more bad ass, if you can believe it."

"I can, so you should probably stay home for a while and leave some awesomeness out there in the world for others to find," Franki replied.

Zoe considered it. "Yeah, you're probably right."

They were still chuckling when the front door swung open with a partial knock and Lemar waltzed in. "She's back, bitches!" he announced, crossing toward them when he paused and narrowed his eyes at the island counter full of fresh coffee, strawberry muffins and homemade breakfast burritos. He sniffed the air. "It smells like man and sex in here."

"Really?" Zoe laughed, beginning to wonder if he wasn't part bloodhound.

When he headed toward her bedroom, she stifled a snort, tucked her tongue in her cheek and gave Franki a smug grin that had the woman's mouth going round in total surprise. Before Franki could ask, they watched as Lemar slowly backed out of the short alcove toward the living room with Hex stalking him down, still in just a pair of slacks, his pale eyes intense and his dark hair sexily mussed. The thick, black coil of a snake curved out from under his slacks at his right hip, before disappearing around his back where it formed a large, lazy 'S' to the opposite shoulder, shot down his underarm, wrapped over the back of his hand, coiled up the front of his arm, made a sideways 'U' over part of his collarbone and throat, disappeared around his nape, and finally ended in the giant snake head across the right side of his neck.

It looked three-dimensional, as if the snake was going to move at any moment, and despite being completely black, its scales were visible—that's how realistic it was. What her employees couldn't see was that it started with the narrow tip of a tail along the outside of Hex's right foot, but she was sure their imaginations went crazy trying to figure out just how much of his body it covered.

"Doe, is there a reason why this. . . man enters your bedroom so freely?" Hex asked, his deep voice edged with a little growl that just made it all the sexier.

Zoe caught his slight pause and knew he'd nearly slipped up and called Lemar a human. She was quite relieved he'd caught himself in time.

"I usually tell him to," she answered, so amused it was taking all of her willpower not to bust a gut.

"I–it's always empty," Lemar stammered.

Hex stilled and then completely relaxed, his seductive smile spreading wide. "I like that answer," he said, then stuck his hand out. "You must be Lemar, Zoe's told me a lot about you. I'm Hex."

Realizing they'd just pulled one over on him, Lemar finally relaxed, but his laugh was nervous. "Uh, I'd like to say the same, but—"

"We just met on my wayward trip," Zoe intervened, then gave Franki a wink. "Told you it wasn't all bad."

"No fucking shit!" Franki laughed, gesturing to Hex. "I mean, damn. What phone?"

Zoe lost it, unable to hold her laughter in any longer. Hex beamed at her, then crossed to the sofa to join them.

"You must be Franki," he said, reaching his hand out to her. After they shook hands, he smiled at Zoe. "She talks like you."

She smirked. "Welcome to New York."

"Where are you from?" Lemar asked with so much interest, Zoe could already picture him traveling to wherever Hex called home to see if there were any more just like him.

"New Orleans," Hex answered. "But I travel a lot."

"You have to travel with the show, huh?" Lemar said, sinking down into the armchair closest to Hex, an avid ear for anything he had to say.

Zoe felt his pain. From night one, she'd never wanted to stop listening to Hex talk.

"The show?" Hex asked, looking back and forth, a little confused.

"Surely you're with some kind of show," Lemar said, looking him over. "A band? The runway? Chippendales?"

Zoe snorted out a laugh. "You wish."

"A man can dream, Zoe Linnea. Why are you such a bubble-popper?"

"Uh, because it's fun," she pointed out.

"What is Linnea?" Hex asked her. "I thought Bankes was your surname?"

"It's my middle name, which I regret that one ever finding out," she pointed at Lemar.

"So what do you do, if you're not in a show?" Franki asked, just as interested, only a lot less obvious about it.

Hex looked at her. "I find the one thing people desire the most and then I give it to them in exchange for their souls."

Zoe almost choked on her coffee, surprised he would be so blunt about it, even if he'd already warned her that he wouldn't lie.

"Oh, so you're in sales," Franki grimaced.

Zoe opened her mouth, even more surprised at how easily Franki had proven Hex right about humans. Of course, the demon wore a smug expression when she glanced at him in disbelief. Good thing they hadn't actually settled on a wager. She'd already lost to Byron, and that was embarrassing enough.

"You're nothing like what I normally picture when someone mentions a traveling salesman," Lemar commented with a slow shake of his head. "I'm going to have to completely readjust my top ten list now."

Hex's smile was slow when he finally seemed to grasp where Lemar was coming from. "I think he's attempting to flirt with me," he said to Zoe, his tone nearly as smug as his expression still.

"Yeah, don't let it go to your head there, big guy, he flirts with anything with a penis," Zoe murmured.

"Girl, please," Lemar returned. "I happen to have very high standards."

"That only works on people who've never gone clubbing with you before," Franki laughed.

Zoe snickered and high-fived her, then clapped her own hands together. "Okay, times up," she announced. "We're on the clock and these hashtags are not going to trend themselves. So, if you're hungry, grab something to eat, grab coffee, thank Hex for both, and let's get some smack-talk going on up in here."

"He cooks, too?" Lemar complained.

"I had one of my personal shoppers get it," Hex said absently as he leaned back and watched everything Zoe did as she started opening all of her social media icons on her laptop.

Lemar stared at her in question, distracting her. "What?" she asked, then the conversation caught up with her. "Oh, yeah . . . yeah, that happened."

Lemar looked Hex over and shook his head as he rose to help himself to the food and coffee. "Make that my top five list."

"Right?" Franki seconded.

Zoe just chuckled and sent Hex a grin, which he immediately reciprocated. Then she dove into her work, never feeling as happy as she did in that moment surrounded by her friends, with her growing business at her fingertips, knowing her bestie was safe and sound, and the demon she loved was right beside her where he belonged. As if he could sense the direction of her thoughts, Hex tucked his mouth into the curls at her ear.

"I have your heart now, little doe," he said.

Zoe tucked her mouth beside his cheek and whispered, "I have yours, too, Hexy."

"Ugh." He smacked his lips dryly and Zoe beamed ear to ear.

Okay. *Now*, she was happy.

THE END

Thank you so much for reading Hexed! If you had fun following Zoe and Hex's wild adventure, I would be super grateful if you'd take a few moments to rate it or leave a review on your favorite retailer's site. It could help other readers find Hexed, too!

But don't stop reading yet, there are bonus goodies up next...

BONUS MATERIALS

Can't get enough of the Seven and all their sorted antics? Then how about a sneak peek at what these Devils will be up to next...

Hell on Earth Series Teaser Previews

Lust

What had begun as a life debt, had turned into the entire Eternal Legion of The Damned Motorcycle Club filling in for Gia Calloway's absentee parents. She was orphan Annie, and her Daddy Warbucks was a brotherhood of stone-cold killers. They called her their lucky penny, gifted with the uncanny knack at sorting foe from friend.

Ash Medai was neither. He'd built his tower of black glass right on the plump artery of Sin City, and then purchased Gia's debt from the ELOTD MC...with interest. *Decadence* was everything it alluded to; sensual and exclusive. A members-only hotel and casino that catered to the sex and gambling addicts.

For Gia, it was just another waystation. A place she'd soon be shuffled from when her life was sold to the next highest bidder. She was everyone's good luck charm, save her own. That proved truest the night she was delivered to Ash, and made the mistake of looking for his aura. It blazed into her mind with the wariness of uncertainty: a white mist doused in Hellfire. Either her new owner was contrived solely of passion, or he wasn't even human.

Was it wrong to hope for both?

Pride

In the City of Angels, Lina had been hiding in plain sight, crawling through the underbelly and frequenting the *Devil's Playground* for years. Who'd she been running from had never been clearer than the night she stalked through the familiar crowd of Kinksters, to find him sitting alone...waiting for her.

He wore a three-piece suit to her black lace, an antique pocket watch to her red leather corset. Everywhere he was polished, she was inked. Yet, the moment his frosty eyes locked with hers, Lina knew which of them was the monster.

He wanted to break her in a bad way. Tear her apart slowly, and savor every soul-ending affliction until nothing remained. If danger was her target, Lina was a shameless flirt, but that didn't mean she was ready to be gutted. And if the malicious vow poised in the curve of his mouth was her only warning; then he already knew her worst nightmares. He was the harbinger, and the executioner. He need only wait. His prey always came begging.

Lina dared him to hold his breath.

Envy

Allyson Renner was a fraud. A bad seed playing the role of the good daughter and gracious citizen of her pathetic town. Voted most beautiful and most likely to succeed, she had brains, beauty and a near psychotic obsession with the ocean. All she ever wanted was to escape her landlocked farm in Nowhereville, Kansas and spend the rest of her life feeling the saltwater breeze on her skin.

Finn was the answer to all of her desperate prayers. Handsome, educated and utterly shallow. On his way to make it big in the Import/Export business in Florida, he was looking for a trophy wife-to-be and Ally happily jumped at the chance to sate her lifelong fascination.

But, the façade was no match for their true desires. A matter Ally's quick to learn, when her very first night in the Keys, lands her in the arms of Thirio Pelagos. The wealthy Greek tycoon may have rescued her from danger, but the threat he poses on her sanity and fragile, fake life is a thousand times worse. Thirio's after a twisted game with her and Finn, one that's straight out of a madman's playbook. Yet, Ally can't seem to fight the powerful pull he has on her. Like the ocean, he is both mesmerizing and deadly, leading his willing victims right into the undercurrents.

If only Ally had ever learned to swim.

Gluttony

No one loved modern technology more than Miranda Blackburn. It allowed her to keep her sanity intact, despite the loneliness. With anything she could ever want or need at the click of a mouse, she rarely had to venture outside of her soundproofed flat in the West Village. Born cursed with the ability to hear the truth behind people's lies, she'd spent all of her formative years being treated like a pariah. Desperate to understand, she'd grown perversely curious about the human psyche.

That curiosity combined with an unerring gift at 'mysteriously knowing' people's real problems and desires, had earned her the reputation of being the youngest and most sought after psychiatrist in the elite circles of New York. Her clients not only paid dearly to keep her confidentiality, but tended to recommend her to their high profile friends. Which, is how Miranda found herself in the living room of Owen Cethridge the day the Devil came to collect on an old debt.

After twenty-four years of never failing to hear the whispers of truth whenever someone spoke, the silence following every one of Mr. Abul's words was like an aphrodisiac to her ears. Until she realized the only explanation was that he'd spoken the truth, and that truth was utterly horrific. Especially, when he turned the psychiatry tables on her and started listing off all of her own deepest, darkest fears, insecurities and desires. For the first time in her life, Miranda got to feel what it was like to be one of her clients, forced to admit truths she'd believed to be hidden, trapped in the vulnerable exposure of bare honesty.

The one thing Miranda never thought she'd be reduced to was craving lies.

###

AN UPCOMING VALENTINE'S TALE:

TWISTED ARROWS
(A Torq Brothers Novel)

Naked trees, slicked with frost, glistened like ice under the beam of headlights. Jag cruised up Cougar Mountain, his car hugging every snaking curve toward Berman Castle; a private residence tucked into the wintry hills of Bellevue. Beyond the spattering of bare maples and alders, thick groves of evergreens turned dusk into treacherous night. He turned up the radio, sank deeper into plush leather and gave the car more speed. Call him what you will: reckless, adrenaline junkie, Jag knew where the line was. He danced all the fuck over it– suavely–and lived to push its boundaries.

Redefining limits was what *defined* him. It was the passion behind his business, his fast lifestyle and without question, his many pleasures. Hence the nearly palpable excitement filling the interior of his car. It was Valentine's Day, his favorite holiday of the year. A night taken back from the dreamy romantics and given to the miscreants of kink with the annual Cupid's Mark Masque; the most exclusive BDSM event to be found. As Jag raced toward ultimate bliss, thousands of hopeless saps were rushing around for last minute gifts, praying they'd be good enough. They wouldn't be. Men who'd been wise enough to pay attention knew that more relationships ended in February, between dinner on the fourteenth and breakfast on the fifteenth, than any other time of year. Guys sweating over the price of earrings, when they should have bought the ring, left with maxed out credit card bills and no sex life come morning.

No fucking thank you.

Limitless sin is what awaited Jag every Valentine's Day, and his demons were foaming at the mouth. He'd gone too long between fixes again, despite telling himself he wouldn't. Work, family, life, these things happened and before he knew it, too much time had passed and he felt feral. At least he was the only victim of his lies. Everyone else got the ironclad honor of his word– whether they wanted it or not.

With a smirk, his gaze flicked to the box sitting on the passenger seat, as he took the final curve off the main road and shot down a private lane surrounded by untouched wilderness. The owner of Berman Castle had built it on a split fifty acre lot to ensure privacy. Thick trees sloped down to his right and rose up to his left, hiding stone walls that encompassed acres of topiary manicured lawns, all monitored by state of the art security. Near the end of the road, he veered left into the drive where wrought-iron gates stood open for the event and climbed the steady slope to the large courtyard already filling up with luxury cars. Jag's contribution was a BMW that belonged to his alias, because anyone who knew him would attest to the fact that he would never drive one. Not that he had anything against the manufacturer, itself, just being *that* unoriginal.

Once parked, he flipped the lid off the box and removed the full-face mask. It was black and featureless with a blood red arrow slashed diagonally across it. After securing it into place, he checked his reflection in the visor mirror, satisfied that his dark green eyes were the only things showing.

He didn't have a face that would go unnoticed in certain circles, and this night was all about anonymity. Just like the car, his invite had been issued under his club alias. He had a name to protect. A business and a family that would burn with him, if his predilections ever made it into mainstream knowledge. Not that his brothers weren't diving headlong into their own kinks, but they each had different tastes and his just happened to be the darkest of the lot. All the wicked, taboo kinks society would waste no time twisting into something they weren't. Which, is why there wasn't so much as a gas receipt placing Jaguar Torq anywhere near Berman Castle tonight.

He grabbed an armored briefcase from the trunk, then headed across the car park, setting the alarm with a silent flash of parking lights. Decked in all black suit, shirt, driving gloves with blood red silk in his breast pocket he was very aware of how much he resembled a comic book villain with the mask. That was fine by him, he was feeling rather villainous.

Under the stone arch of the gatehouse, he provided his invite to one of the guards without an ID, while the other eyeballed the case he didn't offer up for inspection.

"Any weapons?" The man asked.

Jag stared at him, surprised by the question. Deston must have had to fill a new spot recently. "Well, that's a matter of perception, isn't it?" he countered.

"He's clear," the other guard snickered, handing Jag his invite back. "Enjoy your evening, Mr. Carr."

Yeah, his alias was all kinds of fucking funny.

Jag kept his attention on the rookie, as he tucked his invite away. "Don't worry, you're not my type," he assured him, then inclined his head. "Gentlemen."

"We should have checked his case." Jag heard the man grumble, as he headed up the flagstone path.

"Trust me, you don't want to see what's inside." The other responded.

Jag grinned to himself, as he landed on the small stoop of the house and pushed one of the arched, wooden doors open. His brow shot up to find twin beauties standing in the foyer to greet him. Coils of French pink curls were piled atop their heads with long, black and red feathers fanning off the opposite side as the other. Corsets of more black and red pinched their waists above floor-length skirts, complete with bustles. The gaping slit right up the center revealed only striped stockings and silk panties under all the intricate framing. Their masks were only for decoration, frilled lace just around their eyes. No one could mistake Riveted's most popular Burlesque team.

"Sisters DuPrey," he purred.

Their red lips spread into identical smiles. "Welcome to the Cupid's Mark Masque, Mr. Carr. The Arrows Lounge is in the showroom."

No matter how many times he'd heard them speak in perfect unison that way, it still reminded him of the freaking *Shining*. Fighting a shudder, he tilted his head in gratitude and headed across the foyer to the center door in the left wall. Past a guest bath, the hall opened to a split level staircase on his right, but he followed the runner all the way around to another door in the corner of the back wall. Muffled music filled the small anteroom with bass. It vibrated antique oval mirrors hanging on either side of the door to the showroom. Beneath each one, a sub knelt in nothing more than stockings and lace blindfolds, holding sterling silver trays above their heads. One tray held a pile of black, half-face masks with the arrow. The other tray held rows of skeleton keys.

Jag tucked a half-face mask inside the pocket of his suit jacket, then approached the keys. They were all attached to ornate pendants with guest names elegantly scrolled across them. He picked his up and watched the pendant swirl, revealing his name on one side and the number 4 on the other. Another smile spread unseen behind his mask. It wasn't just the number of his suite, but the sub he would spend the whole night wringing every ounce of pleasure out of. And God, it better be *her*.

Through the door, he stepped right into the erotic sounds of leather tails slapping flesh, followed by the gagged cries of the recipient and a Dubstep mix that may have once been Madonna's *Justify My Love*. In the dark, red lights were either set on a slow strobe or steady glow. Jag looked to his right, where the flogging scene was taking place in the largest open area of the room. Two Doms were holding a sub stretched by her arms, while a third worked her bare ass and back with a wicked looking flogger; random metal tips glinting in the minimal lighting. His gaze shifted beyond them, catching the unmistakable red half-mask of Cupid, aka Deston Cassidy, owner of the BDSM club, Riveted and Berman Castle. He was leaning against the far wall, where he'd been watching the scene. Now, his attention was trained on Jag, because he was also known by sight. Not only was he the tallest man there, he never arrived to a Riveted event without his armored case. Jag held up his key, the pendant gleaming red from the only light source. He wanted confirmation that his pick was waiting for him behind door number four. When he got the subtle nod from Cupid, an electric pulse rippled across his shoulders and invigorated his muscles.

Jag pivoted to the left where a row of glass showcases were spaced along the exterior wall. Any other day, they would be filled with all of Deston's Steampunk inventions and costumes. The lights would be on to illuminate his award-winning craftsmanship. The room, with its ribbon dome of stained glass down the center and crystal chandeliers would look more like an underground train terminal than this seedy dungeon of dirty desires. The doors to the solarium across the other side were wide open, a hint of hothouse flowers and plants tinting the air of sin, leather and anticipation. Red pulsing lights captured the silhouettes inside those glass cases where some subs had yet to be claimed.

Jag knew the secret of their temporary cells. Their truest purpose, and his fingers curled from the shot of adrenaline to his system. Too long...fuck he'd gone too long.

He approached the case painted with a number 4, his steps measured for the sake of his own self-control, nothing else. His size blocked out most of the light, making it nigh impossible to see inside the box, so he tapped his gloved finger on the glass. Jag watched the sub step out of the shadows, draped in a silk robe of red with black stockings covering her otherwise bare feet. Her head was bowed, her dark hair too difficult to single out from any other in the dimness. He needed to see her face. When she stopped just on the other side, he tapped the glass again right in front of his chest and waited for her gaze to meet it. Still not enough. He slid his finger higher, pleased when she followed that silent directive, and stopped with his hand obscuring his own vision. Then, he removed it altogether and accepted the fiery punch of lust to his gut, as he watched her blue eyes widen; red lips parting with surprise and fear.

Did she recognize him? There was a chance, since the mask couldn't disguise his height or build. Not that it mattered. She was the one he'd chosen. The woman who'd captured his attention at the fundraiser and had given him every right to stake his claim on her by wearing the golden arrow on her wrist. Jag adjusted the key in his hand and pressed the ornate pendant to the glass, showing her the number. Proving that he was there for her, that Cupid had stole her away in the dead of night and brought her there just for him. Her startled eyes flicked from the key to the matching number painted on the glass and Jag's hidden grin was sinister.

Happy fucking Valentine's Day, sweetheart.

Have you started the Dark Day Isle series yet?

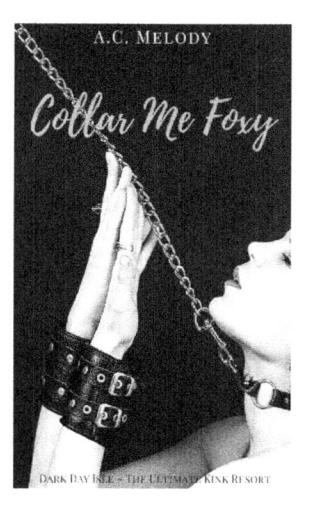

Book 1: **Collar Me Foxy** is now perma-free on most popular U.S. retail sites

Book 2: **Scavenger** can be read free on Kindle Unlimited

Welcome to Dark Day Isle, the Ultimate Kink Resort. They've got sandy beaches, palm trees, tiki bars, azure waters and oh, yeah–lots of kink!

Join Tessa Fauns for a week long getaway in paradise as she puts all of her submissive skills and experience to the test with a Master who isn't shy about pushing her limits in new, creative and often binding ways!

ACKNOWLEDGMENTS

Thank you to all my readers, I can't believe I'm getting the chance to write these notes of appreciation once again. Every time feels like a blessing, because I still remember what it was like to be an 'aspiring writer' daydreaming that someday, someone would want to read my book. This past year has been exceptionally challenging for me, going through trouble with carpel tunnel, tendinitis and just recently learning that I'm most likely battling Rheumatoid Arthritis to boot. It makes typing "Thank You" for reading my book that much more significant for me, so thank you!

To my friend and fellow author, Anna Adler, for always taking my rough drafts in hand and giving me my first round of feedback and critiques!

To my editor, Monique Fischer, who always saves my manuscripts from me and still manages to teach me new things about proper grammar and punctuation. I'm not always the quickest at breaking old bad habits!

I'd really like to thank all of the bloggers and readers who participate in promoting, ARC reading, reviewing or in anyway sharing Hexed with others - you are amazingly awesome and I am so grateful for all of your support!

One last note: Readers, the greatest way possible you can show your enjoyment for your favorite authors is by rating their books or writing a review on your preferred retail site. Just as with any business, word of mouth is an author's best friend. Even just a one line of "I loved it!" goes really far in helping your beloved writers out and your fellow readers with finding a book they will like.

THANK YOU AGAIN & ALWAYS!

ABOUT THE AUTHOR

A.C. Melody is a hybrid author of Erotic Romance and all its savory sub-genres. Confessed javaholic, introverted geeky girl with a twisted sense of humor and a wretched muse. She has a weakness for hard ass Alphas and the strong women who capture their hearts, without damaging their rough edges.

A lifetime lover of fairytales, myths, legends and ancient pantheons, A.C. spends more time researching than writing. Her biggest goal is to provide new, captivating angles on old, favorite tales with enticing twists and characters that redefine preset expectations.
She's 100% guilty of placing all her money on the underdogs, anti-heroes and shameless whores.

Learn more in my Author Interview at:
https://www.smashwords.com/interview/ACMelody

CONNECT WITH ME

Blog: https://acmelodyblog.wordpress.com/

Twitter: @AuthorACMelody

Facebook: https://www.facebook.com/AC.Melody.77

Instagram: https://www.instagram.com/a.c.melody/

Pinterest: https://www.pinterest.com/acmelody77/

Goodreads: https://www.goodreads.com/author/show/9835277.A_C_Melody

Amazon Author Page: https://www.amazon.com/-/e/B011PTY1PO

OTHER TITLES BY A.C. MELODY

Red Sage Publishing:

Hearthstone Alpha: The first in the Úlfrinn series, a Contemporary Paranormal Romance about wolf shifters.

Little Queen: The second in the Úlfrinn series, an Erotic Paranormal Romance about wolf shifters.

Self-Published: *Read free on Kindle Unlimited*

Collar Me Foxy: (Permafree on most U.S. retail sites!) The first novella in the Dark Day Isle series about a Kink getaway in paradise.

Scavenger: The second novel in the Dark Day Isle series about a Kink getaway in paradise.

Avarice: The first novella in the Hell on Earth series, a Dark Erotic-BDSM-Paranormal.

Avarice Unforgiving: The second novella in the Hell on Earth series, a Dark Erotic-BDSM-Paranormal.

Avarice Unleashed: The third novella in the Hell on Earth series, a Dark Erotic-BDSM-Paranormal.

The Avarice Collection: Get the entire Avarice trilogy plus bonus materials with this box set.

ALL SELF-PUBLISHED BOOKS ARE AVAILABLE IN EBOOK AND PAPERBACK!

SPECIAL OFFER FOR MY READERS

Want more free & exclusive stuff? Be among the first to get the inside scoop on all of my upcoming Cover Reveals, New Releases, Giveaways and Blog Tours - Plus, exclusive excerpts, character interviews and other prizes by joining my Elite Readers Group! Just enter the URL below into your web browser to subscribe to my author newsletter and never miss a thing! You can unsubscribe at any time.

Sign up today for the first full chapter of Hayden (Doms of Club Vitalz, Book 1)!

http://eepurl.com/dqg5Bv

Printed in Great Britain
by Amazon